WHERE HER SECRETS LIE

ALSO BY KATIE TALLO

Dark August

Poison Lilies

Buried Road

PRAISE FOR KATIE TALLO

Dark August

"*Dark August* is a tightly paced cauldron of a thriller about small-town corruption, murder, and mayhem, in the vein of *Sharp Objects* and *All the Missing Girls*. A macabre and confidently twisty debut."

—Lisa Gabriele, internationally bestselling author of *The Winters*

"What elevates Tallo's galloping story is the freshness of the writing and the deep explorations of character. An imaginative thriller—as much about family, loss, greed, and a young woman's attempt to find a place in the world as it is about solving a long-buried mystery."

—Peter Heller, *New York Times* bestselling author of *The River*

"Distinctive characters and an intricate plot will keep readers turning the pages."

—*Publishers Weekly*

"Truly inspired piece of writing . . . A mystery of epic proportions . . . Highly recommended for mystery fans, as well as devotees of Margaret Atwood and Alice Munro."

—*Booklist* (starred review)

"One of the best debut novels of the decade. Brilliant characters and a stellar plot make Tallo a talent who should be on everyone's list."

—*The Globe 100*

Poison Lilies

"Moody and riveting."

—*New York Times Book Review*, Editors' Choice

"Seamlessly weaves in threads from the first book and adeptly takes a century-old crime into the present."

—*Library Journal*

Buried Road

"A fast-paced, exciting missing-persons thriller with a heart-pounding, twisty final third that I very much enjoyed. Katie Tallo is a big new talent."

—*New York Times* bestselling author Adrian McKinty

"Katie Tallo's electrifying new novel, *Buried Road*, is a heart-stopping thriller, a sensitive character study, and a riveting follow-up to *Poison Lilies*. Readers will be captivated by the unique landscape of small towns, wealthy vineyards, and stunning scenery in Prince Edward County, all while cheering on a fierce heroine for the ages."

—Amy Tector, author of the Dominion Archives Mysteries

"In *Buried Road*, Katie Tallo masterfully leads readers through a twisted path of riveting clues to uncover the gritty secrets lurking in a picturesque small town. The vibrant setting in this searing mystery will entrance you, and Tallo's enthralling, fearless protagonist will seize your heart in her fist. *Buried Road* is a darkly beautiful, heartbreakingly poignant suspense that is truly stunning."

—Samantha M. Bailey, *USA Today* and #1 national bestselling author of *A Friend in the Dark*

"Katie Tallo writes with a fresh, unique voice, creating a fierce and intimate tale about the power of family love, full of twists, vivid characters, and touches of humor. Enjoy the ride!"

—Barbara Fradkin, award-winning author of the Inspector Green and Amanda Doucette mysteries

"*Buried Road* is a forget-everything-you're-doing kind of book that pulls you in from the first page. With a protagonist you'll cheer on and feel terrified for at the same time, you won't be able to put it down. Smart, twisted, breathtakingly compelling—it's everything you want from a fantastic mystery, and Tallo's storytelling skills mean she's an auto-read author for me. Hands down one of my favorite books of the year."

—Hannah Mary McKinnon, internationally bestselling author of *The Revenge List*

"With an intricate plot and three-dimensional characters, this marks the series' third straight winner. Here's hoping a fourth is on the way."

—*Publishers Weekly*

WHERE HER SECRETS LIE

KATIE TALLO

THOMAS & MERCER

This is a work of fiction. Names, characters, organizations, places, events, and incidents are either products of the author's imagination or are used fictitiously. Otherwise, any resemblance to actual persons, living or dead, is purely coincidental.

Published by Thomas & Mercer, Seattle

www.apub.com

EU product safety contact:
Amazon Media EU S. à r.l.
38, avenue John F. Kennedy, L-1855 Luxembourg
amazonpublishing-gpsr@amazon.com

ISBN-13: 9781662540493 (paperback)
ISBN-13: 9781662540486 (digital)

Cover design by Lisa Amoroso
Cover image: © FTNews, © avtk, © Peyker, © Ihnatovich Maryia / Shutterstock;
© Ryan McVay / Getty Images

Printed in the United States of America

For my dad, Joe.

Autumn 2010

It was a warm September night—too warm for a dead body. The moon was bloodred. Wind whipped the buckthorns into a frenzy of white noise. Lenny was grateful for the cover. Hands trembling from her labors, she opened the shed door and peered inside. It was pitch black. She inched the toe of her rubber boot forward and made contact.

Lenny bent and grabbed his ankles. Even though she was wearing gardening gloves, she could feel he was deathly cold. As she dragged him from the shed, his head bumped the doorframe, but she kept pulling. He wouldn't feel it. She didn't stop until she reached the hole in the back corner of her garden. The corner not visible from her nosy neighbor Mr. Crawley's upstairs window. The hole not deep enough but all she could manage. At least the soil had been easy to dig.

That was because of the mischief.

Earlier that summer, in that very corner, Lenny had discovered rats nesting under her compost bins. A *mischief* was what the exterminator from the pest-control company called the colony. His crew set about laying traps, then fumigated the tunnels for good measure.

No more mischief.

After the slaughter, they excavated the entire back corner and cleaned out the corpses. There were hundreds, mostly babies. *Pups*, he called them. Lenny wasn't fazed. She'd dealt with worse horrors that year. The men brought in truckloads of topsoil and created a new garden bed full of possibilities. Lenny had been debating what to plant in that shady corner ever since. Hostas. Begonias. Part of her knew it didn't matter what she chose. Her garden had always had a mind of its own. She'd tried to make it hers by adding a stone path, a bench, and a metal birdbath, but after decades of diligent weeding, pruning, and mulching, it remained stubborn and unruly—or as Hank liked to call it, *a beautiful mess*.

She knew he wasn't just talking about the garden.

As she stood next to the hole, the wind lifted her long brown hair, bringing it to life Medusa-style. The powerful, destructive forces of life and death snaked her skull, whirling into her belly and radiating up from the stiff body at her feet. Lenny dropped to her knees, braced her hands against the man's torso, and pushed with what little strength she had left. He rolled into the hole and landed with a wretched thud. The sound made her gag.

As she got to her feet and picked up the spade, she glanced toward the house—the modest two-story brick Victorian she and Hank bought a few years after they were married. Through the snarled shrubs, she could make out the yellow pool of light above the back step. Gnats circled the dull glow. She could hear the hum of traffic from the Trans-Canada a few blocks away. Long-haul truckers passing through town in the dead of night, unaware that a woman stood alone in a dark corner of her garden as the claw of grief traced its ugly finger across her chest. Like it did every time she stood still for too long.

She brushed it aside and began filling the hole with dirt.

When Lenny was done, she tipped her Japanese wisteria from its large pot and transplanted it to the back corner. Ten-year-old Juls liked chasing his new puppy through the garden's tangled pathways, so the wisteria would explain the freshly turned earth if her grandson wandered back there. She raked away the drag marks, washed off the gardening tools, and headed into the house. As she tossed the gloves into the garbage with the rest of the evidence, Fender woke from a deep slumber and pawed at his crate. She took the pup for a walk around the block, tossing the garbage bag in a dumpster behind an apartment building up the street.

Back at the house, she tucked seven-month-old Fender into his crate. He watched with drooping eyes as she wiped down the kitchen one more time. When she was done, he was snoring. Lenny dragged herself upstairs and ran a bath. She didn't have much time. They'd be home in a few hours. She could hear the soft cawing of the backyard crows as they began to emerge from their communal roost. That meant the sun would be up soon.

As Lenny sank into the hot water, the sting of violence prickled her skin. She touched her cheekbone where his punch had landed. There was a nasty scrape on the inside of her forearm and a purple bruise on her elbow from when she'd fallen on the patio stones. Lenny gently stroked the welts beginning to form on her neck. She'd have to wear a scarf, long sleeves, cover the bruises with makeup. No one could ever know what had happened, especially the boy. He'd lost too much already.

Lenny closed her eyes as reality seeped into her bones.

She was a fifty-five-year-old housewife, and she'd just buried a body in her back garden.

The last of the rats.

Or so she thought.

PART ONE

1

Autumn 2025

Lenny enters the code on the security panel and lets herself into the memory care unit on the third floor of Maplelawn Manor. She has an *Ottawa Citizen* under one arm and a box of Thyme and Again scones cradled in the other. Store bought will have to do. In what's become a yearly ritual, Lenny once again failed spectacularly in her attempt to bake her mother's famous oatmeal cookies for her father's birthday. She doesn't know why she keeps trying. It's not like at seventy, she'll suddenly transform into a domestic goddess. Her brain has never been wired to follow recipes or chase dust bunnies or separate whites from colors. Hank didn't mind that his dinners were always burnt and his work shirts were yellow. He loved how she was wired.

"Morning, Mrs. Bird. Special day today," says the nurse with a friendly wink.

Lenny gives her a hasty nod as she passes the care station. Lenny's not one for small talk unless it's done over a pint. She heads toward her father's room at the end of the hall. Halfway there, Lenny spots the balloons and **Happy Birthday** sign framing his door. The old Silas would have loathed this sentimental display, but dementia has spun her father's personality into perpetual shuffle mode. One day he's irritated and itchy, the next he's giggly and singing nursery rhymes. Lately, his default playlist is stuck on sweet and corny.

Lenny finds it hard to stomach after a childhood spent walking on eggshells around the old man.

She peers into her father's room. His Sunday best is laid out on the bed. Suit, shirt, pants, tie. Her father is sitting in one of two armchairs under the window, still in his pajamas.

"Happy birthday, Dad," says Lenny.

She walks over and places the box of scones in his lap, then takes the chair across from him. He opens the box and looks at her. His eyes shine.

"Peg, my love, you shouldn't have," he says with a smile, dentures gleaming.

He often mistakes her for her mother even though it's been twenty years since the woman died. Lenny *does* look a lot like her mother, but that's where the similarities end. Peggy was softhearted and whimsical. She played the viola and sang at the top of her lungs in the grocery aisle. She could light up a room. Lenny always preferred the dark, like her father.

"It's me, Dad. Lenny," she reminds him. "Your daughter."

He blinks. It takes him a second, then he sees her.

"Lenny, Lenny, my little Lenny Penny," he sings. "Oh, how I love my Lenny-Loo."

Lenny tries not to cringe. Silas never once in his life said he loved her. Love was not his language. He preferred bugs to people. Silas tugs on Lenny's sleeve.

"It's not my birthday," he whispers, leaning closer.

"Yes, it is, Dad. It's September 19," Lenny reminds him.

Like she could ever forget that date.

He furrows his brow.

"I know what bloody day it is," he snaps, shooing her away. "Who do you think you are? You're just a silly little girl."

There's good old Dad.

Lenny glances into the hallway to see if anyone's within earshot. It's protocol to keep doors open on the third floor. She still can't get used to seeing her once-dignified father lose both his mind and his privacy. Dressing, bathing, even wiping his bum are left to the care of strangers. Lenny wishes she could do more for him, considering she owes him her life.

To ease her guilt, she visits him almost every day, playing the good daughter, hoping to glimpse the man she worshipped as a child. A man who could examine decomposing human remains and determine the time, cause, and manner of death simply by understanding bugs. A man who dismissed her curiosity about his work as girlish audacity. A man whose journals she stole moments with late at night, mesmerized by his postmortem notes about cadaver decay and larval metamorphosis, their margins littered with intricately labeled sketches of tiny creatures. A man she desperately wanted to know, but who didn't seem to want to know her.

And now it was too late.

Part of her wishes he was dead. A kinder fate for both of them. She wouldn't have to endure this half man, half child. But her ninety-five-year-old father's hold on her heart is as strong as it ever was, and the wish quickly melts into a puddle of shame for even thinking the thought.

Besides, he's all she's got.

Lenny helps him dress. She tugs his shirtsleeves over his withered elbows, helps him pull up his trousers and put on his socks, then eases his feet into his dress shoes. He fidgets like a little boy who doesn't want to go to church. Not until she buttons his shirt cuffs and begins to clip on his cuff links does his mood brighten, and he starts to sing under his breath.

And when they were up, they were up,
And when they were down, they were down.

They settle back into their chairs, and Lenny begins reading the newspaper out loud, like she does every visit. Macular degeneration has made it so he can't read. Silas used to never be without a book in his hands. She's never sure her father is listening until she gets to the obits. Then he perks up.

Together, they tease out details from each obituary, upending the carefully chosen words and reimagining them into morbid tales of deaths and misdeeds. There's always a list of suspects, from the so-called grieving wife to the son-in-law with the suspicious surname. It's their favorite game, and it's the closest Lenny has ever gotten to sharing something real with her father.

Eighty-eight-year-old Faith Crockford from across the hall pops by midmorning. She's made Silas a birthday card decorated with cats. She carries a fake one cradled in her arm wherever she goes. She calls the tatty feline Ginger Rogers. Lenny offers Faith her chair. Silas and Faith chat about the weather, even though neither of them goes outside anymore. When the conversation withers, Faith rubs one of Ginger's furry ears, and Silas stares out the window. Lenny is trying to think of a conversation starter that won't bore her to tears when, out of the blue, Silas speaks up.

"Am I old?" he asks.

Lenny's about to state the obvious when Faith jumps in with a better answer.

"Don't let the old man in, Silas," says Faith, looking at him intently.

"Too late," he answers. "He's got his hooks in me."

Faith rests a bony hand on his.

"You're wrong, dear boy. I see you in there," she says. "I see young Silas Flint."

He offers Faith a scone. The pair giggle like first graders, oblivious to the fact that their words have taken Lenny's breath away. She knows all too well the haunting tiptoe of time. How forty slowly becomes fifty, then creeps into sixty, each decade sly yet swift. But last month, turning seventy was different. Seventy was not shy or quiet.

Seventy was a gut punch.

Her father's room is suddenly unbearably hot. Lenny pulls at the collar of her blouse. She slips into his tiny bathroom to splash water on her face. When Lenny looks in the mirror, she can't see her. The child with the gap between her front teeth. The girl with the bruised knees who loved climbing trees. The student who swept her wavy hair into a messy bun when all the girls were straightening theirs, and wore it like that her whole life. The young mother who taught her daughter to ride a bike before she was three. The best friend to a husband who shared everything with her, until he didn't.

Lenny doesn't recognize the face staring back at her.

How did I get here?

She exits the bathroom to find Silas and Faith pecking at crumbs like a couple of old crows. Lenny ducks into the hallway. She instantly feels better in the wide-open space. She walks the length of the hall, striding to get the blood flowing and her brain rehinged. Lenny comes upon Harold Sims, who's pacing near the exit. He's a longtime resident.

"Hello, Harold," she says. "How are you today?"

Dumb question. Harold hates it here.

"You watch for the warden," he whispers. "I think this is the way out."

He points to the exit. Lenny smiles and tries not to glance at the locked door. The back has been painted to look like a bookcase so the residents won't know it's an exit. Harold's a runner. He's seen people disappear behind this bookcase, so he loiters close, hoping to make his great escape.

"I'm not supposed to be here," he says.

That makes two of us.

2

Lenny parks her silver Camry in the driveway of her house at 13 Julian Avenue. She's lived there for over forty years. The house is showing its age in its faded facade. A parcel is waiting on the porch. She picks it up and kicks off her shoes as she enters the house, leaving them where they land. Fender is lying in his usual spot in the hall. He opens one eye, then nuzzles his nose between his paws and goes back to sleep. The old Jack Russell terrier is blind and arthritic, so Lenny forgives his indifference. He only tolerates her because she feeds and walks him, but she's not who he's waiting for.

In the kitchen, she opens the parcel with a steak knife. Inside is a pair of men's high-tops, size 10. She examines the treads, then grabs the Polaroid camera from the top of the fridge. She takes a shot of the treads. As she fans the Polaroid paper, she tucks the shoes under one arm and heads down the narrow stairwell off the kitchen that leads to the back-door landing, then on down to the basement.

Lenny and Hank never got around to finishing their basement. Over the years, it filled with junk. Organizing and decluttering were never Lenny's strengths. It's a large space with rough floors that have deteriorated with time as shifting earth and moisture cracked the concrete. Cobwebbed fissures meander across the floor like a map. There are a gas furnace, water tank, washer and dryer, and fuse box at one end. Metal heating vents criss-cross the ceiling, and exposed water and sewage pipes run down the walls. There are storage shelves jammed with boxes, and propped in one corner are some fishing rods and an old wooden headboard. It looks like most old basements in their quiet Wellington Village neighborhood—except for one thing.

Displayed across the entire length of one of the mortared stone walls is a sprawling collection of photographs and papers. There are newspaper clippings, a map, a garbage collection schedule, Polaroids, and family photos, but what stands out most are the large crime scene photographs.

The strange collection looks haphazard, but there's order to the chaos. Each item has been stuck to the wall with a colored piece of duct tape—green, blue, yellow, pink, orange. And the items have been grouped by color. There's a crime scene photo at the heart of each grouping. These photos depict the same horrific scene from various angles—a woman lying in a pool of blood on a bathroom floor.

The crime scene photo stuck to the wall with yellow tape is a close-up on the tile floor where a bloody tread mark is clearly visible. The family photos grouped around it show a man, woman, and boy at a birthday, on an Easter egg hunt, and at a family barbecue. Scattered among the family photos are countless Polaroids of the soles of footwear.

Lenny steps closer to the wall. She holds up the high-tops and compares them to the family photos. She places them with dozens of other shoes, boots, and sandals, men's size 10, lined up at the foot of the wall. Lenny then compares the Polaroid in her hand to the tread mark in the crime scene photo. When she's completed her examination, she sticks the new Polaroid to the wall with yellow duct tape.

Lenny folds her arms, and she takes in the entire wall.

No luck this time.

She turns out the light and goes back upstairs.

3

The AA meeting is set to start at 8:00 p.m. Lenny gets to the McNabb Community Centre early. It's an unremarkable redbrick building on the edge of Chinatown on a residential street lined with run-down row houses. Close to downtown but off the beaten path. It looks like a high school built in the '60s. The stark room is painted a sickly pale yellow, and the fluorescent lights far from elevate the ambiance. Lenny sits in the last row of metal chairs, away from the others.

He goes to a meeting every Friday like clockwork. Always this location, this time. Predictably, he walks in as the Serenity Prayer ends. He likes to make an entrance. Heads turn. He apologizes for being late. His sandy-reddish hair has faded yellow with age, but the seventy-five-year-old still cuts a striking figure—square jawed and barrel chested. He's already removed his tailored suit jacket and rolled up his shirt sleeves. He's going for a man-of-the-people vibe.

He tips his chin to Lenny as he walks to the podium.

"My name is Reg Caffey, and I am an alcoholic," he begins.

The two dozen attendees answer in unison.

"Welcome, Reg." All except Lenny.

"It's been fifteen years since I last sipped the almighty gargle," he says, leaning heavily into the Irish lilt.

He might be the son of Irish immigrants, but Lenny knows the man has never stepped one of his fancy loafers on Irish soil.

"Fifteen years since I last saw my only son, Vincent," he says, emotion catching in his throat. "Boyo was in the prime of his life. A father himself. All set to follow in his old man's footsteps, he was. Then one day to the next . . ."

He shakes his head and hesitates. Lenny almost feels sorry for him. *Almost.*

"Now you fine folks are well aware of who I am." He smiles. "I might have a wee bit of a reputation about town."

They chuckle.

"But tonight, friends, I stand before you, a humble father. Lord knows I wasn't always a good one. I was hard on the boy, I'm ashamed to admit, but I loved him, and there isn't a day goes by, I don't think on him. It changes a person when they outlive their only child."

He looks at Lenny. She holds his gaze. They do have that in common.

"That's all I wanted to say. I appreciate you lending me your ear," he says, hand to heart.

When the meeting ends, a few people go over to pat Reg on the back. Lenny grabs a Styrofoam cup and pours coffee from a metal dispenser at the refreshment table. She waits for him to come over. He always does. It's their dance. Her, pretending that he's not the reason she's there. Him, acting like they're old friends.

"Eleanor," he says, coming up beside her.

"Reg," she replies with a cool nod.

He smooths his tie as he leans against the table, facing her.

"You should try getting up there to speak sometime," he says. "Cleanses the soul."

"My soul's beyond repair," she says, sipping the weak coffee.

"I doubt that, darlin'," he says with a wink.

Lenny hates that he can still make her blush. Reg folds his arms and sighs.

"Would it kill you to simply ask how the lad's doing?" he says. Reg nods to her cup. "He's the reason you suffer that shite."

Before she can answer, Reg's attention shifts to the exit. Lenny follows his gaze. Billy Rider is standing by the door. He's been Reg's right-hand man for years. He's signaling to Reg.

"No rest for the wicked," says Reg.

Then he's gone.

This is how it goes. A few words exchanged over stale coffee. Sometimes he feeds her a tiny morsel of information about her grandson and his two kids. Once, when Reg was feeling particularly generous, he gave her a photo of the twins from his wallet. The encounters might be fleeting, but something is better than nothing. And the AA meetings are neutral ground. When the meetings end, Reg and Lenny retreat to their separate worlds. In his world, he sees Juls and the girls every day. In hers, she only wishes she did.

Lenny crosses to the window and watches Reg approach his blue Mercedes sedan, Billy by his side. Reg's driver opens the back door for him. Out of nowhere, Reg turns to Billy and grabs him by the ear. Billy wriggles in pain as Reg leans close and says something before letting go. Billy holds his ear as he scurries off to his own car parked across the street.

Just before his driver closes the door, Lenny glimpses Reg's face.

It's not the face of a man who's found God.

But she knew that already.

Sometimes you have to dance with the devil to get what you need.

4

The Carleton Tavern is a circa-1935 fixture of Hintonburg, the neighborhood next to her own. It's a sticky, well-worn bar within stumbling distance of her house. The cozy tavern has a pool hall in the back where local cops gather, including some of the old guard from back in Hank's day.

Today, she drives straight to the tavern from the meeting instead of walking from her house. She needs a drink. Lenny parks across the street. A couple of off-duty cops stand outside smoking.

"Lenny," say the cops in unison, tipping their heads as she walks past.

"Slats. Wyatt," she says. They both trained and worked under Hank.

Inside, Lenny spots Sully in his usual spot at the end of the bar. He's busy typing something into his phone and doesn't see her. She heads over.

The bartender looks up as Lenny takes the stool next to Sully.

"I got a new pilsner on tap I think you're gonna like, Lenny," he says. "Light body. Touch bitter."

"Sounds perfect, Andy," she says. "And I'll take one of those too."

She points to the half-eaten plate of fish and chips in front of Sully.

The bartender nods, then heads to the taps. Sully puts his phone down and drains his Scotch.

"Andy, my man," Sully calls out. "Make it a pitcher and put it on my tab."

Lenny helps herself to Sully's fries. He turns and looks at her for the first time.

"You went again, didn't you?" he says.

She chews slowly and doesn't answer.

"I don't get it, Lenny," he says.

"You don't have to," she replies.

"You could just call Juls instead of begging for scraps from you-know-who," he suggests.

"Shouldn't you be back there playing with your balls?" she says, nodding to Sully's buddies in the pool hall.

Sully laughs. The bartender brings over the pitcher and two glasses. He pours, then heads to the kitchen.

"To a higher power," Sully says, raising his glass.

Lenny knows he's poking fun, but it's not like she ever pretended she was going to the meetings to get sober.

"Let's talk about something other than the almighty Regan Angus Caffey," she says.

"Okay, do-over," he says, holding up his glass. "To Birdie."

They toast. Birdie was Hank's nickname at the Ottawa Police Service. Sully was his partner for years. Real name: Terry Sullivan. Hank once told her he'd take a bullet for Sully.

When Lenny's meal arrives, they watch Formula 1 highlights on the TV above the bar. Sully loves racing. He hollers at the screen when his favorite driver aces his practice session. They order a second pitcher as the volume in the tavern rises with the thickening crowd. The alcohol softens the room, warms her insides, and makes her forget all about what day it is.

Sully heads to the men's room, forgetting his phone. It vibrates nonstop while he's gone. When he comes back, he's smiling.

"I just ran into a guy back there," he says. "Said he knew Birdie when they were rookies with the Vanier Police. Crazy. He still remembers him."

Lenny smiles. She's not surprised. Once you met Hank, he was hard to forget.

"That was Hank's first job," she says. "He got recruited straight out of high school after he didn't make the Carleton U football team. Back then his dream was either the CFL or being a cop. When football didn't pan out, Hank was all in. He never looked back."

"And what was Lenny Bird's dream in high school?" Sully asks.

"I wanted to be a forensic entomologist," she says.

"You?" he asks.

"Studying bugs to solve crimes?" she answers. "What's not to love about that?"

"I can think of a few things," he says with a laugh.

"*I* actually *did* go to university," says Lenny. "I was doing my undergrad in science when we got married, but I took a hiatus when I found out I was pregnant with Kendra."

"I didn't know that," he says. "You didn't go back when your daughter got older?"

"Hank's career took off. I guess mine got grounded somewhere along the way," she says.

"So no crime solving for Lenny Bird," he muses.

"I wouldn't say that. Hank used to bring his case files home all the time," she says. "Friday nights, we'd order Thai and mull over evidence for hours. I loved it. They were like puzzles with pieces missing. If you looked at them long enough, you'd start to see the cracks, you know?"

"That's right, Hank talked about that. Said you had a real knack," he says, smiling. "Said you'd have made a great detective."

"Sometimes I'd stay up late," she continues. "After Hank went to bed. I'd keep digging through all the reports, the witness statements, crime scene photos."

"Guess you weren't squeamish," he says.

"I'd seen lots of photos of corpses," she says.

"I won't ask." He laughs.

"You think some people just never find it?" she asks.

"What?" he says.

"The place where they fit. Hank fit," she says. "It's why he made detective at thirty. He always knew who he was, where he belonged."

"Birdie was lucky," says Sully. "In more ways than one, beautiful."

He gives her soupy eyes. She punches his shoulder, and he nearly falls off his barstool.

"You know what I love about you, Sully?" she says. "You never change."

He raises his glass.

"As Confucius said, *Only the wisest men never change*," he says.

He chugs his lager.

"I think it's *wisest and stupidest*," she says, correcting him.

"Ouch." He clutches his chest like he's been stabbed in the heart.

Lenny grabs the pitcher and pours the last of the lager into their glasses.

Sully's phone buzzes again.

"Antsy girlfriend?" She nods to the phone.

He smiles.

"I better take this, or I'll never hear the end of it," he says with a wink.

She waves for him to go. He heads outside. She wonders how young this one is.

"Come here often?" says a voice behind her.

Lenny turns. Apart from a few lines around her eyes, the petite Latina woman standing behind her looks almost exactly like she did when she was that young clerk Hank brought home for dinner three decades ago her first day on the job. It's what Hank did. He took newbies under his wing.

"Maya?" says Lenny. "Are civvies allowed in a cop bar?"

"You tell me," she says, leaning against Lenny. She's tipsy.

"*I'm* an honorary member," says Lenny. "Besides, this is *my* local watering hole. What's your excuse?"

"They forced me to come," she whispers, nodding to the back room. "I'd rather be curled up on my sofa eating Cheezies and watching my telenovela. But it's Bernsie's retirement party, and you know how that old fucker gets."

She rolls her eyes, then swings her arm over Lenny's shoulder.

"I wish I'd seen you earlier, but I really, really, really have to get home, *amiga*." Her breath is wine laden. "Early shift tomorrow."

Maya hugs Lenny, then backsteps toward the exit.

"But I will see *you* at boxing, right?" She smiles, putting up both fists.

Lenny raises her glass to her friend as Maya heads for the door. Through the tavern's front window, Lenny can see Sully talking on his phone. Doesn't look like it's going well with his latest squeeze. She glances at the TV screen as the racing coverage cuts to a live news broadcast. **Breaking News**. Flashing red-and-blue lights, tactical vehicles, and police tape encircle a warehouse. In the foreground, a clean-cut reporter is talking into his mic. Lenny can't hear what he's saying over the tavern ruckus. A banner pops up on the TV. It reads **Police Operation Underway in Ottawa's East End.**

Lenny is only half watching the screen as a group of men are marched out of the warehouse behind the reporter, cuffed behind their backs, each flanked by two officers dressed in gray tactical gear. She squints at the last man being led out.

Is that my grandson, Juls? Kendra's Juls?

The story cuts back to Formula 1 before she gets a better look.

Sully comes inside and sits down.

"Did you see Maya?" he asks.

She nods. Lenny doesn't tell him what she saw on the TV. She's not even sure she really saw it. Maybe it wasn't Juls. The last time Lenny saw him was sixteen months ago when he stopped by her house with his twins, Flo and Nora. The girls had just turned seven. Lenny had only met his daughters a handful of times. But it was Mother's Day. They came by with flowers. It had always been a hard day for both Lenny and Juls. Kendra wasn't just her daughter—she was his mother. This past Mother's Day, he'd left the flowers on her front porch.

Sully signals to the bartender that he wants to pay up.

"I'm gonna call it a night," says Sully.

"Me too," says Lenny.

Outside, Sully gives her a kiss on the cheek, then opens the door to his waiting cab.

"You sure you don't want me to drop you?" he offers. "It's no trouble."

"I can walk," she says.

"You're definitely not driving," he says, spotting her car across the street.

She shakes her head.

"I'll get it tomorrow," she says. "Don't worry. Now go. It'll be past your girlfriend's bedtime soon."

"See you on the flip side, Lenny," he says.

Sully jumps in and the cab drives off. Lenny crosses the street and checks that her car doors are locked before she heads home. As she steps onto the sidewalk, she notices a sign at the rear of her car. She's parked in a no-stopping zone. She scans the street. All the overnight parking spots are taken. She knows she'll get a ticket or, worse, get towed if she leaves it here. The street is quiet. She glances at the Carleton. No cops are outside smoking. Lenny quickly rifles through her purse for her keys and gets in her car. It's only three blocks.

What's the worst thing that could happen?

A block from her house, Lenny misjudges a turn, jumps the curb, careens across the sidewalk, and drives straight into a granite sculpture of an artichoke. Her head bounces off the steering wheel, then whips back. A car squeals to a stop, a blurry figure runs toward her, someone shouts as her horn blasts, and Lenny closes her eyes.

She had a feeling this day wouldn't leave her unscathed.

5

Three hours later, a nurse is checking Lenny's vitals as the emergency room doctor examines her x-rays.

"No broken bones," he says.

He shines a bright light in her eyes, then feels around her neck. The light makes her dizzy.

"Mild concussion. Whiplash," he says to the nurse.

"High blood pressure," adds the nurse.

He frowns as he flips through her chart.

"Eleanor Margaret Bird. Seventy," he says, pursing his lips.

He turns to the police constable who accompanied her from the scene of the accident. He's a pimple-faced rookie. Just a baby.

"Does she live on her own?" the doctor asks the baby cop.

"I do," says Lenny, trying to catch the doctor's eye.

Lenny's beginning to think she might be invisible. She checks her hands. The doctor fits her with a foam cervical collar and writes out prescriptions for diuretics and painkillers. He tells her not to take them with alcohol in her system. He can smell the lager on her breath. He hands her an AA pamphlet before leaving. *Subtle.*

The baby cop seems embarrassed. He blushes, then glances at the pretty nurse.

"I didn't bother ordering a BAC test," he whispers to the nurse.

Lenny knows what that is. A blood alcohol concentration test.

"No one was hurt," he says, shrugging to the nurse.

The nurse nods sympathetically, batting her long eyelashes.

"Takes all kinds, I guess," she says with a cute shrug.

What's that supposed to mean?

The baby cop turns to Lenny.

"Ma'am, I'm afraid I'm going to have to suspend your license for careless driving," he says in a loud voice like she's hard of hearing.

Lenny's about to protest when a stabbing pain in her neck stops her cold. She whimpers and keeps her mouth shut. She doesn't like it, but the alternative is a DUI charge. The baby cop tells Lenny that her Camry was towed to a scrapyard. He says it's a *total write-off.* She wonders if he and the nurse are thinking the same thing about her.

"I'd like to go home now," she says.

"Is there someone we can call to come get you?" asks the nurse.

Lenny stares at her blankly.

"I'm fine," she says.

"A relative, friend?" says the nurse.

"There's no one," snaps Lenny. "Just call me a bloody cab."

The nurse gives the constable an I-told-you-so look as she exits the exam room.

"My shift's ending," says the baby cop. "How 'bout I give you a lift home, ma'am?"

Before she can answer, the constable tells her he'll be right back. Lenny is pretty sure he's gone to get the pretty nurse's phone number. The second he disappears behind the curtains, Lenny pops a couple of pain pills to dull the humiliation.

She hears voices coming from the bed next to hers. Through a gap in the curtains, she can see a young woman crying. Mascara streaks her face. A man is comforting her, but his tone is impatient. Her father maybe. The woman is wearing a shimmering top and pink spandex leggings. She's just a teenager. The man has his back to Lenny. He says something about appendicitis, and this sets her off crying again. A nurse comes in to examine the girl, and the man steps out from behind the curtains to give them privacy. That's when Lenny sees his face. It's Billy Rider. Lenny tries to close the curtains around her bed, but he spots her.

"That you, Mrs. Bird?" he says.

He walks over, eyes darting left and right. Billy's always been twitchy.

"You don't look so hot," he says.

"You should see the other guy," she mumbles.

She sits straighter, trying to look sober and less pathetic.

Billy shifts from one foot to the other. He's vibrating. Probably high.

"We've missed you down at the Nelson," he says. "Shame you don't come by no more."

He knows why.

"I got busy," she says.

"Too busy to break bread with family?" he asks with a smirk.

Billy isn't family. He's a sewer rat Reg found in the gutter when he was a kid. A low-life street punk who now runs Reg's strip club, the Full Nelson. She's never liked him. He's the one who convinced Juls to quit high school and come work for him as a bouncer.

Billy absentmindedly peruses her chart. His hands tremble slightly. She feels exposed.

"Don't touch that. It's mine," she says, slurring her words.

"Guess the AA meeting didn't take," he says.

Reg must have told him about her being there. Now she feels even more pathetic.

Lenny suddenly feels sick. Her head is spinning. The beer and pills aren't helping her concussed brain.

Where is that damn baby cop?

She swings her legs to the floor but nearly passes out. She grips the bed as nausea rises in her throat. Billy reaches for her arm to steady her. She pulls away.

"You alone?" he asks.

He knows damn well she's all alone. It's all his fault. Lenny sees red.

"You wouldn't dare touch me if Hank were here," she says.

"I meant nothing," he says.

"You'd end up like the other one," she says, glaring at him.

Billy looks at her. Before he can ask her what she's talking about, the constable appears.

"Everything okay here?" he asks, glancing from Lenny to Billy.

"Just a friendly chat, officer," says Billy. "We're old pals. You take care, Mrs. Bird."

Billy gives the constable a salute and slips behind the curtain.

Lenny's ears are ringing. She lets the baby cop guide her by the hand. She lets her mind go numb as drugs and booze slosh around in her bloodstream.

When Lenny gets home, it's well past midnight. Fender is stretched out in the hall, belly up. He rolls over, gets to his feet, and circles. She knows what that means. She also knows she won't make it around the block, so she takes him out to the backyard. The dog disappears into the shadows of the garden.

As Lenny slumps into her wicker chair on the patio, she spots the silhouette of her Japanese wisteria, like a sentry in the back corner. It has grown tall and strong in the last fifteen years. Its vines have crept along the fence, and each spring it makes a spectacle of itself when it blooms. But what rankles her most is the second flush of purple blossoms that cascade down the fence like festive garlands every fall, taunting her.

Fender reappears, and together they stumble toward the house. Just as she's reaching for the door handle, a sound startles her. She turns. It came from the back corner of her garden. She looks in that direction. A tangle of daylilies obscures her view of the old shed, and honeysuckles camouflage the pathways. But high above the trees, she can see that irrepressible wisteria.

She realizes the sound was a memory.

It's the same one that rustles through the buckthorns every September. It comes accompanied by visions of blood and bruises and a trail of drag marks she can never unsee. It is the sound of his body falling into the hole with a wretched thud.

Lenny gags. When she goes into the house, she doesn't notice the blinking light that tells her there're a half dozen new messages on her old answering machine—the one that still plays the original greeting Hank recorded when they first bought it.

You've reached Hank and Lenny. Please leave a message after the beep. We'll get back to you when hell freezes over.

Following the greeting, Hank lets out one of his trademark guttural laughs.

Lenny washes down more painkillers with some amber ale, tosses the neck brace onto the table, and heads for the door to the garage. Fender is back in his spot in the hallway. He lets out a weak growl as she opens the door. He doesn't like when it's opened, and he never goes inside with her. Lenny closes it behind her, turns on the overhead light in the garage, then climbs into the passenger side of Hank's Jeep Renegade. It was brand new when he bought it two decades ago. A gift to himself when he made sergeant. It hasn't been driven in fifteen years. Lenny takes another sip of beer, then turns to look at the empty driver's seat.

"I think I messed up," she says.

Hank doesn't answer.

6

Fifteen years ago

He gave her his jacket. She shrugged it around her shivering shoulders. The tips of her fingers were white. He rubbed them between his own to warm them and cranked the heat in the squad car. It was a blustery, cold day in late January. Tears were frozen to her cheeks and eyelashes. Her new winter coat was ruined. It lay in a puddle of frozen slush in the Walmart parking lot where her boyfriend had tossed it after he tore it off her. He'd driven over it as he left. She thought he'd come back in a few minutes once he cooled off, but he didn't. He left her there without a coat or purse or phone. She'd borrowed a stranger's phone. One of the bystanders who'd watched him yell at her, then shove her against the car. The bystander had tried to step in but backed off when he saw the gun inside her boyfriend's jacket.

The cop had been on a call not far away and came as soon as his daughter called. She begged him not to tell her mother. He promised he wouldn't, like he always did. They sat in the car until her tears stopped and her hands warmed.

Then she asked him to take her back to the apartment where she lived with her boyfriend.

Like she always did.

7

The morning after her encounter with the granite artichoke, Lenny opens her sticky eyes. She hasn't moved a muscle all night. Her body is slumped in the passenger seat of the Jeep, one leg hanging out. Her head and neck are throbbing. Lenny slowly pulls herself from the vehicle, goes into the house, and finds the bottle of painkillers. She can't believe it's already eleven. She washes down three with the dregs of last night's ale, then puts on the brace. The relief is instantaneous as the muscles in her neck relax.

Lenny realizes there's no way she can visit her father. Not for a few days. Not like this. Silas probably won't even register her absence, but it's worth a quick call to Maplelawn. When Lenny reaches for her landline, she notices the answering machine flashing.

She presses play. There are six new messages. All from Juls.

In the first few, he sounds irritated that she's not picking up, but in the last one, his voice is panicked. He's in trouble. Old feelings come rushing back. He might be twenty-five, but he'll always be that beautiful, brown-eyed baby with the shock of curly dark hair who stole her heart the moment she saw him.

Lenny tries his cell, but he doesn't answer. The second she hangs up, her landline rings.

"Lenny, thank Christ," says Juls.

He's always called her Lenny. Not Grannie or Grandma or Gran. Just Lenny.

"I've been trying to reach you for twelve fucking hours," he says.

"I'm sorry," says Lenny.

"Listen, I've been arrested," he says.

Lenny's foggy brain recalls the news story she saw on TV last night. It *was* him.

"I'm at the detention center out on Innis." He goes on. "They're saying I'm going to be here a few days."

"What happened, Juls?" she asks.

"I don't have much time," he says. "My bail hearing is set for Monday at ten a.m. at the courthouse. I need you to go get the girls, right now. Watch them for the weekend, then take them to school Monday morning. That's it."

"Why can't Rudi-Rose?" asks Lenny. "She *is* their mother."

"Listen, can you do it or not?" he snaps.

Rudi-Rose must be up to her old tricks. His girlfriend has a habit of going AWOL every few months. It's always gnawed at Lenny knowing her great-granddaughters probably spend more time in the seedy back rooms of a strip club than they do at home.

"Lenny," he says, his voice shaky.

Juls has never asked her to babysit. Not once. And Lenny never offered. But he's asking now.

"Okay," says Lenny, before she can change her mind. "Where are they?"

"At the Nelson," he says.

Just like she thought.

"Talk to Sugar," says Juls. "She's keeping an eye on them, but I don't want them around that fucking place."

"Little late for that," says Lenny, under her breath.

She regrets the dig. Juls sounds scared. A loud voice booms in the background of the call.

"My time's up," he says. "All you have to do is keep them safe for the weekend, then drop them at school for me. I can get them from there once I get out on bail."

Keep them safe?

"What's going on, Juls?" she asks.

"Lenny, please," he says. "I need you right now. Don't let anyone stop you, hear me? No one. Not even him."

Lenny swallows hard. He means Reg Caffey. Something is very wrong.

"I hear you," she says. "I'm on it."

He hangs up.

That's when Lenny remembers her Camry is in the scrapyard.

8

An hour later, the taxi pulls up to a drab stone building at the sketchy end of Dalhousie, far from the upscale ByWard Market restaurants and nightclubs, down where after-hours clubs and boarded-up shops abound. A neon sign out front says **The Full Nelson**. The double *L*'s are shaped like a pair of women's legs in fishnet stockings.

"You sure this is the place, lady?" the cabbie asks Lenny.

"I'll be right back," she says.

"Your dime," he tells her as he flips on his four-ways.

Lenny jumps out. Her neck aches without the brace, but there is no way she is showing up wearing that thing. Lenny pushes back her shoulders and prepares to enter the lion's den. It's just past noon when she walks through the front doors of the Full Nelson. A bouncer sits in the lobby just inside the door. He looks up from his phone, furrows his brow, then looks back down. This guy's new.

She enters the club. Spotlights zigzag across center stage, where a dancer twirls effortlessly around a pole wearing nothing but a G-string and pasties. The Saturday lunch crowd seems less interested in the woman's acrobatics than jockeying for a spot at the all-you-can-eat buffet.

Lenny holds her breath as she scans the familiar, windowless room. She knows it well.

No lions in sight.

Billy manages the club, and she knows Reg Caffey keeps an office in the back as a base of operations for all of his business ventures—the legitimate and the not so legitimate.

So far, so good.

A few patrons glance her way. A beefy man with tattoos eyes her. He's standing in the corner, arms folded. She doesn't know this one either. She's only ever been to the club after hours for a few of Reg's private holiday gatherings with his inner circle—when she used to be part of that circle. Lenny avoids eye contact with the bouncer. Her heart pounds against her ribs.

Keep them safe.

She searches the dimly lit room for the girls but can't see them. A bartender is polishing a stainless steel draft tower with a rag. He's chatting with two women perched at the wood. One wears a sequin top and matching short shorts. She's rail thin and looks young. The other one is in her late twenties. She wears a skintight leopard print bodysuit. Her ample bosom rests on the bar. The bartender's eyebrows lift when he spots Lenny heading his way.

"You take a wrong turn, lady?" he asks, snickering under his breath.

The women glance over. The older one takes in Lenny, head to foot.

"Looking for a job, dollface?" she asks.

The younger one giggles. Lenny recognizes her. It's the girl who was in the ER with Billy.

"I'm looking for Sugar," says Lenny.

"Ain't we all," says the bartender with a chuckle.

"Lenny!" screams Flo.

The eight-year-old's curly mop of hair pops up from a booth at the end of the bar.

They're here, thank God.

Flo jumps to the floor, races toward her great-grandmother, and wraps herself around Lenny's legs. Lenny struggles to hold on to the girl as her neck screams.

"Easy, honey," says Lenny.

Nora is peeking over the booth to see where her sister's gone.

"You know her, kid?" the bartender asks Flo.

"It's Lenny," says Flo.

"I'm her great-grandmother," says Lenny.

Lenny releases Flo to the floor, leaning close to the girl.

"Get your sister," she whispers in Flo's ear.

Flo scampers away.

"So you're the famous Lenny Bird," says the leopard-skinned woman as she slides off her barstool and struts over to Lenny.

"I'm Sugar," she says, hands on hips.

Lenny can feel her palms sweating.

This will all be over soon. Stay calm. Smile.

"Thanks for watching them," says Lenny, trying to keep her voice steady. "Juls sent me for the girls."

"Did he?" says Sugar, swaying her hips. "Guess he forgot to tell me. Let's check with the boss on that one."

She nods to the bartender. He flicks the skinny girl's arm. She has a nasty bruise on her elbow. She cowers a little at his touch, then skitters off toward a hallway at the back of the bar. Lenny doesn't know if Sugar is talking about Billy or Reg, but she isn't sticking around to find out which lion is in.

Flo is dragging Nora toward Lenny.

"Nora, Flo," says Lenny. "Your dad wants you to come stay at my house for a bit."

"Yay," says Flo, bouncing on her toes.

"Where's Daddy?" asks Nora, arms folded tight.

"I'll tell you later," says Lenny, fake smiling. "Let's get going."

Sugar doesn't take her eyes off Lenny.

"We need to get our stuff," says Nora.

Flo races back to the booth, and Nora follows her sister at a snail's pace.

"You can get it later," Lenny calls out.

The bartender comes out from behind the bar and joins Sugar. He's still holding the rag, only now he's twisting it with his hands like he's about to strangle her with it. Lenny rubs her neck involuntarily. Her hands are shaking.

"What's the hurry?" he asks Lenny.

Lenny glances at the girls. They're shoving their things into backpacks. Nora is taking her time, being meticulous about how she packs her stuff. Lenny spots movement in her periphery. The tattooed ape is slowly making his way through the tables in her direction. Lenny's heart feels like it might burst.

"What exactly did Juls tell you?" asks Sugar.

"Just that he's busy this weekend and needs me to babysit," says Lenny, swallowing hard.

"I think I got that covered," says Sugar.

"We know how to take care of little girls, don't we, Sugar?" says the bartender.

Something about the way he says *little girls* makes Lenny's skin crawl.

The twins appear at Lenny's side. She grabs their hands. As she does, Flo's backpack spills off her shoulder. It hits the floor, and Sugar reaches for it. Lenny does the same. They both tug on it, nose to nose.

"I'm not leaving without the girls," says Lenny, holding Sugar's gaze.

Lenny feels like she might pass out, but she holds firm. The girls stare up at the two women, not sure what's going on. Sugar tips her head to one side, then releases her grip.

"Juls said you were a rare bird," says Sugar. A little smile touches her lips.

The bartender signals to someone over Lenny's shoulder. She turns to leave, clutching the backpack to her chest. She steers the girls toward the lobby. Lenny glances back. She wishes she hadn't. She sees a large silhouette emerging from a dark hallway. A spotlight crosses his face. It's Reg Caffey. Their eyes meet. Billy trails behind him with the girl.

Lenny turns away. That's when she slams into the massive chest of the tattooed ape. The twins look up at him. He blocks the exit.

Don't let anyone stop you.

There's no time to think. Lenny thrusts the backpack into the ape's arms, then clings to one of his giant biceps, pulling him close to her bosom. She gazes up at him with a sweet-as-pie smile as she gently wheels him around to face the exit.

"Oh, it's so kind of you to help, my dear," she tweets. "Thank you so, so much. The meter's running, and Lord knows I can't carry this *and* lasso these two little ones all by my lonesome. Off we go then. Let's scooch. There's a good boy."

The ape looks confused but does as he's told. He ushers Lenny and the girls from the club, past the bouncer in the lobby, and out the front doors. He even helps them into the waiting cab and closes the door for them. Flo waves from the back seat as the cab pulls away.

He waves back, not quite sure what just happened.

9

By the time they get home, the pain in Lenny's neck is alive and kicking. On the plus side, her heart rate has gone back to normal—normal for someone with high blood pressure.

"Why is your house so messy?"

It's the first thing Nora says when they walk in the front door. Typical Nora. Lenny might not have spent much time with the twins, but it's always been easy to tell them apart. From the get-go, their distinctive personalities were fully baked in. Nora Caffey has always been the smart, sensible, serious one, while Florence Caffey was born with a silly, happy-go-lucky, impulsive streak.

From her front entryway, Lenny looks through the living room to her kitchen. Nora has a point. Dirty dishes litter the counter. Random pillows and blankets are strewn across the living room furniture. Circular stains left by beer cans decorate the dusty coffee table, and dog hair gathers in the corners like tumbleweeds. Lenny makes a beeline for the sofa and puts on her neck brace.

"Wowsie," says Flo. "What happened to you, Lenny?"

"Oh, this? It's nothing," says Lenny. "Wrenched my neck vacuuming."

Nora scans the dirty carpet and scrunches her nose.

"Why are *you* taking care of us?" asks Nora, hands on hips.

Fair question.

"Because your mom's away," Lenny answers. "And I want to."

"You don't *look* like you want to," says Nora.

She's not wrong.

"Flo, be a dear and grab me a beer from the fridge," says Lenny. "The cream ale."

"Cream! Yum. Daddy says you like your beer," says Flo, skipping off to the kitchen.

"Where did you say he was again?" asks Nora, folding her arms.

"Toronto," says Lenny. "I told you in the cab. A last-minute job. He'll be back Monday."

It was easier than the truth. She didn't want questions or tears all weekend.

Flo bounces into the room with the beer. Fender trails at her heels.

"I have the best idea ever," says Flo, handing Lenny the can. "*We* should take care of *you*. Not the other way round."

Lenny points to the bottle of painkillers on the coffee table. Flo hands them to her, then starts spinning circles on the living room carpet like a whirling dervish. Fender takes cover. Lenny pops some pills and chases them down with the ice-cold beer.

"Should you be drink—?" Before Nora can finish her sentence, Flo pipes in.

"What do you say, Nor?" says Flo, clinging to her sister. "We can be the grown-ups! It'll be super fun."

Nora does not look amused.

"*You* can be in charge, Nor," says Flo with a toothy grin.

Flo knows her sister. The wheels start turning. The neat freak in Nora wins out.

"Okay, but we start by getting rid of all the yuck," says Nora.

Lenny doesn't care what the girls do as long as she can put her feet up. She settles back and watches Nora through the archway as she tackles the dirty dishes, then wipes down the counters. She even cleans under the toaster with the dishcloth. First time that's been done in twenty years.

Flo isn't pitching in to help her sister. Instead, she's holding Fender's paws and trying to get the poor creature to dance. Lenny feels for Nora.

Her twin sister, Flo, seems destined to float through life. Nora looks like she'll carry the weight of it on her tiny shoulders.

Later, Flo browses through Lenny's ancient VHS collection while Nora takes charge of dinner. She finds a pizza menu on Lenny's front hall table and phones in their order.

"They said thirty minutes or it's free, so I'm timing them," says Nora. "I ordered a large Hawaiian with extra garlic dipping sauce."

"Hula Hawaiian hammy for the whole fammy," sings Flo.

Nora counts out the exact change to the nickel from Lenny's wallet. Meanwhile, Flo has chosen her movie and is busying herself with seeing how long she can stand on her head.

"*Elf*? We can't watch a Christmas movie in September," says Nora, holding up the tape.

"Why not?" asks Flo.

"Because it's not snowing yet," says Nora.

The twins are still arguing about the movie when the pizza arrives. Nora looks disappointed it's on time. After one bite, exhaustion, cream ale, and opioids lull Lenny into a coma.

She has no idea how long she's been out when the sound of Hank's familiar gravelly voice yanks her from the depths. Lenny thinks she's dreaming until she opens her eyes. Nora and Flo are lying on their bellies on the living room carpet facing the TV, chins propped in their hands. They're playing a video on her old VCR. At first, she doesn't know what they're watching, then the footage tumbles her back in time.

The camera is shaky like someone is holding it while they walk. The shot moves closer to the boy as he opens the lid of a box that's sitting in the hallway of Lenny's house. A small brown-and-white furry head pops out. The boy gasps and looks at the camera.

"It's a puppy?" says ten-year-old Juls.

"Now how did that little critter get inside there?" says Hank's voice.

He's the one filming Juls as he lifts the puppy from the box.

"Hank." It's Lenny's voice.

The camera pans to Lenny. She's standing in the hall. Fifty-five. Hands on hips.

"We didn't talk about this," she says, under her breath.

The camera pans back to the boy. He's cradling the puppy, laughing as it licks his chin.

"Can I keep him?" asks the boy, eyes wide.

"He's all yours, bud," says Hank.

A burst of static buzzes across the screen, then another recording cuts in. In this one, young Juls is in the backyard. He has a leash on the puppy, and he's leading him across the patio.

"See, he's getting better at it," says the boy.

The little dog bonks into a chair leg. Hank can be heard laughing.

"Poor little guy should've been born with fenders," says Hank.

Juls looks toward the camera, then back at his puppy.

"Fender!" he says. "That's his name."

The boy kneels and cups the puppy's face.

Lenny wipes drool from her mouth and sits up on the sofa.

"What are you doing?" she asks.

Flo spins around.

"You're awake," says Flo, jumping to her feet.

"We ate the rest of the pizza," says Nora, not taking her eyes off the video.

"Where did you find that video?" asks Lenny.

"There's a whole box of them," says Flo, launching herself onto the sofa.

Lenny spots the cardboard box marked *Bird Watching*.

"But there aren't any birds in these videos," says Flo.

"Duh, it's their last name," says Nora.

Lenny carefully removes the neck brace.

"It was a joke," says Lenny. "It's what Hank called his home movies."

Flo looks at the TV when she hears laughter. In the video, young Juls is lying on his back, and Fender is biting his ear.

"Is this when Daddy came to live with you after his mummy died?" she asks.

Lenny ignores the question.

"Time to turn that off. You girls should get to bed," says Lenny. "It's late."

"You know there's nothing in your fridge but beer," says Nora, not turning off the TV.

Flo turns upside down, legs on the sofa back, head dangling off the edge.

"What's all that stuff on the wall in your basement?" asks Flo.

Lenny stiffens. *Damn it.* They've been in the basement. Of course. That's where she stowed away the box of home movies years ago.

"We were down there looking for sleeping bags," says Flo. "For our campout."

Upside down, Flo points her toe to the blanket fort she's built under the kitchen table.

"It looks like an evidence wall to me," says Nora, eyes still glued to the TV.

Flo tumbles off the sofa and flops down beside her sister.

"Oh, like Pippa's wall," says Flo. "You know, from *A Good Girl's Guide to Murder*."

"I know who Pippa is. I've read the books," says Nora.

Lenny has no idea who they're talking about.

"I bet Lenny's a detective," says Flo. "Like Pippa."

"She's too old to be a detective," says Nora.

Flo shrugs, and both girls' attention is drawn back to the home movie of Juls playing with his puppy. They giggle as they watch their father as a young boy. They're fine. Lenny relaxes. They might have glanced at her wall, but the girls don't seem at all fazed by the graphic images displayed across it. Maybe they thought it was make-believe like in their books. She lets it go.

One more day and they'll be out of her hair.

10

Sunday morning, Lenny takes the twins to visit her father to kill time. They ride the city bus to Maplelawn Manor. Chelsea at reception signs in the new guests as Lenny introduces her great-granddaughters. Chelsea gives each girl a lollipop and pats their heads. Her father's face brightens the moment the twins walk into his room. Lenny can't believe he recognizes them, having only met them twice for Thanksgiving dinner at her house.

"If it isn't Flossie and Freddie," he says with a wide smile.

The girls giggle at his Bobbsey Twins joke.

"Am I Freddie?" asks Flo, smiling ear to ear as she plunks down at his feet.

"You tell me," he says with a grin as he touches her nose.

Flo and Silas trade goofy faces as Nora settles into the other chair. Lenny passes Nora a pencil and the *Ottawa Citizen* she brought from home.

"He likes doing the crossword," says Lenny. "Why don't you read out the clues?"

Nora jumps at the chance to be the one in control. Lenny sits back on her father's bed, watching the girls vie for his attention. He gives it freely, unlike when she was a girl.

"Something with a lot of twists and turns," says Nora, reading a clue.

"Roller coaster!" hollers Flo, bouncing on her knees.

"It starts with an *M*," says Nora.

"Mystery," says Lenny.

"Four letters," says Nora.

"Murder," says Silas.

"Moat?" says Lenny.

"Murder," Silas repeats, louder this time.

"It's *not* murder, Dad," says Lenny.

"It *is*," he shouts. "It *is* murder."

Nora sighs. He's not playing by the rules.

"Wait. I've got it," shrieks Flo. "Maze!"

Nora stares at her sister, stunned.

"That's it, Flo," she says. "Good one."

Silas stares at her.

"'One for sorrow, two for joy, three for a girl, four for a boy,'" sings Silas.

"A poem!" cries Flo, jumping to her feet. "I like poems. Did you make it up?"

"Don't be ridiculous," he yells.

Flo shrinks back.

"It's a bloody nursery rhyme," he says, looking at Lenny. "You remember, Peg. You sang it to Lenny when she was a baby."

Silas scowls and balls up his trembling fists. The twins don't move. They stare at Lenny. She nods to the door. The visit's over.

On the bus ride home, Nora looks up from her book.

"What's wrong with him?" asks Nora.

"Dementia," says Lenny. "He's also ninety-five."

"How old are you?" asks Flo.

Nora elbows Flo.

"It's okay," says Lenny. "I turned seventy this year."

"Wowsie," says Flo. "You don't look that old."

"How old do I look?" asks Lenny.

"Forty-two," says Flo without hesitation.

Lenny bursts out laughing. Suddenly they both can't stop. Nora sinks low in her seat as other riders look over. When their giggle fit subsides, Lenny puts her arm around Flo.

"Thanks, Flo," she says. "I needed that."

They hop off the bus at the Metro Grocery, and Lenny lets the girls pick whatever they want for dinner. Flo chooses cupcakes and Nora, a Greek salad kit. Lenny grabs a frozen lasagna to round things out. They walk home, passing the elementary school where her daughter, Kendra, went. This reminds Lenny that she has to get the twins to school tomorrow. Busing to Lowertown will take hours, but she can't keep them at home. She has somewhere to be. She'll have to hire a cab. Then a better idea comes to her.

There's a perfectly good vehicle sitting in her garage.

11

That afternoon, while the girls play with Fender in the backyard, Lenny walks over to the Petro-Canada at the corner of Parkdale Avenue. She buys motor oil and a plastic can of unleaded gas. Back home, she spends the afternoon tuning up the Jeep.

Without Hank around, Lenny learned how to fix things on her own. Things Hank used to do for her. When the lawn mower broke, she took it apart and put it back together, and it worked better than ever. When the front doorbell stopped ringing, she reconnected it. She even taught herself how to change the oil and swap out the wipers on her Camry. Lenny can't find the Jeep's manual, but it can't be so different. Who cares if it hasn't been driven in fifteen years?

Lenny siphons out the old gas and tops up the tank with the new. The gas station attendant told her this would be a good idea if the vehicle had sat idle for that long. She changes the oil, then does some light cleaning and lubricating. Sitting in the driver's seat, she holds her breath and turns the key. After a couple of pumps of the gas pedal, the engine sputters to life. A few warning lights flicker on the dashboard, but it's running. Just as she thought. *Perfectly good.*

Monday morning, Lenny drives the girls to York Street Public School. It's only when they're on the road that she remembers she doesn't have a license. Somehow this vital piece of information slipped through the cracks of her not-so-perfectly-good brain.

An acidic smell is leaching from the bowels of the Jeep as she pulls up to the school. Lenny is pretty sure it's the battery. The stench has given her a raging headache. Other cars maneuver for spots out front as the bell rings. A school bus pulls up behind her. The driver lays on his horn. Lenny turns to glare at his angry face, then notices she's parked in the bus zone. The girls jump out. Nora's face is bright red; she's embarrassed Lenny has dropped them in the wrong spot. Flo has already inserted herself into a huddle of squealing girls. Nora knocks on the passenger window. Lenny rolls it down.

"Is Daddy in trouble?" Nora asks.

Nothing gets past this one.

"To be honest, I don't really know," says Lenny.

Nora's lower lip trembles. Lenny realizes the girl is looking for comfort, not truth.

"But I'm sure he's fine," says Lenny, backtracking. "He'll pick you up after school."

The bus driver honks again.

Nora opens her mouth to say something, but Lenny hits the gas. The fan belt screeches as the Jeep peels away. The sharp sound pierces Lenny's splitting head. She pops more painkillers on the way to the Ottawa Courthouse.

Lenny finds a spot in the underground parking garage. It's almost ten. She's woozy as she finds her way to the courtroom. She opens the door and spots Juls at the front. She'd know that curly brown head anywhere. He's standing next to a man wearing an expensive navy suit. One of Reg Caffey's high-priced lawyers. Reg is nowhere to be seen, but his sidekick is there. Billy has one hand on the back of Juls' neck. He pulls him close so their foreheads touch. It's an intimate gesture. Then Billy lets go and steps away. She hates that her grandson is close to that lowlife.

The heavy door slams behind her. Heads turn, Juls' included. He shoots her a what-the-fuck-are-you-doing-here look. The room swims. Lenny slides into a bench in the back row.

The justice of the peace calls the hearing to order and begins by reviewing the criminal record of the accused, Julian Vincent Caffey. Assault. Battery. Drug possession. Weapons charges. Disturbing the peace. Juls glances at Lenny, then looks away. He stands up as the new charges against him are read. Carrying a concealed weapon, resisting arrest.

Lenny's throat is bone dry. One of the ceiling lights is flickering, and she's seeing stars. She grips the bench. She feels like she's sitting on a rocking boat. Someone slides down the bench toward her. She looks over. It's Billy Rider. He moves closer, keeping his gaze on the front of the courtroom. He stinks of cigarettes. She feels bile and panic rising in her throat.

"We gotta stop meeting like this, Mrs. Bird," he whispers.

Lenny glances at Billy. He's close to fifty, but his boyish face makes him look younger. She notices small tremors pulsating through Billy's limbs like electricity.

Juls' lawyer is talking, but Lenny's having a hard time focusing on his words. The lawyer is saying something about Julian being a family man with a good job. An upstanding citizen. Ties to the community. Poses no flight risk.

"How's the neck?" says Billy.

She ignores him.

"I been thinking a lot about the other night in the ER," he says. "What you said."

Now the justice is speaking, but her words sound like mud. Lenny's attention is laser focused on Billy. Sweat forms on her upper lip.

"I wasn't myself," says Lenny.

"Now that's where I think you're wrong," he says. "I got the feeling that was the real Lenny Bird I was talking to for once."

The justice raises her voice, and it brings both their attentions back to the room. She's addressing the entire courtroom, but neither of them heard what she said. The justice repeats her question.

"Is the person responsible for Mr. Caffey present in the courtroom?" she asks, an edge of impatience in her voice.

Billy whispers in Lenny's ear.

"Nice chatting with you, Mrs. Bird," he says. "We'll pick this up later."

He rises and straightens his wrinkled suit jacket.

"That'd be me, Your Honor," says Billy. "Mr. Billy Rider, madam."

Before she can stop herself, Lenny is on her feet.

"Or me," she says, holding up her hand.

Billy turns to look at her. Juls stares at Lenny.

"And you are?" the justice asks.

"I'm his employer, Your Honor," says Billy. "I represent the Caffey family. I'm here on behalf of his paternal grandfather, Reg Caffey."

"I know who you are, Mr. Rider. I wasn't talking to you," says the justice.

She nods to Lenny.

"Eleanor Bird," says Lenny. "I'm Julian's grandmother, on his *mother's* side. I raised him since he was ten."

"And I took over when he was sixteen," mutters Billy.

The justice glares at Billy.

"Kindly sit down and be quiet, Mr. Rider," she says. "Clearly you were not paying attention during my previous instructions."

He hesitates, then sits. The justice continues.

"As I stated, the accused has been granted bail on the condition that he not go within one hundred yards of any business or residence owned by the Caffey organization or within one hundred yards of any known *associate* of Mr. Regan Angus Caffey. Which means, Mr. Rider, that *you* cannot be responsible for Julian Caffey under these conditions since, as you said yourself, you represent the Caffey family."

Billy opens his mouth to speak but thinks better of it.

"Mrs. Bird," says the justice.

The justice looks down at a document in front of her and reads from it.

"Are you willing to take responsibility for the accused, ensure that he shows up for all court appearances, and honors the conditions of his bail as laid out by this court, and furthermore, are you willing to house the accused at your place of residence until such time as his trial has concluded?" she asks.

Lenny grips the bench in front of her.

"Mrs. Bird?" repeats the justice.

Juls is looking at her, shaking his head.

Lenny nods to the justice.

"I'll need verbal confirmation, Mrs. Bird," says the justice.

This is a mistake. It should be Billy.

Lenny looks to her right. Billy is gone.

"Mrs. Bird?" says the justice.

"I am," she says. "I am responsible."

Juls lowers his head.

"Very well, bail is granted," says the justice. "You're free to go, Mr. Caffey."

The justice bangs her gavel.

The sound echoes in Lenny's ear.

12

Fifteen years ago

The nurse directed him to the examination room. She was sitting on the edge of the bed with her back to him when he approached. She glanced up. Her long, dark hair covered half her face. He spotted the splint wrapped around her index finger. A dark-purple bruise splayed across the back of her hand, which shook violently. She couldn't control it. The boy sat in a chair across from his mother. He was biting the skin around his fingernails. His legs swung as his gaze stayed fixed on the shiny floor. The doctor came in and handed her a prescription for painkillers. At first, she refused it. He told her the finger was broken. The car door crushed multiple bones in her hand. She'd need it for the pain. She took the prescription from him, but when he left, she tossed it in the garbage can in the corner. He knew why. She couldn't risk putting any drugs in her system.

He didn't drive them back to their apartment, like she asked. Not right away. Instead, he took them out for pizza at Heartbreakers. The boy ordered a small pineapple pie. She didn't want anything. They sat together at a window table watching the snow fall. When the boy was done eating, he ran outside to go see a golden retriever. Through the window, they watched as the boy knelt next to the dog and petted its head. The dog's entire body wiggled with joy. A young boy about the same age was walking the dog. The two boys talked and laughed as the dog jumped at their chests. Tears filled her eyes as she watched her son.

When she finally spoke, she said it was her fault.

All he could do was put his arm around his daughter. He was too angry for tears.

13

After taking care of the paperwork at the courthouse, Juls and Lenny had swung by his apartment to pick up a few things for the girls, and to get his Mustang. Technically, Juls wasn't supposed to go there since Reg Caffey owned the building where he lived, but the Jeep was spewing black exhaust, and Juls wanted his own car.

Now that they're back at her house, reality is sinking in for both of them. Juls tries to help Lenny put on the neck brace. She pushes his fumbling hands away. She wishes he'd stop fussing. Ever since she told him how she got the nasty bruise on her forehead, he's been treating her like a geriatric patient.

"Just get me a beer, Juls," she says.

"Aren't you on pain meds?" he asks.

Lenny glares at him. Juls does as he's told.

"There should be a couple of spiced brown ales in the fridge door," she shouts.

Juls brings two cans into the living room and sits next to Lenny on the sofa. Fender has been trailing after him ever since he came through the door. The old dog rests his chin on Juls' knee. Juls scratches his scruffy little head.

"You gonna tell me what *really* happened?" Juls asks.

"I told you. It was a minor fender bender," she says.

"You took out a giant avocado and totaled your car," he reminds her.

"It was an artichoke," she says. "I did the neighborhood a favor."

"What did they say in the ER?" he asks, his leg bouncing. "Should you even be driving?"

Lenny takes a sip of her beer and doesn't answer.

Why should she? It's not like he's told her anything about his arrest.

"And driving around in that Jeep. What were you thinking?" he says. "What if something had happened?"

"To the girls, you mean," she says.

His leg stops bouncing.

"I was worried about you, Lenny," he says. "I couldn't reach you for hours. I told you to get a cell phone."

"Like you ever call me," she grumbles.

"What if you fell or something?" he continues.

"Fell?" she says, with a snort. "I'm not on the verge of breaking a bloody hip."

Lenny slams her beer on the coffee table. Her neck tweaks, which makes her even angrier.

"Why is everyone treating me like an invalid?" she says. "Like I shouldn't be living in my own house or driving my own car. I am not *invalid.* I am completely and utterly *valid.* And my driver's license should be too."

Juls tips his head like he's not sure he's heard her right.

"Tell me you still have your driver's license," he says.

Lenny waves her hand like she's swatting at a fly.

"Jesus, Lenny." He sighs. "Were you drinking when you hit that artichoke?"

"For your information, I did get a cell phone," she says. "I simply chose not to take it out of the box because there's nothing wrong with my landline."

Juls gives up. He leans back into the sofa cushions and takes his first sip of beer.

"Tastes like carrot cake," he says, holding up the can.

A peace offering. He knows beer is the way to his grandmother's heart.

"Thanks for taking care of the girls this weekend," he says.

"They took care of *me*," says Lenny.

"I bet they did," he says.

His expression changes when he talks about his girls. It suddenly dawns on her that it's not only Juls who's been ordered to live with her. It's a package deal that includes Flo and Nora. Lenny only went to the courthouse so she could see her grandson. It had been so long. But Billy threw her off, and now she's stuck with all of three of them for God knows how long.

"I should have kept my bloody mouth shut in that courtroom," she says, almost to herself.

Juls bites the skin around the nails of his fingers, a nervous habit he hasn't shaken since he was a skinny little kid being bullied at school. Only now he's all muscle, and his large hands are marred by scars and nicotine stains. His hands tell a rough and tough story, but in this moment, he seems fragile. She regrets her words. Juls gets to his feet and rummages through his pockets for his car keys. Fender whimpers. The dog doesn't want him to go.

"The girls'll be getting out of school soon," he says. "I should go get them."

"I better come with you," says Lenny.

Juls motions for her to stay put. His jaw tightens.

"Look, Lenny, I know that thanks to you I'm not still sitting in some cell right now, but this arrangement isn't what either of us wants," he says. "And to be clear, I don't need an escort, and I'm not under house arrest, so I'll come and go as I fucking please."

Lenny is stung. She bites back.

"The justice made *me* responsible for you," she says. "So I'm coming."

He laughs.

"You haven't been responsible for me since I was ten," he says. "Why start now?"

Juls nearly steps on the dog as he storms out of the house. Fender barks at the door when he's gone. Lenny hears the Mustang's engine rev, then fade into the distance.

She gets why he's angry. His life has been taken out of his hands once again by a court—just like when he was a boy.

Fender nestles into his spot in the hall and waits. The house is quiet. Too quiet. A bad feeling takes root in the silence. Lenny doesn't remember exactly what she said to Billy Rider in the ER, but she knows it was careless. Open-a-fifteen-year-old-can-of-worms careless.

She tries to focus her mind on something else. Anything else. She zeroes in on the sound of the ticking clock on the kitchen wall. The dull hum of the fridge. The rumble as the furnace comes to life. That rumble shifts her gaze to the stairwell that leads down to the basement.

Then she remembers what's down there.

And the bad feeling grows.

14

It's been just over a week since Juls and the girls moved into Lenny's house. The bruise on her forehead has faded, and the neck brace has been retired. She's overdue for a workout. Lenny punches the large aqua bag hanging by a chain from the ceiling. Electronic music blasts from the speakers in the dimly lit garage-turned-studio that sits on a paved lot on Scott Street, about six blocks from Lenny's house. Maya is one bag over. Lenny can see her tiny frame reflected in the mirrored wall. Maya is pushing hard, face red, torso twisting with each blow.

"Three-four-five-six, three-four-five-six," hollers Ashley, their favorite instructor at the Rig.

The fiery, fit blonde strides the floor between the row of bags.

"Let's get extra spicy, people," shouts Ashley. "That's it. Keep it up. Ten more seconds. You got this."

Lenny repeats the combination, over and over, lactic acid burning her biceps.

"Time," calls Ashley.

"Motherfucker!" says Maya, bending forward, panting hard.

Lenny is out of breath and lightheaded, but she got through the workout.

Maya comes over, and the two women bump their boxing gloves together in triumph.

"You got something against that bag?" asks Maya.

Lenny smiles, sweat drenching her tank top.

"You try living with two third graders," she says. "One of them smarter than you."

"Nora's not buying the story about the apartment flooding, I take it?" asks Maya.

"Not for a hot second. She wants to go home," says Lenny. "And little Flo wants her mom. Rudi-Rose is still MIA. And Juls is a barrel of laughs. He still won't talk about his arrest."

"Sounds like a hoot," says Maya.

"Let's just say I really needed to punch something today," says Lenny.

They make their way to the Rig's change rooms. Maya sits on a bench and starts unlacing her gym shoes. Two women at the far end of the room head into the showers. Maya looks around to make sure they're alone.

"Speaking of your Juls," says Maya. Then she pauses.

"What?" asks Lenny.

"After you called last week and told me what happened, I did a little poking around," she says. "I hope you don't mind."

Lenny sits on the bench next to Maya.

"Tell me," says Lenny. "*He* is definitely not going to."

"The guys in Guns and Gangs were pretty tight lipped, but I ran into the team lead of the tactical unit that kicked in the door that night. He told me it was a royal fuckup. They were on the verge of something big. They thought they had Reg Caffey dead to rights this time, but when they got there, the warehouse was empty. Reg wasn't even there. There was a scuffle with Caffey's cleanup crew. A few of the guys were carrying weapons. Julian included."

"What were they expecting to find in the warehouse?" asks Lenny. "Drugs? Guns?"

Maya pulls off her shoes and socks. She doesn't look at Lenny.

"It's messed up," says Maya, lowering her voice. "The warehouse was a holding pen. At least that's what the intel was. It's one of a half dozen industrial buildings Reg owns across the city. The commander said it looked like they'd cleaned it out in a hurry. He figured they got tipped off. But they didn't get everything out. There were still some cages, collars, and chains, that sort of thing."

"For what? Dogs?" asks Lenny.

Maya looks at Lenny.

"Women. Girls," she says. "It was a holding pen. It's where they keep their new stock until they're seasoned and ready for distribution."

Lenny doesn't understand.

"They're human traffickers, Lenny," says Maya.

"Who?" says Lenny. She can't be talking about her Juls.

"From what I understand, Reg Caffey is the main connect for some high-level foreign exporters. Bad dudes," says Maya. "He's part of a network of domestic buyers and serves as the go-between with the international players."

"You said the holding pen was where he—what did you call it? Seasoned?" asks Lenny, unable to get the word out of her head.

"It's what they do to the girls to ensure compliance," says Maya.

Lenny grips the locker door as she clues in. Cages, collars, chains. She feels sick. All Lenny can see is that bruise on the young dancer's arm and the scars etched across her grandson's knuckles.

"I'm sorry," says Maya. "He was a good kid. I'm sure part of him still is."

Lenny heads for the showers. She stands under the stream of cold water, still wearing her tank top and shorts, her entire body shivering.

Lenny isn't so sure Maya is right about Juls.

Maybe a ten-year-old boy who finds his mother's dead body on the bathroom floor is destined to grow into a man capable of terrible things.

15

After a slow walk home from the Rig, Lenny enters the kitchen as Juls is putting dinner on the table. Bowls of his homemade chili and a plate of garlic bread. Since moving in, he's fallen into a rhythm of evening routines. Most days, she has no idea where he goes after he drops the twins at school, but at night he cooks and spends time with the girls. Fender circles his feet as usual. Juls smiles at her like everything's normal.

"Just in time," he says.

Lenny notices dark circles under his eyes. He hasn't been sleeping. She takes her usual chair at the kitchen table as the sound of running feet thumps down the stairs.

Flo bursts into the kitchen ahead of her sister.

"I don't care," she cries, her face a storm of emotions.

"Then why are you crying?" says Nora, with her nose in a book.

"What's going on, Flo?" asks Juls, touching her arm gently.

"Nothing," Flo sobs.

"She's being a baby," says Nora.

Juls taps Nora lightly on top of the head.

"Be nice to your sister," he says. "She's tired."

"I'm not tired, and I'm not a baby," bellows Flo.

Flo plunks into her chair, arms folded tight, chin bowed. Juls dips garlic bread into his chili and starts eating. He knows it's best to ignore her when she gets like this. Nora digs into her dinner, and so does Lenny, ravenous from her workout.

"How was boxing?" asks Juls, trying to lighten the mood.

Lenny shrugs. She can't look at him, let alone talk to him right now.

"Eat up, Flo," he says. "No cookies if you don't finish your dinner."

"I don't want any of Lenny's bloody cookies," she sobs. "I don't want anything."

She shoves her bowl away, and it topples to the floor. Flo bursts into tears and runs upstairs. Nora rolls her eyes, picks up her book, and starts reading as she continues to eat.

A door slams upstairs.

"She misses her mum," says Juls.

Juls stares at Fender, who's begun licking up the mess. Lenny keeps eating. Not her problem.

"You okay?" asks Juls, trying to get Lenny to look at him.

"Tough workout," Lenny mumbles into her food.

"Listen, I need to do some laundry," he says.

Lenny looks over and follows his gaze to the back stairs. He knows her washer and dryer are down there. She swallows a mouthful of chili. He can't go into that basement. Last week, Lenny had hastily hung rope across the basement stairs, telling them all it wasn't safe to go down there. The steps were rotten. She assured Juls she'd booked a handyman to fix them. It was a temporary fix to a problem she'd been ignoring for days. Her wall.

"There's a laundromat in Hintonburg," she says. "Sudsey's, I think it's called."

He sighs. She can tell it's not the easy solution he was hoping for.

"I think the washing machine is on the fritz anyway, so—" she says.

"Like everything else around here," mutters Nora, not looking up from her book.

Lenny rises, wanting this conversation to be over.

"I'll go check on Flo," says Lenny, leaving her half-eaten bowl on the table.

Upstairs, Lenny doesn't check on Flo. Instead, she goes into her own bedroom. She needs to put some space between her and Juls, to keep from saying something she'll regret. Lenny can hear the girls talking in Kendra's old room. The room looks exactly like it did when Kendra was a teenager. Lenny never got around to redecorating it, and when Kendra died, she couldn't bring herself to change a thing.

A while later, she hears the twins brushing their teeth, then Juls' voice as he tucks them in for the night. His footfalls pass by her door, pause, then continue on to the spare room. Fender usually goes with him.

Once she's certain everyone is asleep, Lenny tiptoes downstairs, grabs a blanket from the sofa, and goes into the garage. It's not heated, and the autumn temperatures are dropping. In the darkness, she feels for the Jeep's door handle and opens it. She nestles into the passenger seat, leaving the door open so the soft glow of the dome light keeps her company.

Lenny rests her hand on the driver's seat.

"Oh, Hank," she whispers. "What do I do now?"

Lenny closes her eyes.

16

Fifteen years ago

He waited until there was only one car parked outside the gym. Then he tossed a chunk of ice at the streetlamp closest to the building. It shattered, and darkness enveloped the snow-covered parking lot. The gym was located in an industrial park that was pretty much deserted this late at night. Her boyfriend liked the twenty-four-hour access. He liked working out late when no one else was there. He had some kind of phobia about watching other guys pump iron. At least that's what she'd told her dad once. He'd filed that tidbit of information away for the right time.

Now was the right time.

He pulled the ski mask down over his face and grabbed the baseball bat. Then he waited in the shadows. Her boyfriend came outside, wearing headphones and singing to himself off-key. The guy wasn't wearing a winter jacket, just an expensive sweat suit that he probably thought made him look like a gangster. The guy even wore a gold chain. His combat boots were unlaced and hanging open, gym bag slung over his shoulder.

He waited until the man got close, then he came up behind him fast and hard, driving the bat into the guy's rib cage, then slamming the bat across the back of his knees. The guy dropped, shielding himself as the bat struck him in the arms and torso, over and over again. The guy tried to lift his head, tried to see who it was. He took aim and swung the bat right at the guy's jaw. Crack. His head hit the ground hard. Blood gushed from his mouth, splattering across the white snow. The guy moaned and held up one hand in surrender.

He lowered the bat, spat in the guy's face, and walked away.

Message delivered.

17

In the middle of the night, the chill in the garage wakes Lenny. She's disoriented at first, then she hears the sound of muffled voices. As she enters the house, Lenny looks down the front hall and sees a blue light coming from the living room. She peeks in. Juls is sitting on the sofa watching TV. Lenny gasps when she looks over and sees her daughter's smiling face.

Juls turns. He sees Lenny wrapped in a blanket, trembling.

He rises and comes over to her. He touches her arm.

"You're ice cold," he says. "Come sit."

He grabs a second blanket and pulls it around her. He sits close to her, one arm over her shoulder, sharing his warmth.

"Were you outside?" he asks.

Lenny stares at the TV, mesmerized.

"This was their engagement party," says Lenny. "They'd only been together a few months. We thought it was too soon, he was the wrong guy, this was the wrong family. Maybe deep down Kendra knew it too. There never was a wedding. No plans, not even a date. She kept putting it off. Even when you were born three years after this party, she still wouldn't marry him."

Juls looks at the screen.

"I couldn't sleep," he says. "I found this box over there."

"The girls dug them up," she says.

"You told me you lost them," he says.

He pulls his arm away, staring at the images of his mother.

"Why the fuck didn't you ever show this to me?" he asks.

"It was Hank's camcorder," says Lenny, knowing it's not an excuse. "He was the one always taking home movies. After he died, I couldn't bear to look at them. I packed them away. I guess I forgot about them."

"Sounds like you," he says, rocking back and forth.

Her gaze is drawn to the screen.

Hank's lens zooms in on Reg Caffey, mid-fifties, finely tailored suit, cigar in hand. He's standing near the bar on a stone terrace. Smoke billows from his mouth. Behind him is a view of a rolling golf course. Vincent and Kendra are standing next to him. Kendra looks beautiful in a lavender chiffon strapless dress that clings to her slender frame. A matching shawl drapes over her bare shoulders and arms. She's pulled her long, dark hair to one side, and it flows down her shoulder. Reg snuffs his cigar in an ashtray, then clinks his champagne flute with a spoon. The crowd quiets.

"May your glasses be ever full. May the roof over your heads be always strong. And may you be in heaven half an hour before the devil knows you're dead," says Reg, raising his glass to the couple.

Everyone hoots and hollers. The camera pans the crowd. Billy is there, leaning on the bar off to one side. He downs his champagne in one gulp. The view pans to Lenny, who's standing next to the camera. She sticks her tongue out.

"Be nice, Lenny. The guy's footing the bill for this shebang," says Hank. "You're not one to turn down an open bar, after all."

Lenny shoos Hank away. His lens scans the crowd. Reg is coming right for him. As he gets closer, Reg grins and looks directly into the lens.

"We're almost family now, boyo," he says.

Reg moves on, and Hank continues to film, searching the crowd for his daughter. He finds her and zooms in just as Reg slips his arm around her waist and pulls her close. Her chiffon wrap floats to the floor. She smiles and tries to pull away from Reg, but he holds tight. From the look on Vincent's face, he doesn't like it, but he bites his lip and does nothing. Reg's eyes search the room, then his gaze fixes on Hank's lens as he slowly moves his hand down Kendra's hip.

Lenny looks away from the TV.

"Those are track marks," says Juls, almost to himself.

He pauses the video. He spotted the marks on her forearms when her shawl slipped off.

"It's not what you think. I mean it *is*, but she wasn't—" says Lenny, hesitating.

"Wasn't what? A junkie?" he says.

"No, she made a mistake, that's all," says Lenny. "Listen, when your mom was a teenager, she never got into any trouble. Good grades. Captain of the volleyball team. I used to go to all her games. She had lots of friends. Once in a while, she broke curfew or talked back. Typical teenage stuff. The thing is, she had this fearless streak. Kendra would try anything. And she hated missing out. She had some at a party in high school. Everyone else was doing it. But it took hold of her."

"Meth?" he asks.

"Heroin," says Lenny. "We got her help, and she got clean. She was doing okay until she met Vincent. He was from a different world. He was exciting, dangerous. That's what she liked about him. Things began to change. She changed. Kendra didn't see her old friends anymore. And once she moved in with Vincent, we barely saw her. When we did, we knew she was using again."

"Fuck," says Juls.

"They'd been together three years when she got pregnant with you," says Lenny. "She stopped the second she found out. Kendra even came home for a while. We got her through the worst of it, but then she went back to him."

"You should have stopped her," he says, shaking his head.

"She thought she was in love with your father," says Lenny. "What were we supposed to do?"

Juls picks up the remote and turns off the VCR. A blue screen appears on the TV.

"You were supposed to help her. She was your flesh and blood," he says.

He looks at Lenny.

"And you've got the fucking nerve to judge me and Ru for how we raise our kids," he says with a bitter laugh.

Lenny doesn't say a word. Juls tosses the remote.

"Why did you bother fighting for custody?" he says. "You weren't capable of being a parent. You checked out after she died. That's why I got the fuck out of here the second I could."

Lenny reaches out to him, but Juls rises and pushes past her.

"Maybe it's why Hank got the fuck out too," he says without stopping.

Lenny bristles. Juls disappears upstairs, leaving her sitting alone in the cold blue light.

A restless autumn wind rattles the house as decay wafts in through the cracks of the old bay window. It's the first day of October. Winter is creeping closer. She can feel it in her bones. The familiar pain of that cruelest of seasons.

Lenny pulls the blankets tight around her and stares into the blue screen.

18

The next morning, Lenny stays in bed until she hears Juls and the girls leave for school. He doesn't come back. As soon as it's open, Lenny seeks comfort at the Carleton. When Sully slides onto the stool next to her, Lenny is already three pints in.

"Hey, beautiful," he says. "Don't usually see you in here before happy hour."

Lenny tips her glass in his direction but barely looks at him. The lunch rush has been and gone, so the Carleton is empty save for a few regulars.

"Been a while. Where *you* been hiding?" asks Sully.

"I had family stuff to deal with," says Lenny, keeping her eyes on the bar.

She wonders if the gossip has found its way to Sully.

"Yeah, I heard about Juls," he says.

He points to Lenny's pint and holds up two fingers to the bartender.

"Am I a shitty person, Sully?" she asks.

"The shittiest," he says, leaning into her and bumping her shoulder.

The bartender brings over the pints. Sully takes a swig.

"What's going on, Lenny?" he asks.

"I was thinking about this time I went by their apartment. They weren't expecting me. I was in the neighborhood. Kendra was standing at the counter with her back to me, making a sandwich. She wouldn't look at me. Vincent was all chatty. More than usual. He sure got me out of there fast. Said they had somewhere to be. I think he'd hit her or she was high, I don't know which. It wasn't the first time. I'd seen bruises before."

Lenny looks at Sully.

"I knew, Sully," she says. "I knew and I did nothing. I didn't protect her."

"Not true," says Sully. "You and Birdie both tried, and she pushed you away."

"We should have pushed back harder," says Lenny. "We knew what he was. Who his family was."

"And Kendra knew it too," says Sully.

"Do you think he did it?" asks Lenny.

He sips his beer.

"All I know is, he had a solid alibi," says Sully. "Gun was never found. No witnesses came forward. Shit was stolen from the apartment."

"Right, a robbery gone wrong," says Lenny.

She downs her pint.

"A week before she died, Kendra told me she was leaving him," says Lenny. "They'd been living together on and off for thirteen unbearable years. I'd heard it so many times, I brushed her off."

"You're not a shitty person, Lenny," says Sully. "Whoever killed her was."

Lenny runs her finger across the rim of her beer glass.

"You should take a page from Birdie's playbook," says Sully. "He had these lessons he always passed on to new guys training under him."

"Oh, I'm well aware of Hank's lessons," she says. "Trust your instincts, keep your cool, do the right thing, and remember, nobody's perfect."

"That's right, Lenny, nobody *is* perfect," says Sully. "You did your best. Stop beating yourself up. It wasn't your fault."

Lenny signals the bartender for another pint.

"What brought all this on?" he asks. "Seeing the kid again?"

"I didn't do right by Juls back then," she says. "And now he's in trouble. He could go to prison. Lose his kids. And it feels like it's happening all over again. There's nothing I can do."

"He was lucky to have you, then and now," says Sully, placing his hand gently on hers. "But the kid *is* a Caffey."

"What's that supposed to mean?" asks Lenny, pulling away.

"I'm just saying, he grew up around some heavy shit," he says. "Maybe he's more at home in their world than yours."

The bartender brings Lenny another pint. She sips her beer.

All she can see is the Juls she used to know.

"You remember how scrawny he was?" she says. "Then he had that growth spurt around fourteen and started playing sports, lifting weights, and really bulked up. The girls loved him."

"Good-looking kid," says Sully. "Looked like his mother. And she looked like you."

"His hockey coach said he was a natural," says Lenny. "He had the skills to go pro but would never make it because he was too soft. Didn't have the killer instinct."

"He might not have been born with it," says Sully. "But from what I hear, Reg Caffey's got his own special way of training his guys to be anything but soft. And *his* playbook is all about bringing out that instinct—one way or another. That's not on you."

Lenny flips her hand and stares into her beer glass.

Sully knows when she's done talking.

He turns his attention to the afternoon baseball game on the TV.

"Hey, Andy, can you turn that up?" he calls out. "I got action on this one."

The volume goes up, and the two settle into a comfortable silence as they watch the game. Only Lenny's not really watching. Something else is playing out in front of her eyes.

That video of Kendra's engagement party.

She can see Reg Caffey slowly moving his hand down Kendra's hip.

She can see him looking right into Hank's lens.

The crime boss was sending the cop a message.

His daughter now belonged to the Caffeys.

Lenny wonders if the same is true of Juls.

After the custody hearing, she remembers what Reg said to her and Hank. He couldn't sway the judge on his son's behalf, but Reg held his head high and came over to shake Hank's hand outside the courthouse. He gave them both a warm smile.

"Take good care of that lad for me," he said. "He'll be mine one day."

19

Fifteen years ago

He buzzed the apartment, but no one answered. He quickly ran around back to check the parking lot. Their car was gone. The school had called when the boy hadn't shown up that morning and they couldn't reach either of his parents. He was the other emergency contact on their list. He'd left the station, telling his partner he needed to take an early lunch. That's when he found the note on his squad car. YOU DID THIS. *That's all it said. All caps like a scream. He knew who wrote it. He punched the steering wheel, called her phone. It went straight to voicemail. He drove over to the Spaniel's Tale bookstore where she sometimes picked up shifts. He stopped by the Full Nelson. No one had seen them. He called his wife. She hadn't heard from their daughter. Panic set in as he drove around, calling her old friends, checking her favorite spots.*

His partner called to see if he was coming back. He said he needed to take the day. He didn't tell him what was going on. All he could think to do was to go back to her apartment, maybe break in, look for any clues as to where they might be, hoping and praying something worse wasn't waiting for him. His mind reeled. He buzzed again. He was waiting for someone to come out so he could duck inside when he heard a voice behind him.

All she said was "Dad," but he nearly passed out. He'd been holding his breath all day. He turned and there she was. Her son was beside her. And right behind them was her boyfriend. A small scar on his cheekbone was the only sign that he'd had his jaw wired shut for two months. The boyfriend draped an arm across her shoulders, hooked it around her neck, pulling her close.

Her smile disappeared when she saw the look on her father's face. She explained they'd gone up to the cabin for the day. Her boyfriend's last-minute idea. She asked if something had happened. He shook his head. Said he'd just stopped by to say hello, that's all. The boyfriend ruffled his son's hair. The boy squirmed away from his touch. She asked her father to come in, but he told her he had to get back to work. She followed her son inside, waving goodbye. As the boyfriend brushed past him, their eyes met, and the boyfriend winked.

Message received.

20

After leaving the Carleton midafternoon, Lenny doesn't head home. Instead, she takes the O-Train downtown. The rocking of the light-rail car sloshes the beer in her belly to a nauseating swill. When she steps out of Rideau Station, she's glad of the crisp fall air and begins the six-block walk to the Full Nelson.

It's only when she's out front that she hesitates, listening to the faint pulse of music from inside. As she reaches for the door, it flies open. Lenny crashes into the person coming out. It's Billy Rider. She steps back as he squints into the bright sun. In the light of day, he has the chalky pallor of a guy who's spent his life in a windowless nightclub, smoking and drinking too much.

"You" is all he says, as he collects himself.

She notices a fresh shiner under his left eye. The eye is bloodshot.

"I'm here to see Reg," she says, hoping to get past him quickly.

"He ain't in," he says. "But if you're looking for a sponsor, I'd be happy to step up."

"You've done enough, thanks," she mutters.

"You don't like me much, do ya, Mrs. Bird?" he says.

"You're the one who got my grandson mixed up in this horrid business," she says.

Billy lets the door close behind him. He lights a cigarette.

"True, I might be the fucktard who gave the kid a job when he came begging for work, but I'm also the fucktard who watches over him. I been doing that since he was a sad-ass little punk crying over his dead mama."

Lenny goes to slap his face, but before she can, a group of men burst from the depths of the club and crowd their way out the door. Billy gives them room, and Lenny steps back. Billy makes small talk with his customers. He seems to know them well, and they seem to like him.

She notices a small tremor in the hand holding his cigarette. As much as she loathes the man, part of her can't help but pity him—the way he trails after Reg like a skittish puppy waiting to be kicked.

The men head off down the sidewalk, and Billy turns his attention back to Lenny.

"Juls is gonna be fine," he says. "The arrest is nothing. Reg'll take care of it. He looks out for family."

"When will Reg be back?" she asks.

Billy shrugs.

"Didn't say," he says. Billy's thumb wanders to his black eye.

He flicks his half-finished cigarette into the gutter.

"I don't get you. You got your boy back," he says. "Come all the way down here to rub it in the old man's face? Or are you really here to see me?"

She knows he's talking about her slipup at the ER. Lenny looks down the street.

"What is it you really want, Mrs. Bird?" he says, stepping closer to her.

He's too close.

"I need to use the ladies' room," she says.

He smiles.

"Have at it," he says, opening the door and waving her inside.

Lenny enters the sticky-floored club and makes a beeline for the back corner. She knows exactly where it is. From Reg's *family* gatherings. She remembers them well. He'd dim the lights, pull together the tables to make one large one, and lay out cloth napkins and candles. He made it so it didn't feel like a strip club. Reg would belt out Irish songs, and the twins would run behind the bar and spray soda from a wand. Juls would slow dance with Rudi-Rose. Billy was always there, with a few other strays. Reg's gatherings were warm and friendly on the surface, but underneath there was tension. The kind that comes when two very different worlds bump up against each other. Lenny never belonged. The cop's wife. The outsider. She went for Juls' sake, but the laughing and dancing and holiday cheer got under her skin. Juls noticed. And the unsaid was finally said out loud, in front of everyone.

Just be happy I came at all.

You hate it so much, don't come back.

And she didn't. That was over a year ago.

Inside the ladies' room, Lenny retreats to a stall and empties her bladder. She stares at the scratches and dents in the stall door. Lenny has no idea why she's here. A beer-soaked impulse to have it out with Reg? But now her boozy courage has faded. She's sober and sad.

Lenny hears a tiny whimper coming from the stall next to hers. She dips her head and sees a pair of feet. The woman has kicked off her high heels. There's a run in her nylons.

"You okay in there?" asks Lenny.

"Oh, sorry, yes, I'm fine, sorry, sorry, missus," says a small voice.

"Do you need help?" asks Lenny.

"No, no, I mean not to bother you," says the woman. She has an accent Lenny can't place.

Lenny hears her blow her nose. Then the main door to the washroom squeaks open.

"Becks," shouts a woman. "I know you're in here."

Lenny lifts her feet to hide. Heels click across the floor. Lenny peeks through the crack of the stall door. It's Sugar. She's wearing a lime-green swimsuit with a matching sequin-studded collar and stilettos.

"Move your skinny ass, girl," says Sugar. "I don't have time for this shit."

Becks picks up her heels and exits her stall. In the mirror, Lenny catches a glimpse of her face. It's streaked with mascara. It's the young teenager from the ER. The one who was sitting at the bar when Lenny came to get the twins. The one with the bruised elbow.

"I'll cover for you this time, Becks," says Sugar. "But that guy's a regular, and you're gonna have to learn to go with the fucking flow. Now clean your face up."

Lenny comes out of her stall. Becks spots her in the mirror, and her eyes go wide. Sugar turns to look at Lenny. Something in her eyes makes Lenny regret showing herself.

"Go," Sugar tells Becks.

The young woman grabs her high heels and scurries back into the club.

"You lost?" asks Sugar.

"I was just using the washroom," says Lenny.

"You shouldn't be here," says Sugar.

"I'm worried about what Juls has gotten himself into," replies Lenny.

"He's a big boy," says Sugar. "Best you talk to him."

Sugar turns and struts toward the door.

"Is that girl being forced to work here?" Lenny calls out.

Sugar stops, then slowly turns around to face Lenny.

"You are way out of your depth, grandma," says Sugar. "I suggest you go home and bake some fucking cookies."

"How old is she?" asks Lenny. "Fourteen? I want to know what my grandson is—"

Lenny doesn't get the words out before Sugar comes at her. She slams Lenny into the stall door. It flies open, and Lenny loses her footing. She sprawls back onto the toilet. Sugar hovers over her, hikes her leg, and jams the heel of her stiletto into Lenny's throat.

"Now listen to me, you nosy old hag," says Sugar. "Stay the fuck out of it, or you're gonna get someone killed. And it could be your grandson. You hear me?"

Lenny can't speak.

"*Do you hear me, Lenny Bird?*" shouts Sugar.

Lenny nods. Sugar releases her stiletto and walks away.

Lenny doesn't move until the sound of Sugar's footsteps is long gone. When she does try to stand, a wave of nausea hits her.

Lenny turns and vomits into the toilet.

It automatically flushes.

She just wants to go home.

21

When Lenny steps off the bus in front of the thrift store at Harmer and Wellington, a block from her house, she glances at her reflection in the store window. There's a welt forming on her throat from Sugar's stiletto. She goes into the thrift shop and buys a secondhand nylon scarf to hide it.

The Mustang is parked in the driveway. Juls hasn't left yet to get the girls from school. She was hoping he'd be gone. They haven't seen each other since last night. When she walks into the house, Fender is asleep in his usual spot. Juls isn't in the living room or kitchen. She glances out the kitchen window. He's not in the backyard smoking. Then she spots the rope lying on the back landing.

Her heart sinks.

Juls has his back to Lenny when she comes down the basement stairs. He's staring at the wall. There's a laundry basket of dirty clothes at his feet. The last step squeaks as she reaches the bottom. He knows she's there, but he doesn't move a muscle.

She slowly walks over to him, hoping to explain.

"It's an evidence wall—sort of," she says. "But I think of it more like a story."

Lenny glances at him, hoping to read his face.

His expression is blank. He still hasn't moved.

"I've been working on it for years," she says. "Ever since you moved out."

Lenny steadies herself, then approaches the wall. She runs her fingertips across it.

"These are from family albums," she says.

Then she points to one of the crime scene photos.

"These larger ones, I got from Hank's partner, Sully, years ago," she says. "And the Polaroids—they're like a record of the data I've been collecting."

She points to the most recent Polaroid of the high-tops.

"I've been trying to pinpoint the exact shoe that made the print in this crime scene photo," she says, tracing her finger across the bloody tread mark. "See?

"I'm trying to match the type of shoe to one of these old photos. But that's just one thread in the larger story." She motions from one collection to another.

Lenny looks back at Juls to see if he's following her train of thought. He isn't. Tears stream down his face, and his glassy eyes are fixed on a spot on the wall. Lenny follows his gaze. He's staring at the wide shot of Kendra's lifeless body.

Lenny is numb to the horror after all these years. She no longer sees her daughter lying there. She sees a crime. An unsolved case that needs to be examined from every perspective. A puzzle with pieces missing that need to be found. But that's not what her grandson is seeing. He sees the worst moment of his life on full display, from every gruesome angle.

Juls sinks to the floor. She's broken him. Lenny realizes she's made a terrible mistake. She should have taken everything down days ago when the girls first went into the basement. She should have hidden it all away.

"I'm so sorry," says Lenny. "I wasn't thinking."

Juls looks down at the basket of clothes.

"Nora wanted to wear her blue sweater, but there was a stain on it, so she couldn't," says Juls, his voice barely a whisper. "I—I had to do laundry. I thought I could fix the machine."

"I never meant for you to see it," says Lenny.

"What is this?" he asks, looking up at her. "Are you trying to prove my dad killed her?"

She stares at the wall. Lenny's gaze wanders across the family photos of her beautiful daughter. Blowing a kiss to the camera, hugging her little boy, laughing with her arm around Vincent, standing with her eyes closed as she dances in a crowd at an outdoor concert.

"I needed to know the truth," says Lenny.

Juls wipes his wet face with his shirt. He gets to his feet.

"Of course he fuckin' did it," says Juls. "And I hope he rots in hell for it, but this?"

He paces the basement floor.

"You don't understand," says Lenny.

"What's there to understand? Look what you've done to her," he cries. "It's sick."

Lenny reels back, stung by his words. She can't breathe, she's so angry.

"If this is sick, then I'm sick!" she shrieks at her grandson.

Juls stares at her.

"Because this is *me*. This is the only way I know how to do this," says Lenny, pointing to the wall. "*This* is how I can stand to live without ever seeing her smile or hearing her voice again. *This* is how I get out of bed every day without her or Hank or you. This is all I have. Without it, I might as well be—"

Lenny walks over to the wall and presses her hands to it, trying to calm her racing heart. Juls is dead quiet. She can hear him breathing behind her.

"I gotta get out of here," he says, heading for the stairs.

Lenny runs over and blocks his way. She doesn't want him to leave. Not like this. Juls tries to get past. She grabs hold of him, but he pulls from her grasp. He tries again. This time she shoves him hard in the chest. Something snaps inside him. He cocks his arm, fist raised, eyes blazing. Lenny shields her face. Juls freezes.

He slowly lowers his arm. He might be a man who was taught to use his fists, but as Lenny looks at Juls trembling in front of her, she sees the sweet, gentle boy he once was.

"I hate you," he whispers.

"I *love* you, Juls," she says. "I've loved you since the day you were born."

Juls shakes his head.

Lenny wraps her arms around him. At first, he resists and tries to pull away.

"I'm here now," she says. "I've got you."

She holds him tight. She can feel his heart beating fast. He gives up trying to get free.

Juls rests his cheek on her shoulder as his body goes limp.

He has no fight left in him.

22

The next morning when Lenny gets to Maplelawn, Silas won't look at her. It's been days since she last visited with the twins in tow. The personal-support worker changing his sheets even seems put off by her absence, like it's any of her business. Silas refuses to wear his hearing aids. Lenny tries reading the obits, but he won't play. When she switches to the crossword, he stares out the window and starts singing to himself.

"'Five for silver, six for gold, seven for a secret never to be told.'"

Her father stops singing and looks at her for the first time since her arrival.

"Do we have a secret?" he asks, sitting forward in his chair.

Lenny glances at the PSW. She looks lost in her work, but she's probably listening. Lenny touches her father's hand and shakes her head. She puts the newspaper aside and doesn't speak until the PSW finally leaves the room.

"Juls saw my wall yesterday," she says.

Her father looks at her blankly. He doesn't have a clue what she's talking about. She's never shown him the wall, or anyone else for that matter, but it feels good to talk about what happened with someone.

"He was upset, but he didn't ask me to take it down." She goes on. "We put the rope back up so the girls wouldn't see it. I didn't bother telling him it was too late for that."

Silas puts in his hearing aids.

"Last night Juls even asked me about the map on the wall," she says. "When I told him the dots were all the locations of break-and-enters in Kendra's neighborhood over a five-year span, he almost seemed impressed."

Silas squints at her. Lenny leans closer to her father.

"We don't have a secret, Dad," she whispers, wishing it were true.

He sits back with a sigh. He seems visibly relieved.

Lenny wonders if remnants of their shared secret lie buried somewhere deep inside his mind. If the past haunts him too. Maybe the dreadful is never eradicated. And even as her father's memory fails him, perhaps those shocking moments don't fully disappear but continue to grow like mold in the dark corners. She can't know.

Lenny spends the morning with Silas, then heads home. It's just past noon when she rounds the corner onto Julian Avenue and spots someone walking down her driveway. At first, she thinks it's Juls, but the man's gait is wrong. He doesn't see her. She's too far away to make out who it is. He heads in the other direction toward a parked car a few doors down. A black Lexus. The engine is running. She can see the exhaust swirling from the tailpipe. He jumps in. As he drives past, shadows cross the windshield, obscuring his face. But she does catch the license plate.

Lenny imprints the plate in her mind, repeating it over and over—a habit she developed while strolling the neighborhood with baby Kendra. She'd memorize license plates and locations, hoping one day there'd be a bank robbery or a triple homicide in the area, and she'd be the one to crack the case. The habit scratched an itch for a bored housewife.

She's seen the car before. It was across the street when Juls dropped her at Maplelawn this morning. She's certain of it. Someone is following her—or Juls. The Mustang isn't in the driveway, so Juls is likely still at the gym—at least that's where he told her he was going.

When Lenny opens the door, she knows an intruder has been in the house. She can smell his aftershave. The scent is familiar. She drops her purse on the entryway table and searches the main floor, then upstairs.

Nothing seems to be missing. When she comes back down, Lenny's heart stops. The dog. He's not in his usual spot in the hall.

"Fender!" Lenny shouts, fear tightening her throat.

She yells louder. Then she hears a distant bark coming from outside. Lenny shoves open the back door and races into the yard.

"Fender!" she hollers.

The barking comes from deep in the garden. She runs along the snarled path leading toward the old shed. She hears him scratching at the wooden door. He's inside. The rusty padlock lies broken in the dirt. The one she put on the shed door years ago after scrubbing away the bloodstains. Lenny yanks open the rotting door. It nearly comes off its hinges. Fender leaps from his prison, launching himself into her arms. She cradles the shivering dog as he licks her chin, panting doggy breath up her nostrils.

"It's okay, buddy," she says. "You're safe."

But it's not okay. Someone was inside her house—*and* her shed. Lenny pushes the rotting door closed. The intruder must have been looking for somewhere to stow Fender so the neighbors wouldn't hear the barking.

Lenny weaves through the garden back to the house, Fender in her arms. Inside, she carefully places him down. He immediately pees on the kitchen floor. Lenny wipes up the mess as Fender cowers near the door leading to the garage. He scratches at it. He never does that. She opens the door, and his nose sniffs the stale air inside. The dog lowers to his belly, resting his chin on the threshold. He wants Hank. So does she.

Lenny steps over the dog and goes into the garage. Fender stays put at the threshold.

Lenny roots through some boxes on the shelves that line the far wall.

She finds what she's looking for under some of Hank's old police uniforms.

Then she goes back into the house and calls Maya.

23

A few hours later, outside the Rig, Maya and Lenny lean against the concrete wall of the boxing studio, still sweating from their workout. Mist wafts from their heads into the cool night air. Maya's boxing gloves are slung over her shoulder. They both take swigs from their water bottles.

"That license plate you asked me to run," says Maya, handing Lenny a piece of paper.

Lenny reads the name written on it.

William Thomas Rider. That's why the aftershave was familiar. It was Billy.

"You said the car was weaving down your street?" asks Maya.

Lenny can't believe he was in her shed. *Damn it.*

"You know the name, don't you?" says Maya. "This wasn't about some erratic driver, was it?"

Maya knows her too well.

"It's nothing. It's just Billy," says Lenny. "He runs the club where Juls works."

"Juls isn't supposed to go near those guys," says Maya. "Is he breaching bail?"

"No. Billy was probably dropping off a paycheck," says Lenny.

Maya presses her hands into the wall and leans in to stretch her calf.

"The guy's harmless," says Lenny.

She drains her water bottle.

"Listen to me, Lenny," she says. "No one in Reg Caffey's orbit is harmless. Don't forget about the headless corpses."

Lenny spits water from her mouth.

"Granted, it was twenty years ago," Maya continues. "You remember. Four headless dudes were dredged up by a maintenance crew raking weeds from the Rideau Canal."

"Vaguely," says Lenny.

"The whole city was in shock. People couldn't conceive of shit like that going down in their sleepy little government town," says Maya. "But you and I both know there's a sleazy criminal underbelly in every city, and Reg Caffey is head sleazeball in this one—he was then, and he is to this day."

"I get it," says Lenny.

"Do you?" says Maya, as she finishes her stretches and turns to face Lenny.

"Those four horsemen were Reg Caffey's main competitors," says Maya. "For a while, he was the prime suspect, but they couldn't pin the murders on him. He had more lawyers on his payroll than the service did. Still does."

Lenny wishes Maya would stop talking, but she doesn't.

"The man's been involved in gangs since his street-fighting days back in the seventies. And right now, he controls one of the largest criminal syndicates in the country," says Maya. "And Caffey's only become more ruthless over the years. So do not underestimate him or his people."

The two friends finally go their separate ways, but Maya's words follow Lenny home. As she walks down Hinchey Avenue in the dark, Lenny feels eyes on her. She picks up her pace. Maya's story has her spooked. She's glad when she finally gets home, closes the front door, and locks it behind her.

It's late. The girls are probably in bed. The house is dark. Juls must have gone up early.

As Lenny grabs a beer from the fridge, she notices light coming up from the basement stairwell. It dawns on her that she never checked the basement after Billy's break-in. She's only halfway down the steps when she sees it. The remnants of her wall have been scattered across the basement floor. Whoever did this didn't simply pull them off the wall and leave it at that. Every photo has been ripped, every document torn to bits. Every piece of Kendra's story lies in ruins.

This took time and effort—and a whole lot of rage.

Juls is picking up pieces, one by one, and carefully placing them in a garbage bin. Lenny sits on the bottom step. All those years were for nothing. She solved nothing. She proved nothing. Kendra's wall is gone.

"Was this you?" she says to Juls.

He turns, startled. He hadn't heard her come down.

"Fuck no," he says. "I thought it was you."

Lenny shakes her head. She knows who it was. That fucktard.

"It was Billy," she says. "He broke into the house."

"What the hell, Lenny?" he says. "When?"

"This morning while we were out," she says. "I saw him leaving when I got back from visiting Silas."

"Billy?" he says. "It doesn't make sense."

Lenny has her theories as to why he broke in. Billy is suspicious. He's on the hunt.

"Reg must have put him up to it," says Juls. "The old man won't like that I'm here. He's fucking with me. He's letting me know he has eyes on me."

He looks rattled. Lenny starts helping Juls pick up the pieces.

"You could just walk away," says Lenny. "After your trial. Be done with him."

"It's not that simple," he says. "I can't right now."

"I don't understand you," she says.

"Nobody asked you to," he says.

Juls continues to clean up. Lenny picks up one of the torn photos and stares at it.

He's right. Nobody did ask her. She brought all this on herself. None of this would have happened if she'd kept her distance. Stayed away. Protected herself.

Lenny spent fifteen years building an impenetrable fortress around her heart, but ever since Juls and the girls moved in, cracks have begun to form. And just like with her father, the past, which had been tucked away in the shadows, is threatening to come out.

She doesn't know how to stop it.

24

Rudi-Rose is the last person Lenny expects to see standing on her doorstep the next day. It's late afternoon. Juls has gone to get the girls from school. The young woman's kimono-style chemise hangs open. Under it she's wearing a cropped tank that exposes her midriff. Her faded jeans sit below her pierced belly button. Her long sandy hair is braided with gold beads. The tip of her nose is burnt. She's been somewhere warm.

"Juls isn't here," says Lenny. "Does he even know you're back?"

"I was hoping to surprise them," says Rudi-Rose with a smile.

Lenny doesn't invite her in. Instead, she leaves the front door open and heads into the living room, where she takes a seat on the sofa. Rudi-Rose follows her into the house.

"What was it this time? A sick friend?" asks Lenny. "Or did you need some me time?"

Rudi-Rose wanders into the living room and sits on the edge of the coffee table.

"You haven't changed a bit, Lenny," she says. "Still all warm and fuzzy."

"I see you got some sun," says Lenny.

The coffee table creaks, and Lenny nods to the sofa. Rudi-Rose stands, twirls, then plops down opposite Lenny. Just like Flo.

"How are my angels?" asks Rudi-Rose. "Oh, and I heard about the whole court thingy. How is Juls doing?"

Lenny hears the rumble of the Mustang's engine.

"Guess you're about to find out," says Lenny.

A few minutes later, Flo spills through the front door.

"Mama!" screeches Flo when she sees her.

Flo races into her mother's arms and wraps herself around her like a baby monkey. Nora and Juls are behind her. They stand in the entryway staring at Rudi-Rose.

"Daddy is making breakfast for dinner. Bacon and eggs and everything. It was my idea," says Flo, kissing her mother's face. "Do you want breakfast for dinner?"

"Sounds peachy," says Rudi-Rose, glancing at Juls. "If you'll have me."

He looks away and helps Nora take off her backpack, even though she doesn't want help. Then he disappears down the hall without a word.

"I'll take that as a yes," says Rudi-Rose. "Nor-Nor, come say hello to Mama."

Rudi-Rose reaches out a hand.

Nora carefully lines up the two backpacks alongside the hall table.

"I'll help Daddy," she says, heading to the kitchen.

Rudi-Rose turns her attention back to Flo.

"How's my little Polkaroo?" says Rudi-Rose. "Tell Mama everything."

Flo gives her mother a motormouthed rundown of her school day while Lenny slips into the kitchen. She grabs two cans of beer from the fridge and offers one to Juls.

"She showed up at the door a few minutes ago," says Lenny.

Juls is cracking eggs into a bowl, and the shells keep falling in. Lenny places his beer on the counter next to him when he doesn't take it. She can tell he's still rattled by Billy's B&E. And now Rudi-Rose has made an unexpected return. Earlier that day, Juls arranged to have all the locks changed. He even insisted Lenny charge her cell phone and carry it with her. He set up their phones to track each other in case he couldn't reach her. She didn't fight him on it because it seemed to ease his frayed nerves.

"Let me do it, Daddy," says Nora. She takes the bowl and carton of eggs away from him. Juls takes a long pull of his beer, then starts putting bacon in the frying pan. Flo pulls her mom by the hand into the kitchen.

"No bacon for Mama," says Flo. "Remember, she's a vegetarian."

"We know," says Nora, not looking up. "She's only been gone two weeks."

Juls leans against the counter, waiting for the bacon to heat. He chews on his finger.

"The girls told me you're a detective, Lenny," says Rudi-Rose.

Lenny nearly chokes on the beer.

Juls looks from Lenny to Rudi-Rose.

"When was this, Ru?" he asks.

Rudi-Rose smiles. She's got him talking. She crosses the room and leans against the counter, pushing her hip against his. She grabs the can of beer from his hand and takes a sip.

"I might have seen them the other day at recess," she says, batting her eyes.

Juls takes back his beer. She rolls her eyes.

"Chill, babe," says Rudi-Rose. "Anyway, Lenny, I think it's really cool that at your age you're still making yourself useful. It's super inspiring."

Lenny grits her teeth.

"You're never too old to do anything," says Nora.

Nora smiles at Lenny for the first time since they moved in. Lenny returns the favor.

At dinner, Flo and her mom do all the talking. No one asks where she's been. They've grown up with their mother drifting in and out of their lives. When Juls is done scarfing down his dinner, he gets up without a word and goes into the backyard. Rudi-Rose follows him.

The twins head upstairs to do their homework, and Lenny lingers by the kitchen window, pretending to wash the dishes. Juls is smoking and pacing. He's gesturing with his hands as he talks. She can tell things are heated. Juls finally sits in one of Lenny's wicker chairs. Rudi-Rose pulls the other chair close to him. Not a good sign. His head is bowed. Rudi-Rose runs her fingers through his curly hair. He doesn't pull away. Another bad sign.

Rudi-Rose lifts his chin and kisses him. He pulls away at first, but then he kisses her back, placing a hand on the back of her neck and pulling her close. Lenny looks away. She knows where this is headed. Juls could never resist Rudi-Rose. He's been crazy about her ever since he saw her dancing at Reg's club when he was sixteen.

As Lenny crosses through the living room, she passes the framed photographs she keeps on the bookcase—Kendra as a newborn, Hank and Sully in dress uniforms at a police charity ball, the twins on their third birthday, ten-year-old Juls on a dock holding up a fish, and Hank and Lenny's wedding photo. Lenny lingers a moment, staring at the picture of Hank.

She knows what it feels like to be young and crazy in love.

Then her gaze falls on the photo of baby Kendra. It's one of the few she has left of her daughter now that Billy's torn up most of them. Then she remembers the cardboard box in the corner by the TV. The box marked *Bird Watching*. She walks over, kneels in front of it, and starts looking through the collection of VHS tapes. Hank labeled the tapes with a Sharpie. *First Birthday*, *High School Graduation*, *New Puppy*, *First Day of School*, *New Baby*, *Engagement Party*. There are dozens of tapes. Lenny chooses one and puts it into the VCR. She sits back on her heels, turns on the TV, and presses play. The video comes to life on the screen.

A nurse is wheeling Lenny out the sliding front doors of the Civic Hospital. Lenny looks like a teenager. No makeup. A baby in her arms, swathed in a pink blanket.

Hank's lens moves closer.

"Hank, I'm a mess," says Lenny.

She has dark circles under her eyes. Her hair is gathered into the usual chaotic nest on top of her head. Hank's voice chimes in.

"You look beautiful. More beautiful than you've ever looked."

Lenny rises slowly from the wheelchair. She thanks the nurse.

"I'm a dad," says Hank.

The nurse smiles in the direction of the camera.

"Yes, you are," she says before wheeling the chair away.

The view follows Lenny as she makes her way to a red Toyota Tercel. The back door sits open. There's a baby seat in the back. The camera hovers close to the baby. Her big brown eyes squint up at the sunlight.

"That's the sky, little bird," says Hank.

The baby coos.

"Well, hello to you, too, Kendra Margaret," says Hank.

Lenny gently places the baby in the car seat.

The video cuts to a new clip of Lenny as she approaches the front door at 13 Julian. She's holding the baby. The camera backs into the house as she steps across the threshold.

"Welcome home," says Hank.

Young Lenny smiles. The camera bobbles as Hank turns the lens, leans into the shot, and kisses the baby, resting his forehead against Lenny's. He's in his twenties too. Clean cut and grinning.

"Look what we made," he says, his eyes filling with tears.

He kisses Lenny on the lips.

"Love you forever and back again, Lenny Bird," he says.

Lenny pauses the video on Hank's glowing face. She stares at it. She knows that face so well, but in those final months together, it was like she didn't know him at all. He was no longer this Hank. He was someone else. She had lost him somehow.

Hank wasn't the same after the death of his daughter.

None of them were.

25

Fifteen years ago

He raced down the hall toward the open front door of the apartment. The officer standing there put his hand out, barred the door, and shook his head, his face ashen. They knew each other. When he didn't back off, the officer sighed and handed him a pair of rubber gloves and some booties for his shoes. He put them on, then the officer let him pass.

He made his way down the narrow hall. The pungent smell of nitroglycerin hung in the air. The ident team was scattered around the apartment. As he got closer to the bathroom, another odor hit him. Metallic blood. An ident guy holding a camera stepped out of the bathroom to take a wider shot of inside. When the guy saw him, he lowered his camera, hesitated, then stepped aside.

He emptied his mind like he did anytime he was about to take in a violent crime scene. He steadied himself, then looked through the doorway. He examined the scene in snapshots. The gunshot wound near the heart. The wrist twisted against the tub. The bruise. The half-open eyes. The blood pooling near the torso. The splatter on the mirror, sink, and wall. The scratches on the windowsill. The bare feet. The chips of paint under the fingernails. The sweep of dark hair spread like a wildflower on the tiles. The necklace with the pendant in the shape of a K.

He looked away, had a quick word with the ident guy, then walked out of the apartment. He needed air. Outside, the fragrant spring air flooded his senses, making his eyes tear up. He rubbed them dry, then scanned the surrounding area, taking more snapshots in his mind. The vehicles in the visitor parking, their makes and models. The faces in the gathering crowd—age, ethnicity, gender, clothing. Litter on the grass. A blue bike in the metal bike rack out front. A flyer on the lobby window for math tutoring services. Neighbors peeking out windows or standing in doorways, curious about the police cars, the ambulance, the crying boy.

Then he stopped taking snapshots and focused on one man who was leaning against the building. An officer was talking to the man and taking notes. The man being questioned looked in his direction. Their eyes met, and the man winked.

That's when he knew for sure.

26

After watching the video of baby Kendra, Lenny has to get out of the house, away from Juls and Rudi-Rose, away from the memories. She walks all the way down Gladstone and finds herself standing across from the McNabb Community Centre. It's Friday night, and he'll be here for his AA meeting. Maya made it pretty clear Lenny shouldn't mess with Reg Caffey, but there'll be people around. It's their neutral territory. Maybe she can reason with him in a safe environment. Get him to let her grandson go.

The meeting has already started. She can see Reg in the window, talking to the group. Lenny is about to cross the street when she spots Billy Rider standing next to Reg's blue Mercedes, talking to his driver. She ducks behind a stone wall by the soccer field, hoping he didn't see her. Every inch of her wants to run over and strangle him for what he did to Kendra's wall, but she can't risk provoking Billy. Instead, she turns and walks away, heading to where she should have gone in the first place.

Lenny arrives at the Carleton just past nine. She grabs her usual stool and orders a draft. The tavern is humming with end-of-the-week revelers.

"He been in tonight?" she asks the bartender, nodding to Sully's empty stool.

Andy points to the poolroom.

Lenny grabs her pint and heads back. She spots Sully deep in conversation with a curvy brunette half his age. A young guy playing pool is giving Sully the evil eye.

"Wha'd I tell you, old man?" says the guy. "She's with me."

"Take a pill, Franco," says the young woman. "We're not doing nothing."

"Shooting the shit, man," says Sully. "That's all."

When Sully turns his back, the guy pokes Sully with his pool cue. The cops at the other table pause their game. Franco's buddies nudge each other and stand at the ready. These guys clearly have no idea they're in a cop bar.

Sully turns to face the guy. He spots Lenny over the guy's shoulder.

"There's my girl," he says, smiling.

He ignores Franco and walks toward her. Franco sticks his pool cue out, blocking Sully's path, but Sully pushes it aside. He's not in the mood for a fight. He approaches Lenny and kisses her cheek. Then he puts his arm around her and leads her toward the bar.

"That's right, keep walkin', gramps," calls out Franco.

Sully stops. Lenny looks at him and shakes her head. He shrugs. Maybe he is in the mood. He turns and heads for the guy. Before Franco knows what's happening, his face is bouncing off the side of the pool table, and a couple of his teeth are rolling across it. His friends don't move a muscle as blood gushes from Franco's nose. The brunette rushes to his side. Franco pushes her away and looks down at his cupped hands as blood pours into them. He passes out.

The cops at the next table continue their game.

Sully heads back over to Lenny, and they take their stools at the bar.

"A pint of your finest ale, good sir," he calls out to the bartender.

"Having fun, I see," she says.

"Always." He smiles.

The bartender brings over a pint for Sully as the brunette leads her bloodied boyfriend toward the door. She mouths a *fuck you* to Sully. He gives her a wink.

"Can I ask you something?" says Lenny.

"Fire away," he says.

"How did Hank seem to you back then?" she asks. "When Juls came to live with us? Did he seem different?"

"Memory lane again?" Sully asks.

"Indulge me," says Lenny, sipping her beer.

Sully rubs his chin like he's thinking.

"Birdie?" he says. "Considering what happened, I guess he was holding up as best he could. But it wasn't like I saw him all that much."

Lenny looks at Sully.

"What do you mean?" she asks. "You were his partner. You saw him every day."

Sully shakes his head.

"He wasn't on the job," says Sully. "He took leave after she died."

Lenny furrows her brow. He's dodging the question.

"Sure, for a couple of weeks," she says. "I'm talking about when he went back to work that summer. How was he then?"

"Birdie never came back, Lenny," says Sully.

Lenny stares at him.

"He extended his leave into the fall," says Sully.

"No, he didn't," says Lenny.

"I'm sorry, Lenny, I figured you knew," he says.

"But he left the house every day," she says. "He told me he was working a case."

A laugh bursts from Lenny, and she covers her mouth to stifle it. "He was pretending to go to work," she says. "Oh my God, I'm such an idiot."

"I'm sure he had his reasons," mumbles Sully.

"For lying to his wife?" asks Lenny.

Sully stares at his beer.

Lenny rises from her stool. It falls back and clatters to the floor. Sully stands and helps her pick up the stool. He touches her arm, but she pulls away. The bartender drifts their way as Lenny grabs her purse.

"Everything copacetic here?" asks Andy.

"All good." Sully nods.

Sully follows Lenny outside.

Lenny stumbles onto the sidewalk.

"Can I at least walk you home?" he asks.

She waves him off.

"Lenny," he says. "Birdie wasn't cheating on you if that's what you're thinking."

"I almost wish he had been," she says, turning to face him. "Then I could blame *him*."

"Don't do that," he says.

"Sully," she says. "My husband couldn't even tell me what was going on in his life. What does that say about me?"

Lenny backs away.

"I have to go, Sully," she says, then turns to leave.

He doesn't try to stop her.

"Good night, Lenny, I'm sorry," he calls out after her. "Shit."

Lenny crosses the street without looking back. Once she turns the corner, she starts running. She runs all the way home. The house is dark when she walks in. Rudi-Rose and Juls have gone to bed. She heads straight for the garage and climbs into the Jeep. Lenny sits there until her breathing steadies. Then she reaches out and rests a hand on the driver's seat.

"I'm so sorry, Hank," she says softly. "I was so lost. I wasn't there for you."

Juls might have been right about her.

Maybe it's why Hank got the fuck out too.

27

Fifteen years ago

He told his wife she didn't have to come with him. It was a few days after the custody hearing. He arrived a half hour before the court-appointed pickup time. He parked in the visitor lot out front and made his way around the side of the residential building, scanning for kids or dog walkers or window gazers. Luckily it was a rainy Sunday, and the housing development was deserted. He hadn't been back to the building since his daughter's murder.

Her boyfriend's car was parked in spot number six. Kendra's car had already been sold. He stood against the brick building, below the balconies, watching a woman juggle several bags of groceries as she headed for the back door. He went over and offered to hold it open for her. Security in the development was minimal. A buzzer out front, a key-card-operated back entrance. No cameras. He wore an oversize sweatshirt and baseball cap pulled low to hide his face, just in case the man looked out the window.

Once the woman was inside, he closed the door, then pulled the device from his pocket and headed for the car. He shot a quick glance back toward the building, then knelt beside the rear wheel. He reached inside the wheel well and attached the magnetic GPS tracker, then he quickly jogged for the side of the building and retraced his steps around front.

He checked his phone. Fifteen minutes until the appointed time. He opened the tracker's app. A blinking dot indicated the location of the tracker in the back parking lot. He closed the app and pocketed his phone, then he entered the building's front foyer and pressed the buzzer marked Vincent Caffey. *Her name had already been removed like she'd never existed.*

Ten minutes later, the boy stepped off the elevator alone. No surprise the man wasn't going to show his face. He'd lost this latest round, and he'd be stewing. The boy had a large duffel bag slung over one shoulder and a backpack stuffed to bursting on his other shoulder. The ten-year-old looked like he was carrying the weight of the world on his back.

In a way, he was.

28

After another sleepless night in the garage, Lenny sits at the kitchen table sipping her morning coffee. It's the weekend, so the twins aren't up yet. Juls stumbles into the room, sleepy eyed, a half smile curling his lips. Fender follows at his heels. The poor sap has no clue Rudi-Rose has already flown the coop. Lenny saw her leave before dawn. She'd looked out the front curtains just in time to see her beaded head hop into a cab. Like a summer storm, Rudi-Rose has done it again. She's blown through town, suddenly and without warning, leaving damage in her wake.

Juls feeds the dog, then pours himself a coffee. He glances out the back window to see if his girlfriend is in the yard, then his eyes search the living room behind Lenny. He's about to ask where she is when he sees the look on his grandmother's face. His smile dissolves. He sits across from Lenny and runs a hand through his thick dark hair. Lenny's about to tell him he's better off.

"Don't," he says, staring into his coffee.

She keeps quiet.

"Why do the girls think you're a detective?" he asks.

Before she can answer, the doorbell rings. Juls is up and out of his chair in a flash.

"I got it," he says. He thinks she's come back.

Lenny hears the front door open, then the sound of a woman's voice. It's not Rudi-Rose.

"How'd you get this address?" Juls sounds angry.

Lenny rises and quickly crosses the living room.

"I'm just trying to do my job," says the woman.

"My kids are here," says Juls. "Fuck off."

Lenny spots Nora on the stairs, eyes wide. She sees a brunette woman in a blazer and jeans standing at the threshold, holding out her phone. She's recording. She must be a reporter. Juls is looking past her, scanning the street.

"I know you think I'm the enemy, but I'm not out to get you," says the woman. "I actually feel for you. It can't be easy—one grandfather a cop, one a criminal?"

"He's a businessman," says Juls.

Juls flinches when he feels Lenny behind him.

"If Reg runs a legit operation, why were you arrested the other night?" asks the woman, placing one hand against the open door. "What was going on in that warehouse?"

"Move your fucking hand," says Juls.

Lenny sees his fist clench at his side. The woman turns her attention to Lenny.

"You're Eleanor Bird, right?" she says. "How do you feel about your grandson being a Caffey? I imagine your husband's rolling in his grave."

Lenny wishes she hadn't said that. Before she can stop Juls, he yanks the door hard. The woman tumbles forward, landing on her knees. Her phone flies from her hand. Juls grabs her elbow, lifts her in one motion, and shoves her out the door. She tumbles to the porch. He tosses the phone at her. Lenny's next-door neighbor, Mr. Crawley, is standing on the sidewalk staring.

Juls slams the door. He turns around and sees Nora running back upstairs, past her sister, who is only now coming down. Flo rubs sleep from her eyes.

"I'm hungry," she says.

Juls slams his fist against the door.

"Wha'd I say?" says Flo.

Juls storms past Lenny, down the hall, and out the back door. Lenny looks at Flo.

"He's upset that your mom had to go," she says.

Lenny figures she might as well tear that Band-Aid off. Flo's lower lip quivers. Lenny coaxes Flo into the kitchen, pours her a bowl of cereal, then heads out to the backyard.

She finds Juls smoking. His hands are shaking.

"What was that all about?" she asks.

"She had no business showing up here," he says, exhaling his cigarette smoke sharply.

"You know her?" asks Lenny.

"She's a fucking journalist. She's been working a story about organized crime," says Juls. "She's come by the club. Harassed some of the dancers. She's been dogging Reg for months."

He flicks his cigarette butt onto the patio.

"Me talking to her won't look good," Juls says. "He won't like it."

Lenny realizes Juls is more scared than angry. It's the second time she's seen that look on his face. The first time was when he found out Billy had been in the house. He's afraid of Reg.

Juls phone pings. He pulls it from his pocket and checks the screen.

Without another word, he picks up the discarded butt and goes inside the house.

Lenny hates that he's scared, and she hates that she doesn't know why.

But she is going to find out.

29

Lenny props her phone in the cup holder and keeps an eye on the small map on her phone. Juls' location pin moves along Churchill Avenue going south. Just like last Saturday morning, he's driving the girls to their swimming lessons at Dovercourt Recreation Centre. Nora took some convincing. Juls apologized for getting angry and told the girls everything was okay, and their mother would be back soon.

Lenny stays well behind his vehicle. After dropping off the twins, he continues on. Today he's not staying to watch them swim. She suspected as much. No doubt that text he got was from Reg or Billy or one of Caffey's crew. Lenny is certain he's been in contact with them since making bail. She needs to know what he's been up to. What he won't tell her. What's got him so on edge. As Lenny follows him, she's dogged by Sugar's threat.

Stay the fuck out of it, or you're gonna get someone killed. And it could be your grandson.

Juls heads down Carling, then takes Fisher to Prince of Wales Drive, where he turns right onto Colonnade. It's an industrial area running alongside a set of train tracks, mostly factory outlets and office buildings, but at one end, there's an outdoor minigolf park. His location pin stops at the park. She reaches the entrance and drives in.

As Lenny is rolling through the parking lot, she spots Juls. He's standing in the shade of some trees near the railway line at the back of the property. He looks deep in conversation with two people—a man and a woman. Lenny reverses into a parking spot between a large van and a black SUV. She gets out and peeks around the van. They're still talking. The man is facing her. It's not Reg or Billy. It must be one of their guys. The woman turns. It's Sugar.

Out of the corner of her eye, Lenny spots a police cruiser pulling into the entrance. It begins to circle the lot. Juls can't be seen with Caffey's crew. If the cops run their IDs, they'll find out he's breaking his bail. He could be arrested.

As the cruiser gets closer, Lenny decides the only thing to do is create a diversion. She jumps into the Jeep and backs straight into the side of the cruiser as it passes. The two officers look stunned. They get out, examine their vehicle, then approach her window. One of the cops is in his late fifties, and the other looks to be a fresh-faced rookie.

Juls and his coworkers hear the crash, and their meeting breaks up.

When the cops see who's in the driver's seat of the Jeep, the older one seems more concerned about Lenny's well-being than some minor dent in their vehicle. Lenny pretends to feel faint as he helps her from the Jeep. The rookie asks Lenny for her license, insurance, and proof of registration. He's all business. She suddenly realizes three things.

She doesn't have a driver's license.

The Jeep's permit and insurance are long expired.

And, worse than that, she has Hank's revolver in her purse.

After Billy broke into the house, she dug it out of the box of Hank's old things in the garage. She's been carrying it around ever since. Lenny pretends to search her purse but instead tucks the revolver deeper, then admits she doesn't actually have a license or insurance. The rookie shakes his head and flips open his ticket book. Lenny reaches for the copy of the vehicle permit that Hank always kept tucked under the visor, held with an elastic band. She hands it to the older cop, who examines it.

"What's your name, ma'am?" says the younger one.

"Eleanor Bird," she says. No point in lying.

"I'll run the plates," says the rookie. "See if we get a hit on the name."

A hit. *Does he really think I'm on some most-wanted list?*

The rookie heads back to the cruiser. This is bad. They're going to book her, take her down to the station, search her, find the revolver, and lock her up. What was she thinking?

"Hold up there, Travers," says the older cop. He turns to Lenny. "You were married to Hank Bird."

She nods. He looks at Hank's name on the permit, then back at Lenny.

"Sit tight for one sec, Mrs. Bird," he says.

He goes over to talk to the rookie. She can't hear what they're saying, but the two appear to be at odds. The older cop looks like he gets his way when the rookie jumps into the cruiser but doesn't touch the radio or laptop. Instead, the rookie just sits there drumming his fingers on the steering wheel. The older cop comes back over to Lenny. He smiles and tells her they're going to take her home.

She can't believe it.

The cop's name is Nelson. He knew her husband, and he remembers her from the annual Christmas parties. He says if she promises not to drive until she's renewed her license, insurance, and registration, they'll let her off with a warning. It's the least he can do, he says. He tells her not to worry about the damage. It's an old cruiser that's seen better days. He drives her home in the Jeep, and the young rookie follows in the cruiser. When they reach Julian Avenue, Lenny spots the Mustang parked in the driveway. Juls will have seen her. He'll know she followed him, and he won't be happy. Lenny invites the officer inside for tea, but he politely declines.

Thank God.

Lenny waves as they drive off, then closes the front door. She grips the entryway table for support. Lenny breathes a huge sigh of relief. Because of Hank, she's not in the middle of getting her mug shot and fingerprints taken. Instead, she's home.

Lenny looks around the house for Juls. She spots him out the kitchen window, sitting in the backyard. Lenny opens the fridge. She's down to her last two cans of beer. She makes a mental note to do a beer run, then grabs the cans of IPA. A peace offering. She goes out back and sits in the wicker chair next to Juls. He doesn't look at her. He takes a long drag from his cigarette. She hands him one of the cans.

"Sunsplit?" she says.

He looks at it and sees the name on the side of the can.

"Little early, no?" he says. He takes the beer anyway. "But hell, you don't seem to have any boundaries, so what the fuck?"

He pops the lid and takes a swig.

"You should be thanking me," she says. "If I hadn't distracted them, those nice police officers would have caught you doing *exactly* what you're not supposed to be doing. I know those were Reg's people. So if it weren't for me, you'd be sitting in a jail cell right now."

He shakes his head.

"I'll give you this much, Lenny," he says. "You're ballsy as fuck."

She takes a gulp of ale for courage.

"Juls, I need you to tell me what you really do for Reg," she says. "All these years working for him, I doubt you're still a bouncer."

He drains the beer, then drops his cigarette in the can.

"You don't want to know, Lenny," he says, looking at the ground.

"I know it has something to do with human trafficking," she says, sipping her beer.

His Adam's apple bounces. He wasn't expecting that. He tries to change the subject.

"Sugar said you were down at the club," he says. "Asking questions."

Lenny can still feel the welt on her neck. She doesn't answer.

"Maybe the girls are right about you being a detective," he says. "Guess we've both been hiding things."

Juls stands up. He looks out into the garden, his back to Lenny. She keeps at him.

"I know you don't think I have any right to be, but I'm worried about you, Juls," says Lenny. "You've told me diddly-squat about your arrest, and I can tell you're scared. All I've been trying to do is find out what the hell is going on."

Juls turns around.

"Diddly-squat?" he says, trying not to smile.

"It's not funny," she says, slamming her can on the table. "I don't care how bad it is. You can tell me. I'm tougher than you think."

Juls sighs. He sits back down next to her. Fender emerges from the bushes. The dog sniffs his way over to Juls and leans against his leg. He scratches the dog's scruffy head.

"That guy I was meeting with. He's not one of Reg's men," says Juls. "He's a cop. Works in Intel. He's my handler. I've been giving him information on Reg going on six months."

Lenny stares at her grandson. She's stunned. Lenny knows all about confidential informants from Hank.

"Sugar's undercover," he continues. "She's the one who recruited me."

Sugar wasn't threatening Juls. She was trying to protect him.

"You're right about the human smuggling," he says, picking at his fingernails. "Reg got in with these dirtbags about a year ago. He started down a dark path. He's been trying to drag me along with him. Billy has kept me out of the worst of it. Thing is, it's my girls I worry about. Reg has customers who like them young. And he acts like he owns me and my kids. I was scared for them. I felt like I was drowning, then Sugar tossed me a lifeline. A way out. A way to protect them—so I grabbed it."

Juls' hands tremble as he lights another cigarette. It reminds her of Billy's tremors. All of a sudden, his frayed nerves and short fuse make so much more sense. Juls has been lying to the people closest to him for months. Pretending. Spying. And if they caught wind, they'd kill him.

"I got arrested with the other guys so as not to blow my cover," he says.

Lenny's heart aches for him, but it is also full to bursting.

"I knew you were a good boy," she says.

He looks away.

"Today at the meet, they said Reg is worried someone's talking to the cops. They think he's just sniffing around," says Juls. "But I'm walking a tightrope, Lenny. So from here on out, you have to trust me. I need you to lay low, back off, and let me do my thing. Can you do that for me?"

Lenny nods.

"I should have dragged you back home when you were sixteen," says Lenny.

"I wouldn't have come," he says.

Juls meets her eye.

"I'm sorry for what I said the other night," he says. "About Hank. I didn't mean it."

"I know I wasn't the easiest person to live with back then," she says. "Maybe now too."

"I was an asshole," he says.

"None of that matters," she says. "What does is that you're doing the right thing."

"I'm no fucking saint," he says. "Maybe I deserve whatever I get."

"Don't say that, Juls," she says.

"He's my grandfather," he says. "He's family, and I'm stabbing him in the back."

Lenny takes Juls' hand in hers.

"*This* is family," she says, squeezing tight.

There's sadness in his eyes. Despite everything, he loves Reg. She understands why Juls is drawn to the man. Maya called it Reg Caffey's orbit—like everything and everyone revolves around him, drawn to him by some unseeable gravitational force. Lenny has fought its pull for years.

But in this moment, she feels something else.

The universe has shifted.

The people she loves most are under threat.

And her world and Reg Caffey's seem destined to collide.

PART TWO

30

A week has come and gone since Juls confessed to being a police informant. Tensions have eased between grandson and grandmother. Lenny has done as he asked. She's been lying low, staying away from the Carleton. Lenny even gave up beer. Partly because she was all out and figured sobriety might ensure she didn't mess up. Juls jumped on the wagon in solidarity.

It's Thanksgiving weekend, and Lenny goes to visit her father. Guilt comes along for the ride. She's been so preoccupied with Juls' situation, Silas has been the last person on her mind. As she hops off the bus outside Maplelawn, Lenny wishes she'd brought the twins. She realizes it hasn't been the worst thing having Juls and the girls around. Flo's silliness lightens the mood, when she's not sobbing. And Nora keeps everything shipshape. She's even been teaching Lenny how to use her phone. She's quite the tech-savvy kid. The house feels different. More alive. Fender feels it too. The old dog has more pep in his step.

Silas is lying on his bed when Lenny enters his room. He's fully clothed but fast asleep. She waits a few minutes and then decides to check in with the staff. It's not like Silas to nap this early in the day. The nurse at the care station informs her he's been up all night pacing the halls. *Sundowning*, she calls it. Then she goes back to cutting paper leaves for a holiday garland. Lenny decides to leave. As she walks away, the nurse tosses her a parting shot.

A loss of routine can cause it.

Lenny pretends not to hear. She feels like a child scolded.

A half hour later, Lenny is standing in line at the checkout at the Beer Store. She is using all her willpower to stop herself from opening one of the cans in her cart and downing it right in the store. When she reaches the counter, Lenny places her selection of craft beers in front of the cashier, who scans them through. Lenny spots a stray can at the bottom of her cart. An oatmeal stout called the Darkness. She doesn't remember choosing that one. It's from a local brewery she likes. When she picks up the can, she finds a note under it.

I got proof.

That's all it says. She stares at it. *Proof of what?* It comes to her. She's forgotten all about Billy being in her house. And her shed.

Lenny drops the can. It rolls across the floor.

Credit or debit? It's the cashier.

You dropped this. It's a woman holding out the can of stout.

The other customers stare. The cashier points to the pay machine. Lenny rummages through her purse. Her fingers graze the revolver. She panics and rushes from the store.

Ma'am, your beer!

Lenny glances up and down the street for Billy. It has to be him. The bus whizzes past, so she sets off quickly on foot, looking behind her every so often to see if he's following.

He can't have proof.

He doesn't know anything.

If he had proof, he'd take it to the cops.

The long walk home begins to settle her shaken nerves. As she turns onto Julian Avenue, she reasons it out. The fucktard is just fishing. Trying to throw her off balance, but she won't let him. Lenny walks in her front door, drops her purse on the table, and looks into the living room.

She stops cold.

Reg Caffey is sitting on her sofa, arms outstretched, fancy loafers resting on her coffee table. He's made himself at home. So much so that she almost offers him a beer in jest.

Beer. She looks behind her. It dawns on her that she left the store without her supply. Lenny laughs out loud. Everything about this moment seems absurd. She knows the outburst is her nervous system trying to stave off panic.

Laugh or scream. Flight or fight.

She considers bolting out the door or grabbing Hank's revolver from her purse. She does neither. But she does stop laughing.

"There's our gurl," says Reg, curling his tongue. "The lad said you'd be back in no time."

Lenny hasn't noticed Juls until this moment. Through the archway in the living room, she can see him sitting at the kitchen table. His expression tells her nothing. Fender is at his feet, and there's a guy in a wrinkled suit sitting next to Juls. On the table is a black chauffeur's hat. Reg's driver. She can hear the girls giggling upstairs in Kendra's room.

"C'mere so I can get a better look at you, lass?" says Reg.

He lifts his feet off the table and pats the sofa next to him.

Lenny settles onto the sofa at the far end. She can smell the smoky aroma of cigars coming off his double-breasted suit. Fender scampers over to Lenny and jumps up. The dog sniffs in Reg's direction. He doesn't growl. Even the dog is fooled.

"You're awfully quiet, Eleanor. Thought you'd be happy I came by, seeing as the two of us haven't had a good *craic* in a while. You didn't so much as wave hello when you came into my establishment a few weeks back to whisk away my great-grandbabies," he says, sprinkling in the old Irish charm. "I have to say, it hurt my feelings a touch."

"That wasn't my intention," says Lenny.

Lenny sits on her hands so he doesn't see them shaking.

"I thought we'd developed something of a friendship, you and me," he says. "A meeting of the minds. But, lo and behold, next thing I know, you're down at the courthouse, and once again, you're weaving your way into my affairs."

"I was looking out for my family," she says. "Which is why you can't be here."

Out of the corner of her eye, she sees Juls shift in his chair.

"And why exactly is that, my gurl?" he says, smiling.

"The court order," she says, her mouth bone dry.

"Ah, the infamous court order," he says. "You know, *that* is precisely why I came by."

Fender ambles across the sofa to Reg and sniffs the gold ring on his finger. Reg scoops the dog up in one massive hand and places him on his lap. He gently strokes the dog's head.

"I felt it was best to sit with you a spell—to remind you of the terms of our little agreement." He nods toward Juls. "The one where I keep you in the loop, so to speak, about the boy and his kin—and you stay on your side of the street, *so to speak*."

Lenny glances at Juls. He meets her gaze. This is news to him.

"Now when that justice of the peace, God love her, asked the court who was responsible for the lad, and *you* stood up, well, that brought you over to *my* side of the street," says Reg. "And now here we are."

Reg's hand loops around the dog's neck. Fender's little tail wags. Lenny can't breathe.

"I've always liked you, Eleanor. You're good people. Hell, you were copper's wife. I bet you never so much as jaywalked in your life." Reg looks over at Juls. "That's what you're always saying, isn't it lad? Your grandma's a real straight arrow?"

Juls doesn't answer.

Flo comes tumbling down the stairs and into the room. She startles Lenny and the dog. Fender jumps off the sofa and scurries back over to Juls.

"Lenny! You're home," squeals Flo as she belly flops onto the sofa between her and Reg. "Daddy says we can order pizza for dinner."

"That's nice. Now you go on back upstairs and play with your sister," says Lenny. "I'm not done talking to your great-grandpa."

"He can stay too," says Flo, turning to Reg. "You like pizza, don't you, Pops?"

"Oh, that I do, sweet dove." Reg smiles. "But didn't your dada tell you? Me and him, we've got some business to deal with tonight."

"You do?" she says, sticking out her lower lip.

"Another time, I promise, darlin'," he says, pinching her cheek.

Flo giggles.

"As you wish, Lord Regan." She smiles, putting on her best British accent. "Lady Eleanor, I bid you adieu."

Flo twirls, then bows to Lenny and Reg before scampering back upstairs.

Lenny makes sure Flo is gone before she speaks.

"Juls can't go anywhere with you," she says quietly.

"You see, there it is again, you acting all responsible for the lad. I don't doubt your moral conviction on the matter, Eleanor. But I, *too*, have responsibilities."

Reg brushes dog hair from his trousers as he continues talking.

"Customers who expect merchandise to be properly packaged and delivered, you get me?"

It's not a question.

"Now tonight, there happens to be an all-hands-on-deck sort of meeting that I'm afraid can't be rescheduled," he says with a smile. "And I expect the young lad to be in attendance."

He nods to Juls.

"And *you*, lovely Eleanor, now that you're *on my side*," he says with a smile. "*You* are going to make sure he shows. After all, the court did make you responsible, didn't they now? And I know you're not one for shirking."

Reg slaps his knees and looks over at Juls.

"I best shove off so you can spend the rest of this fine Saturday with those precious little girls of yours," he says. "I'll text you the when and where once everything's set."

Reg is heading out the front door before his man even realizes the get-together is over. The chauffeur grabs his hat and follows fast. Lenny peeks around the front curtains. Reg walks down the laneway and crosses the street to his Mercedes. She didn't notice it parked there when she came home. She was too distracted with thoughts of Billy.

Mr. Crawley is weeding his garden. He's not hiding the fact that he's watching Reg. Crawley better watch *himself.* It's one thing to mess with Lenny, but it's a whole other ball game messing with Reg Caffey.

She's learning that lesson fast.

31

After they finish their pizza, Juls and the girls go outside to play hide-and-seek through the maze of pathways in the garden. Still no text from Reg about tonight's meeting. The sun burns orange as it drifts below the horizon. When it's too dark to see anymore, they come inside. The girls' cheeks are flushed, their knees grass stained, their curly hair adorned with twigs and leaves. The twins change into their pajamas, then cuddle on the sofa with their dad.

Lenny takes Fender around the block, hoping Reg was messing with them. Maybe there is no meeting. When she gets back, Juls is reclined deep in the cushions, his arms around Flo and Nora on either side of him. Flo looks like she's asleep, and Nora is yawning.

Lenny goes into the kitchen and fills Fender's bowl with water. As he laps it up, she sits at the table. Juls untangles himself from the twins. The girls curl into the warm spot left behind. He joins Lenny at the table and checks his phone again. Still nothing.

"I found out something about Hank the other day," says Lenny, hoping to distract him.

"Okay," he says.

"You remember how he was always working late?" she asks.

"I guess," says Juls. "It was a long time ago."

"You'd only been living with us for a couple of months," she says.

"Yeah," says Juls.

"Turns out he *wasn't* working," she says. "He was spending his time somewhere else."

"Doing what?" asks Juls.

"I have no idea," she says.

"An affair?" asks Juls.

"No, that wasn't Hank," says Lenny, shaking her head. "If I had to guess, it had something to do with your dad. There's just no way Hank would have let it go."

"You think he was going after him?" he asks.

"I don't know. I remember a few months after your mom died, Vincent was accused of killing a security guard. It was some bank robbery that happened a year earlier, but some new evidence surfaced, and he was arrested."

"Yeah, Billy said something about that once," says Juls. "Turned out to be a bogus charge. He got released. It was just before my dad skipped town."

"Maybe Hank was mixed up in that somehow," says Lenny.

Juls' phone pings. He checks the screen, then pockets it. He stands up.

"Gotta fly," he says.

Lenny's heart sinks. Reg wasn't posturing. There is a meeting.

"Sugar's going to be there to watch your back, right?" she asks.

"I'll be okay," he says. "He's just flexing. Letting everyone know the raid didn't rattle him and he's still the shit."

"Be careful," she says.

"I won't be long," he says.

Before he leaves, Juls kisses both girls on the forehead. Flo doesn't wake, and Nora doesn't take her eyes off the TV. As he's walking out, he glances back. Nora doesn't notice him looking. She doesn't know what he's thinking.

Lenny can guess. As Juls said, he's living on a tightrope.

He's hoping this isn't the last time he sees his daughters.

32

By lunch Sunday, Juls still isn't home. He's been gone all night. Lenny tried tracking his phone, but no location was found. It must be powered off. Lenny wishes Hank was here. He'd know what to do. Her mind is spiraling. It's been more than twelve hours. How long can a meeting last? She calls the Full Nelson, but the voice message says the club is closed. Of course it is. It's Thanksgiving. She considers calling Sully or Maya, but what would she say? She'd just get Juls in trouble. He's not supposed to be anywhere near Reg Caffey. And Juls might be a CI, but that doesn't mean anyone but his handler knows about it.

It's a warm autumn day, so Lenny takes the girls on a walk along the river with Fender. The twins take turns holding his leash. Nora knows something is off. That morning, Lenny told the girls that Juls left early to go play golf. That's why he wasn't there when they woke. It's the first thing she could think to say. She knew Reg belonged to an exclusive golf club. But the excuse hadn't passed Nora's smell test. She'd scrunched her nose, and now she was pouting.

The four of them wander down to the river's edge and collect stones on a small beach at the end of Carleton Avenue. Then they make their way through Tunney's Pasture, stopping by the Beer Store on Scott Street. It's closed. Damn Thanksgiving. Lenny would give her left arm for an ice-cold beer.

As they head home, they make a pit stop at the playground on Parkdale Avenue. Vendors are selling pumpkins and gourds and mums at the outdoor market. A brewery is selling craft beer at one of the stalls. Lenny gives thanks and buys two six-packs. Flo and Nora play on the swing set. Lenny sits on a bench and lifts her chin to the sun, hoping the warmth untangles the knots in her stomach. She's killing time. Hoping he'll be home when they get back. He's not.

As they head up the front path, a car pulls to the curb in front of the house. Lenny turns and spots the journalist jumping out. Lenny hurries the girls toward the front steps. She tells Flo and Nora to take Fender inside, then she turns as the woman heads for her.

"I think my grandson made it clear we have nothing to say to you?" Lenny says.

Her neighbor, Mr. Crawley, has stopped raking his leaves. Why is that man always around at the worst time?

"Was that Florence and Nora Caffey?" asks the woman as she pulls out her phone.

"Don't you dare," says Lenny, pointing to the phone.

The journalist nods and puts it away.

"Okay, off the record. I'm not here to harass you, Mrs. Bird," says the woman. "I'm here because, frankly, I'm concerned. Something's going down. And I doubt your grandson wants his family in the cross fire. Maybe he *is* a good guy. But I can't know unless I speak to Julian."

"Get off my property, or I'll call the police," says Lenny.

Lenny is about to turn away when she spots Crawley filming them with his phone. She gives him the finger.

"A body was found floating in the Ottawa River this morning," says the woman.

Lenny freezes.

"We think there's some kind of turf war heating up," says the woman. "Some of Reg Caffey's associates were seen around town. These are bad people, Mrs. Bird. Julian should think about those little girls and get on the right side of this thing before it's too late."

Lenny turns and grips the porch rail as headless corpses bob across her brain.

"Either he's one of them or he isn't," the woman calls out.

Lenny squeezes her eyes shut. It can't be Juls. Her limbs thaw, and she starts to climb the steps. She can hear the journalist behind her. Lenny turns, and the woman shoves her card into Lenny's hand.

"For when he's ready to talk," says the woman. Then she leaves.

Lenny catches movement at the living room window.

Nora ducks out of sight. The window is open.

She heard everything.

33

Fifteen years ago

He waited on the far side of the casino parking lot with a clear view of the main doors. He'd tracked the car to the location a few hours earlier. No sign of its occupant. He must be inside. The man came here most days, usually in the afternoon. He stayed a few hours. It was obvious from the way he carried himself when he came outside if he'd had any luck or not. Shoulders hunched, hands deep in his pockets, scowl on his ugly mug if he'd lost. Chest puffed, girl on his arm, smug mug if he'd won. The man finally appeared. Today, he'd clearly lost. The loser squealed out of the parking lot. He followed.

Twenty minutes later, the car stopped at an auto-body shop. He pulled onto the dirt shoulder a few hundred feet away. He grabbed his camera and pointed the long lens as the loser got out of his car. He took rapid photos of the loser banging on the garage door with his fist. The place looked closed. After a few seconds, the garage door opened, and a small, wiry young man stepped out. The young man cowered. The loser shouted in his face and pushed him inside. The garage door closed behind them.

About twenty minutes later, the loser came out, rubbing his hand like he'd punched something or someone. The loser had a spring to his step as he jumped in his car and sped off.

He waited there, not bothering to follow the loser just yet. It didn't take long for the young man to come outside. Using his long lens, he took a series of shots as the man hastily fumbled with his car keys, looking over his shoulder as he did, occasionally pressing a dirty cloth to a bleeding gash over one of his eyes. The man finally got into his car and drove away. The camera caught his license plate. When the car was out of sight, he pulled his vehicle off the shoulder, drove toward the building, and parked across the street. He took a photo of the sign on the front of the body shop. Tento's Garage.

Then he checked the GPS tracker and drove in that direction.

34

Thanksgiving is ruined. Lenny doesn't bother cooking the turkey. It's still sitting in the fridge, likely spoiled. She feeds the girls mac and cheese instead. Sunday rolls into Monday, and still no word from Juls. No text, no call, nothing. He promised the twins they would carve pumpkins together. Flo and Nora try doing it themselves, but Flo slices her finger, which leads to tears and an early bedtime. Lenny insists. The girls have school tomorrow, and Great-Grandma needs some alone time.

In the garage, Lenny has one foot on the glove box, and the other leg dangles out of the Jeep. She drains her fourth beer. This one is a hazy pale ale with a hint of lime. It goes down smooth, but like the others, it doesn't help. Juls has been gone two days. This can't be good for her blood pressure.

Lenny glances at the driver's seat.

"I don't know if I can do this. Not again," she says. "What if he doesn't come back? What if I've lost him too?"

Hank doesn't answer, as usual.

His silence is deafening, and it makes her blood boil.

Lenny whips the empty can across the garage. She starts kicking the Jeep as hard as she can, over and over, denting the dash until it cracks and the glove box pops open.

She can't help but laugh. That glove box has been jammed shut for years.

She stops laughing when she sees what's inside. It's Hank's cell phone. She couldn't find it after he died. She thought it was lost or at work. The charger is still in Hank's bedside table, where he kept it. She put his watch, wedding ring, and wallet in along with it when he died. Tucked them away fifteen years ago. And like the voice message on her answering machine, they are pieces of him she can't bring herself to part with. Sometimes, Lenny takes out his wallet and smells it. Maybe it's her imagination, but she's certain traces of him linger in its folds.

Lenny picks up Hank's phone and presses the screen. Not surprisingly, the phone is dead. She places it on the dash, then roots around inside the glove box. She finds a pair of sunglasses, a small ice scraper, a pen, and the Jeep's manual. An envelope is sticking out of the manual. She pulls it out. Inside are some photos and papers. One is a newspaper clipping of an obituary for someone named Paul Choi. The other paper is an autopsy report for Choi. As she leafs through the manual, she sees handwritten notes scribbled in the margins. Hank's barely legible handwriting. She'd know it anywhere. She flips through the photos. Most are of Vincent Caffey. It looks like Hank was following him.

The rumble of a car's engine grabs her attention.

It's the Mustang. It's Juls.

Lenny tosses the manual and jumps from the Jeep. She races into the house and dashes to the front door. A key turns the dead bolt. The door opens.

She sees Rudi-Rose first, then she sees him. Rudi-Rose is holding him up. He can barely walk. In the dim hallway, with his head hanging, she can't see his face. Rudi-Rose looks at Lenny with bloodshot eyes.

"We're going to need a first aid kit," says Rudi-Rose. "And a needle and thread."

Lenny doesn't think. She takes the stairs two at a time, dashes down the upstairs hall, rummages through her linen closet and bathroom for supplies, then races back downstairs.

She finds them in the kitchen. Rudi-Rose is standing over Juls. He's seated in a chair, head tipped back. She's holding a bag of frozen peas over half his face. Lenny spots a deep gash across his cheek. Blood stains the front of his T-shirt. When Rudi-Rose lowers the bag, Lenny gasps in horror. She barely recognizes her grandson. He's been badly beaten. One eye is swollen shut, and his lips are puffed out and caked in dried blood.

Lenny drops the first aid kit on the table. Rudi-Rose takes the sewing kit from Lenny. She threads one of the needles, then starts sewing the gash in his cheek closed.

"You got any painkillers?" asks Rudi-Rose.

Lenny gets some of the leftover pills from when she crashed her car. She brings Juls a glass of water. He opens his mouth. She puts the pills in and holds the water close to his lips. He sips the water, coughs, and winces. Lenny can hear wheezing. He must have broken ribs.

"He needs a hospital," says Lenny.

"No," says Rudi-Rose. "We can't."

Rudi-Rose finishes sewing him up. Lenny hands her a clean dishcloth that she's run under warm water, and Rudi-Rose dabs the dried blood from his face. Lenny sinks into the chair across from Juls. His knuckles are a mess of bruises and cuts. His T-shirt is torn in places, and she can glimpse bruises on his torso and a nasty scrape across his chest.

Lenny gently touches his hand.

He's home.

35

The next morning is littered with more lies and bribes as Lenny makes the girls' lunches and hustles them into the Mustang.

"Daddy caught a bad cold when he was golfing and needs to rest," she tells the girls.

"Is he hungover?" asks Nora.

"No, but he might be contagious," says Lenny. "Best you leave him be."

She doesn't tell them their mother is back.

Last night, after Rudi-Rose patched him up, she and Juls went to his room, and they hadn't come out since. Lenny didn't want the girls peeking in. They couldn't see him like that. And if Flo knew her mom was there, Lenny would never get them out the door.

At school, Lenny watches the twins across the yard. Flo is doing pirouettes to the delight of her friends. Nora is standing alone, fidgeting with the straps on her backpack. Lenny used to linger like this and watch Kendra in the schoolyard after dropping her off. Hoping she had nice friends, hoping she was happy, hoping the world was being kind to her. As Lenny looks at Nora and Flo, she worries their world might have something else in store for them. Something cruel—like it did for Kendra. As she watches them, she vows to do everything she can to make sure that doesn't happen—not this time.

Back at the house, Lenny finds Rudi-Rose sitting at the kitchen table. Her hair is damp. She's wearing one of Juls' shirts. She looks like a child. Her eyelids are heavy. Both hands are wrapped around her mug of coffee like she's trying to warm them. Her cigarettes and phone sit on the table next to her. Lenny pours herself a cup and joins Rudi-Rose.

"How is he?" Lenny asks.

"He'll live," says Rudi-Rose.

The young woman takes a sip of her coffee. Her hands are vibrating so much that she spills some. Lenny gets a cloth and wipes up the spill. She's desperate to know what happened to Juls, but she doesn't push it. She waits for her to get there.

"It was fucked up, what he did," says Rudi-Rose.

"Who?" asks Lenny.

"Who do you think?" she answers.

She's talking about Reg. A darkness swims in the young woman's eyes.

"Everyone was there. Reg's inner circle. About twenty guys and eight women. He took all our phones. Stowed them behind the bar like always. At first, we thought it was a regular meeting. Then he dropped a fucking bomb. He said he knew someone on his crew was working with the cops. None of us could believe it. He said no one was leaving until he rooted out the rat. Then he laid out the rules. This was no meeting. This was going to be a good old Irish *cath*."

"I don't know what that means," says Lenny.

"It means a battle. Reg is obsessed with this sport called *bataireacht*. It's a type of Irish stick fighting, and it's fucking brutal," she says. "I'd seen a few of the guys sparring before. Reg got into it in his street-gang days. It's how he trains them to be tough. But this felt different. This wasn't practice. Reg said if they were loyal, they should be willing to fight to prove it. Not one of the guys wavered or backed down."

Rudi-Rose notices blood under her fingernail. She scrapes it away.

"Did he find his rat?" Lenny asks.

"I don't think he was ever looking for one. It was one of Reg's games. I knew it the second his Toronto and Montreal connects walked through the door with their guys. This was a fucking tournament. Reg even brought in some girls from his stable to keep the other bosses entertained at intermissions. I got lucky. He put me on the bar."

Her lower lip trembles.

"It went on for two days," says Rudi-Rose. "Then everything went to shit."

"How so?" asks Lenny.

She bites her lip as she picks up her phone and taps the screen.

She slides it across the table to Lenny.

"See for yourself," she says. "This is who Reg Caffey really is."

Lenny looks at the frozen video image on the phone.

She doesn't move at first, but then her hand reaches out.

She has to know.

She picks it up and presses play, and the video comes to life.

36

The angle is low like Rudi-Rose has propped the phone on a shelf or box near the floor. It's an unobstructed view across a large open space with concrete floors and high ceilings. It looks like a warehouse. Much of the room is in shadows except for a large two-foot-high platform, flooded with light, at the center of the room. Dark stains streak the surface. It looks like a boxing ring but without guard ropes.

Folding chairs are arranged at the far side of the ring, where a collection of bloodied and bruised men sit waiting their turn. Sugar is holding a towel to one guy's nose. Most of the men are bare chested, either slumped back or doubled over.

In the foreground is a row of fancy leather barstools where four men in suits are lounging, cocktails and cigars in hand. Clouds of smoke hover around them. Billy stands nearby at a table where money is stacked.

Juls is sitting on the edge of the platform, his bare chest heaving. His muscles glisten with sweat and blood. Reg is standing in front of him, leaning over Juls, talking to him, one hand on his shoulder. Juls is nodding as he listens. Reg ruffles Juls' hair, then approaches the other bosses with a shit-eating grin.

"Gentlemen," says Reg, rolling up his shirtsleeves. "We're agreed? Each of us puts up our toughest lad. No holds barred."

"All fighters in the ring at once?" asks one of the bosses.

Reg smirks.

"As you like. You want to play dirty, have your lads team up against my best fella," he says, nodding to Juls. "Suit yourselves, but the ante just went up fifty K."

There are grumblings from the four bosses.

"Gentleman, I can hear your feckin' balls shriveling," says Reg with a snort. "Allow me to sweeten the pot. Let's say we toss in all our winnings—and seeing as my boy's won more than all your lads combined, I'd say that's one helluva sweetener."

"Winner takes all?" confirms one of the bosses.

"The whole colcannon," says Reg.

The bosses look at each other. Nods are exchanged. Reg smiles. He turns to face the room, arms outstretched, voice booming.

"Looks like we got ourselves one helluva feckin' finale, lads!" he bellows.

Cheers erupt from above. In the shadows beyond, there's a metal staircase leading to an upper level. Men are seated on the steps, and some are hanging over the railings above. They're chanting *Caffey, Caffey, Caffey* as they bang their fists on the metal. Reg has invited more than just the bosses and their fighters. He's invited spectators to his little tournament.

Juls remains with his head bowed, a thick wood stick resting across his knees.

Billy is stacking cash on a table as the other bosses' bagmen empty their carrying cases. Each boss signals to their best fighter to get to his feet as Reg grabs the stick from Juls and steps onto the platform. He raises the weapon. It's the length of a sword with a large knob at one end. Reg lifts the stick to those watching above.

"What I hold in my hands might look like a simple walking stick made from the mighty blackthorn," he shouts, displaying the stick. "But this here is the shillelagh—a symbol of the good old Irish love of fighting. Yet make no mistake, friends, the shillelagh ain't about something as trivial as violence. No, lads. It's about the ancient warrior tradition of toughness, strength, endurance, and mastery. *That's* the feckin' shillelagh, and that's why we love to feckin' fight."

The audience cheers.

Reg holds out the stick to Juls, who rises to his feet and steps onto the platform. His entire body tenses and flexes. Juls shakes out his arms, awakening his muscles. Reg hands him the stick. When he takes it, Juls spins it like a baton, with ease and grace, then grasps it with both hands. The other fighters join him on the platform. They line up opposite Juls, each with a stick at the ready. Reg remains between them.

"Fighters ready," says Reg. "Let the games begin."

Reg steps off the platform, and the other four fighters try to spread out so they can surround Juls, but he quickly blocks the path of the fighter at one end, lunging and jabbing his stick into the man's chest. The man tries to sidestep Juls but stumbles and knocks into the man next him. The four men crash into each other like dominoes as Juls thrusts his stick with lightning speed into the first man's gut. The man's stick lowers. That's when Juls strikes, delivering a crushing blow to the man's jaw with the knobby end of the stick. Teeth and blood fly as the man does a face-plant. He's out cold. Cheers echo from above.

Juls takes a blow to the lower back from the second man and drops to one knee as the third fighter jabs him in the ribs. Juls rolls onto his back, driving his stick upward, hooking the knob of one fighter's stick. He yanks it hard, and the man drops his stick. Juls picks it up and jumps to his feet, now wielding two sticks. He attacks both men, striking quick blows, in and out, like a sword fighter. The man without a stick raises his arms to protect himself. Juls slams the stick down on his arm, and the sound of bone cracking is met with a wail. A piece of the man's radius sticks out of his forearm. More cheers erupt as the injured fighter staggers off the platform, cradling his broken limb.

Juls spins around and lands a blow to the other attacker's face. The fourth man dekes out of the way as the other man moans. Blood pours from his nose. He's dazed. Juls kicks his feet out from under him, and the man falls onto his back. Juls stomps on his chest a few times, then digs his foot under the man and rolls him off the platform.

The crowd whistles and hoots.

The fourth man, who looks more like a kid, has been waiting for Juls' back to be turned. The kid comes up behind him and uses his stick to get Juls in a chokehold, dragging him backward. Juls twists but can't get free. Juls drops one of the two sticks and drives the other into the kid's foot. The kid shrieks and loosens his grip, and Juls breaks from his hold, spins, and slams the kid across the ribs. The kid drops his stick, and it rolls off the platform. He doubles over, clutching his chest. Juls raises his stick high, but the kid is fast. He dekes out of the way, then high kicks the stick from Juls' hand. Juls goes after it, but the kid charges at him. They grip each other, bending and clasping necks like wrestlers.

The bosses are on their feet. Reg is pounding the edge of the platform.

"You got him now, boyo!" he yells.

Juls drops to one knee, slides under the kid, gets his arm through his legs, and grabs hold. He yanks the kid across his back, then rises. The kid's feet come off the ground. Juls lifts him high across his shoulders like a fireman, then slams him to the ground. The kid lies on his back groaning as Juls picks up his stick. He spirals it over his head in an elegant arc as he straddles the kid. Juls raises it high and aims the stick at the kid's face. The crowd chants.

Caffey, Caffey, Caffey.

"Finish the fecker," Reg hollers. "Kill him!"

Breathing hard, Juls looks at Reg. For a moment he's frozen, then Juls lowers the stick and tosses it aside. The crowd goes silent. Juls and Reg stare at each other. The first fighter that Juls knocked out has managed to drag himself to his feet after coming to. He's right behind Juls.

"At your back," yells Reg when he spots him.

Juls turns. It's too late. The man drives the knob of his stick into Juls' face. Juls hits the floor, blood pouring from a gash in his cheek.

"Get up!" yells Reg.

The man who hit Juls staggers to the center of the ring.

One of the bosses approaches the edge of the platform.

"We have a winner," he shouts. "It's over."

"It's not over till I say it's over," hollers Reg.

Reg jumps onto the platform and grabs Juls by the arms. He hauls him to his feet. Juls sways as Reg hands him a stick and pushes him toward the other man. Juls wobbles. The man looks at his boss, then at Reg. He strikes Juls in the chest, and Juls drops to his knees. Reg grabs the stick from Juls and jabs it straight into the other fighter's eye. The man falls, clutching his face. Reg starts beating him with the stick across the head. He hits him over and over until he's no longer moving. The whole place goes dead quiet.

Reg looks around. His eyes are wild. Panting hard. A string of spit drips from his mouth. His face and dress shirt are splattered with blood. The kid tries to sit up, but when he sees Reg standing over the beaten man, he lies back down. Juls is flat on his back, blood pooling beside his head from the gash. Reg moves to the center of the ring. He raises the bloody stick in victory.

The audience erupts.

Caffey, Caffey, Caffey.

Reg salutes the spectators, then he signals to his men. He hops off the platform, still holding the stick. Caffey's men take up positions around the other bosses as Reg starts shaking their hands whether they want to or not. A couple of his guys stand guard at the table of money. Billy comes over and whispers something in Reg's ear. When Reg makes a move like he's going to crack Billy with the stick, Billy cowers. Reg laughs. A young woman brings Reg a towel, and he wipes his face. Behind him the other crews are already dragging their men from the ring. One of the bosses has gone up on the platform, and he's kicking the kid who's curled in a ball. Sugar is helping Juls sit up. He spits blood. She waves in the direction of the camera. She's signaling Rudi-Rose to come help.

The video tips sideways, then stops.

37

Lenny places the phone on the kitchen table. She feels numb, yet at the same time, rage bubbles inside her. Rudi-Rose just stares at it.

"All eyes were on the ring, so I grabbed the phone from under the bar," she says. "I thought if Juls ended up dead, I'd have proof of what Reg did to him."

"*Did* someone die?" Lenny asks, remembering what the journalist said about a body.

"I don't know," says Rudi-Rose. "The bosses were royally pissed, but most of them are scared shitless of Reg. They let him have the cash. Some took out their frustrations on their fighters. Once everyone was gone, Reg made us clean the place. Most of the guys hadn't slept in two days, but he made them mop up their own blood. Juls included."

"Wait, why were *you* there?" asks Lenny.

"Reg wanted all his people there," she says. "No one was allowed to sit this one out."

"But you stopped working for him when the twins were born," says Lenny.

Rudi-Rose laughs.

"That asshole's owned me since I was thirteen," she says.

Rudi-Rose grabs her cigarettes and goes out into the backyard. As Lenny watches her go, it's like she's seeing her for the first time.

Someone's daughter, girlfriend, mother.

Another casualty of Reg Caffey.

Lenny makes some toast and takes it outside for Rudi-Rose. She refuses it, so Lenny leaves it on the table between them. They sit looking out at the garden. Rudi-Rose smokes with deep inhales and exhales. Just like Juls does when he's anxious. Lenny pushes the slightly burnt toast closer.

"You should eat something," says Lenny.

Rudi-Rose leans forward, elbows on her knees. She doesn't look at Lenny.

"My folks kicked me out when I was thirteen. We lived in this town called Clayton on the Saint Lawrence in upper New York state. For a while, I couch surfed with friends, then I met these guys who were running contraband smokes across the border. I needed money. They offered me a job in Canada. They introduced me to their boss. Reg Caffey. He paid my way to Ontario, then he took my passport. He said I could work off my debt by dancing in his club.

"Five years later I was no closer to paying him off. Then I met Juls. My knight in shining armor. When I got pregnant, I thought Reg would let me go—being the mother of his grandson's kids and all. But when the twins were a year old, Reg told me mat leave was over. He had a new role for me in Florida, recruiting and training new girls for these private retreats he hosts for his international connects. My US passport came in handy, I guess. Ever since, I've been his American bottom bitch."

She drops her cigarette butt and stands up.

"You've seen who Reg is," she says. "Well, now you know who I am."

"Juls has no idea, does he?" asks Lenny.

"If Juls ever found out, he'd try to end Reg," she says. "He'd get himself killed. I might be a terrible mother, but Juls has good in him. He's not like me. The best thing I can do for those girls is make sure they still have their dad."

Lenny feels a surge of tenderness for Rudi-Rose.

"Take care of them for me, Lenny," says Rudi-Rose.

She heads for the back door, and Lenny runs after her.

"Wait, where are you going?" Lenny asks.

"To our apartment to get some things," she says. "Reg said I could drive Juls home, but he wants me back today for a new job. Don't tell Nor and Flo I was here."

Lenny grabs Rudi-Rose by the arm.

"I can't let you go back," says Lenny.

"Seriously?" says Rudi-Rose, glaring at Lenny's hand.

"It's too dangerous," says Lenny.

"I have no choice," says Rudi-Rose.

"You don't understand," says Lenny.

"You're the clueless one, you old bat," says Rudi-Rose, trying to yank her arm free.

"You can't run away like you always do. Not now," says Lenny, holding tight.

Rudi-Rose slaps Lenny's face. Lenny is stunned. She slaps Rudi-Rose across the face. The young woman wasn't expecting that. Tears pool in her eyes. Lenny instantly regrets hitting her. Lenny pulls her into an embrace.

"Let me go," says Rudi-Rose.

Lenny pulls her closer and whispers in her ear.

"Reg was right. One of his crew is working with the police," says Lenny. "It's Juls."

Rudi-Rose pushes away from Lenny's grasp, shaking her head, her tears spilling out.

She sinks to the back steps and sits there, shaking her head.

"No," she says softly. "Not Juls."

38

Fifteen years ago

According to the tracker, the car was stationary near a diner in the Carlington Park area. He headed in that direction, keeping his eye on the location marker on his phone. As he got closer, the marker started to move down Clyde, then turned east on Carling. He rerouted and followed until it stopped at a storage facility near Westgate Mall.

He parked in the mall and walked to the facility on foot with his camera over his shoulder. The drive-in bay was sitting open, so he ducked inside. He spotted the man's car parked on the far side of the large bay. The man wasn't in it. Through the glass windows of guest services, he spotted him talking to the woman at the counter. His back was to him.

He hid behind a parked van just as the man turned around and came back out. A gym bag in his hand, the man headed through a set of double doors. A chime sounded as the doors opened. He dashed over before the doors closed and slipped through. He entered a long hallway. On either side of the hallway were rows of locker doors, each the size of a small garage. The man was up ahead, turning a corner. He hurried after him. At the intersection where the man had disappeared, he slowed, peeked around, and spotted the man standing at a locker. The man seemed to be having trouble entering the code in the keypad of the door.

Camera aimed, he zoomed in to a close-up on the keypad. The man tried the code again. This time it worked. There was a whirring sound as an electronic lock disengaged. The man lifted the door and stepped inside.

He lowered his camera and waited. A few minutes later, the man exited the locker. The man had the gym bag over his shoulder, only now it looked deflated and empty. As the man started pulling the door closed, he retreated fast in the other direction so the man wouldn't catch up to him. He turned a corner, then another, going deeper into the maze of hallways, away from the exit. Then he stopped and waited. He could hear the man's footsteps echoing, then the sound of the chime as the main doors opened and closed.

When he was certain the man was gone, he retraced his steps back to the man's locker and entered the code. He opened it. There wasn't much inside. A metal chair and a small table with some rubber bands and an old kitchen scale sitting on it. But what caught his eye was the large hockey bag on the floor. He walked over to it and unzipped the bag. It was full of cash. Bundles of hundreds. There had to be a few million in the bag.

He heard the distant chime of the main doors. He zipped the bag, checked the hall, then closed the locker quickly, leaving the cash where it was.

Footsteps were heading in his direction.

He took off the other way.

39

It takes Rudi-Rose almost a full hour to recover from the shock of Lenny's revelation. She's finally able to pull herself together enough to call Reg. She tells him she has a stomach bug. He gives her a day to *get her shit together*.

Injuries and exhaustion keep Juls in bed, which gives Lenny time to work on Rudi-Rose.

As the end-of-day school bell rings, Rudi-Rose and Lenny are waiting by the curb for the girls. Flo is giddy to see her mother in the driver's seat of the Mustang. But when they tell them they're not going back to Lenny's to see their dad, Nora screws up her face and refuses to speak.

They drive to a small motel tucked on a side street in Westboro, halfway between Lenny's house and Maplelawn Manor. Lenny has passed it many times on her way to see Silas. She chose it because it's completely random but still close by.

Lenny books them a room with a kitchenette and living room, and a separate bedroom. She checks them in under a fake name and pays cash. As the girls get settled in, Lenny pulls Rudi-Rose outside and fills her in on the real plan. They're not here just to keep the girls out of sight. When Lenny heard about the private parties for Reg Caffey's international connects, it came to her.

"There's a journalist I think you should talk to," says Lenny.

Rudi-Rose's face drops.

"She's on her way here," says Lenny, handing her the journalist's card. "Her name's Christie Coote. She's been working on a story about organized crime. She's after Reg."

"She's coming here? Now?" asks Rudi-Rose, eyes wide with panic.

"I told her to come alone," says Lenny. "She knows to watch her back."

Rudi-Rose leans against the doorframe and glances inside at the twins. They're sitting on the bed sorting through the vending machine treats she bought them. Lenny touches her arm.

"Juls has risked a lot," says Lenny. "Now it's your turn."

Rudi-Rose pulls away sharply.

"Don't do that," she says. "Don't try to fuck with my head. You should have asked me."

A car pulls into the parking lot, and the journalist gets out. Christie nods to Lenny.

"I'm not gonna do this," says Rudi-Rose. "Not for him. Not even for them."

She looks at the girls. Christie walks over.

"You must be Rudi-Rose," she says, hesitating before holding out her hand. She heard what the young woman said.

Rudi-Rose folds her arms. She turns to Lenny.

"I'm going to do it for that thirteen-year-old girl," she says. "That girl whose life he stole. I'm doing it for her. *Me.* For all of them. Let's fuck this guy hard."

Lenny likes Rudi-Rose more by the minute.

"I like the sound of that," says Christie, shaking her hand. "Let's talk inside."

Before leaving the two women alone, Lenny pokes her head into the bedroom to say goodbye to the twins. Flo is bouncing on the bed, chewing M&M'S. Nora is perched in a chair, hugging her knees.

"I'll see you girls tomorrow," says Lenny, giving them a wave.

"When's Daddy coming?" asks Flo.

"He's staying at home tonight with me, but he'll see you soon," says Lenny.

"Everyone lies to kids," says Nora, scrunching her nose.

"They *do*?" asks Flo, looking at her sister with wide-eyed astonishment.

"Why can't we go home with you?" asks Nora.

Lenny doesn't want to lie.

"Your mom has to talk to someone," says Lenny. "And it needs to stay secret."

"Secret from who? Daddy?" asks Flo, plopping on her bum.

Lenny regrets saying anything.

"There's pay-per-view," says Lenny. "How about you girls pick a movie?"

"Yay, maybe they have *Elf*?" exclaims Flo as she rolls onto her back.

Nora gets up and walks over to Lenny.

She glances back at her sister, who's doing bicycle kicks on the bed.

"Is Daddy a bad man?" whispers Nora.

Lenny feels a rush of affection for the little girl. She hugs Nora.

"Your daddy's one of the good guys, honey," she whispers in her ear. "I promise."

Lenny lets go of Nora. The eight-year-old turns and leaps onto the bed.

"We are *not* watching *Elf*," says Nora, tucking under the covers with her sister.

"How about *Home Alone*?" asks Flo.

Nora buries her head under the covers.

Lenny's chest aches. As much as it scares her and as much as she's fought it—it's happened. These two lovely creatures have burrowed their way deep into her heart.

40

Lenny leaves the Mustang at the motel for Rudi-Rose and takes the city bus back home. The second she's in the door, Lenny checks on Juls. He's still asleep in his bedroom. He looks like he's been run over by a truck. She refills his water and pulls the duvet over him. Juls snores deeply. His body has been through so much, he needs rest and time to heal. Definitely out for the count.

It's early evening, and the house feels too quiet, too empty. Lenny goes out to the garage to feel less alone, and that's when she spots the manual and phone lying in the Jeep where she tossed them. In the chaos of Juls' return, she completely forgot about her discovery.

Lenny gets the charger from the bedside table, brings it down to the kitchen, and plugs in Hank's phone. She tries to power it on, but the phone won't come to life. It dawns on her that phone batteries probably don't last fifteen years. She'll have to buy a new one. Lenny skims through the notes and photos but quickly gives up. She doesn't have the bandwidth right now to decipher Hank's scribbles, and she really needs a drink. With Juls tucked in bed, she considers heading over to the Carleton. Then she gets a better idea. Lenny shoves everything into her junk drawer and makes a call.

After changing clothes, applying makeup, and pulling her hair into a messy bun, Lenny catches a cab.

Irene's is a small pub in the Glebe, only a few blocks from the Rupert Street house where Sully has lived for decades. She wanted to meet somewhere with a good selection of beer but without a cop on every other barstool. When she arrives, Sully is already seated at a corner table, sipping a dark ale. His face lights up when he sees her. Sully rises.

"I'm glad you called," he says, kissing her cheek. "Thought you'd written me off after last time."

"You did nothing wrong," she says, taking her seat. "You just told the truth."

He pushes in her chair.

"You look amazing," he says.

Lenny is wearing tight black jeans and a flowy emerald blouse that flatters her cleavage. She blushes, suddenly feeling like she's on a date. The server comes over.

"You hungry?" asks Sully.

She hasn't eaten all day.

"Famished," she says.

Lenny orders a pilsner and hot-honey wings. Sully goes with a brisket sandwich and fries. As the alcohol flows into her bloodstream, Lenny feels the muscles in her shoulders loosen. Sully leans in a little too close and lets his eyes linger a little too long. She doesn't mind. It's been a long time since someone's looked at her that way. The lights dim, and the cozy pub purrs with the sounds of laughter, music, and the light clink of glassware. For a moment, the specter of Reg Caffey fades into the background. They settle into comfortable small talk. He asks about her dad. She tells Sully about her father's dementia and about his cloistered life on the third floor at Maplelawn Manor. Sully knows the place. Before his mother died, he'd looked into it when her Alzheimer's got bad.

As she sips her third beer and the server clears away their dinner plates, Lenny remembers that she called Sully for more than company. She wants to pick his brain. She sits back in her chair, more relaxed than she's felt in weeks.

"I found some photos of Hank's," says Lenny. "Looks like he might have been following Vincent."

"Still digging through the past, I see," he says. Sully takes a sip of his beer as he ponders this. "Makes sense. Birdie was looking into the guy he thought killed his daughter. I'd expect no less."

"What if he got too close?" she says. "Maybe Vincent told Reg he was being followed, and when he disappeared, they suspected Hank."

Sully downs his beer. He has to swallow hard.

"What is it, Sully?" she asks.

"You remember how I told you I didn't know what Birdie was up to?" he says. "It was only half true. I didn't know at first, but a couple weeks into his leave, I reached out. Right after Vincent Caffey got nabbed that summer."

"For shooting the security guard," she says.

"That's right. Something about it didn't smell right," he says. "Vincent getting nabbed for a cold case right after what happened to Kendra."

"I was thinking the same thing," she says. "Hank had something to do with it."

"I went to see Birdie and asked him outright," says Sully. "You're right. He'd been tailing Caffey for a while. But what you don't know is that Birdie got his hands on a bullet casing from evidence. He planted it in the trunk of Vinny's car. Then he called in a tip, cops found the casing, and Vinny was arrested."

"Hank set him up?" asks Lenny.

"He wanted Vincent to go down for murder, nothing less," he says. "He asked me to look the other way. He was my partner, but he was also my friend."

"But the case fell apart," she says.

"Someone figured out the evidence box was tampered with. Rumors started to circle Birdie," he says. "PSU opened an investigation, and his leave got flipped into a suspension."

"Professional Standards Unit?" says Lenny. "So he didn't extend his leave."

"I didn't want to tell you," says Sully. "Don't think badly of him, Lenny."

"Funny thing is, I don't," she says. "He was trying to make things right in a world where everything had gone wrong."

"He was probably too ashamed to tell you," says Sully. "I'm sorry I never did."

Sully squeezes her hand. Then he lets go.

"There's something else," he says, his mouth tight.

Lenny isn't sure she wants to hear it.

"There was cash in the trunk when he planted the casing," he says. "Two million."

"Jesus," she says.

"Lenny," he says. "Birdie took it."

Lenny's mouth drops open.

"I'm guessing from the look on your face, he didn't tell you that either," says Sully.

Lenny shakes her head.

"When Vincent made a pit stop at a casino, Birdie saw his chance to plant the casing. Said he wasn't thinking when he saw the money. He grabbed it. He didn't know how to walk it back, then PSU started sniffing around. Birdie thought he was about to lose everything. Career, reputation, family, you. He knew he'd messed up real bad. I'd never seen him like that."

The server walks past, and Sully points to their empty glasses. Lenny leans closer and lowers her voice.

"This proves my point," she says. "If Reg found out any of this, he would have had Hank killed."

Sully tries to take a sip, but his glass is empty.

"You can't rule it out," she says. "It's motive."

He bows his head.

"Fuck, this is my fault," he says. "I shouldn't have told you all this shit. I know what you're trying to do."

"What's that?" she asks, lifting her brow.

"Birdie said you were good at this," he says. "But his isn't some case that needs solving. There's no mystery here."

Lenny tries to pull away, but he holds tight.

"We know what happened," he says softly.

The server returns with two more beers. Lenny pulls her hand sharply away and folds her arms tight across her chest. The server makes a quick exit.

"Lenny, we both saw what he did," he says.

"Don't," she tells him, willing him to stop talking.

"I can still taste the fumes," he says, his voice faltering.

Lenny pushes her chair back.

"I can see the rag in the tailpipe of his Jeep," he says. "I can't get it out of my head. I wish I could."

Sully chokes on his words.

"Please stop," says Lenny.

"If I could go back, talk him out of it, get him to see reason, make him understand how much he was needed, how much I loved him, how much you loved him," he says. "If I could, I'd beg him not to do it. But he did it, Lenny. He fucking did it. He took his own—"

Sully's eyes fill with tears. He stands abruptly and heads for the washroom. As Lenny watches him go, she can't bring herself to hate him for what he's just said. Deep down, she knows he's right. She was the one who found Hank in the garage. And Sully was one of the first cops to arrive at the scene. He was devastated. They both were.

Lenny picks up her beer and takes a long pull.

When Sully finally returns to the table, his eyes are bloodshot. She doesn't know what to say. Lenny looks around the pub at the smiling faces and feels nothing but sadness. Sully sips his beer as he tries to collect himself. Lenny reaches out and grazes his hand with her fingertips. He looks at her.

"You don't know this, but the night before he died, we came here," she says. "I told him we were going out. I dragged him down here. He didn't want to come, but after a few beers, it was like old times."

She glances at the bar. She can almost see them sitting there, barstools pulled close, Hank's hand on her thigh as they debated the merits of each beer. Brown versus pale. Hoppy versus smoky. Fruity versus spicy.

"We got very drunk," she says. "On the cab ride home, Hank was ranting on about all sorts of nonsense—how to change the spare tire, what to do if a fuse blew. He said there was a trick to the fuse box. I remember, he called it *persnickety*. I laughed, but he insisted on explaining how the wiring was ancient, how he'd been meaning to get the whole thing replaced. He was yammering on and on, so I finally had to shut him up by kissing him."

Sully smiles.

"A few weeks later, I thought about that night," she says. "I realized he was tying up loose ends. Making sure I knew how to take care of myself. Hank knew he wasn't going to be around."

A wave of heartache washes through Lenny.

"You know the only thing Hank despised more than Vincent Caffey?" she asks.

"What was that?" asks Sully.

"A dirty cop," she says. "Hank would have hated himself."

Sully sighs deeply. Lenny downs her beer. He follows suit, then he looks up at her.

"This has been fun," he says.

They both laugh.

Lenny lets her sorrow drift into the cozy shadows of the pub as she looks into Sully's familiar green eyes. She reaches out and cups his face. She pulls him close.

Lenny kisses him tenderly on the lips.

Sully returns her kiss.

41

Fifteen years ago

He parked in a wooded area across from the driving range. He watched the two men through his long lens. The older one was giving the younger one pointers. Adjusting his stance and his grip. The younger man was a quick study. This seemed to make the older one happy as he lit a cigar and smiled, nodding his approval as the younger man took a swing. Even from a distance, it was clear the father and son were having a bonding moment.

Two middle-aged women were practicing in the stall next to the men. One of the women waved away the cloud of smoke that wafted in their direction. She put her hands on her hips, then stormed over to the attendant at the mini clubhouse. The attendant came over and said something to the men. The older man ignored him. When the attendant didn't leave, the older man butted out his cigar. The women practicing in the next stall thanked the attendant as he passed by. The older man walked over to the two women, said something in one woman's ear. She looked horrified, and the women quickly gathered their clubs and left. The younger man laughed, and the older one lit his cigar again.

The two men took turns driving balls for over an hour until their buckets were empty. The older man rested a hand on his son's shoulder as they walked to their cars, their golf bags trailing behind them on pull carts. They left their bags standing next to them as they talked awhile in the parking lot. The younger man leaned against his car while the older man imitated a golf swing. They looked like they didn't have a care in the world until they heard the sirens.

Before either of them could make a move, four squad cars peeled into the lot and surrounded them. Guns were drawn. The younger man was made to lie face down on the pavement. The older one lifted his golf shirt to show he wasn't carrying. The cops seemed more interested in the younger one. He was patted down, then the trunks of both vehicles were popped and searched. One of the cops bagged something, and the younger man was cuffed and put in the back of a squad car. Yellow tape was strung around his vehicle, and the older man was being encouraged to leave. He tossed his business card at one of the cops, then he got in his car and drove away.

42

It's late when Lenny stumbles across the threshold. The house is dark. She teeters into the hall table. Then she hears a sound in the living room. Lenny tiptoes into the dark room and switches on a lamp. Juls is lying on the sofa. Fender is curled by his side. Neither of them wakes. On the coffee table are her pain pills and a half-eaten ham-and-cheese sandwich. Somehow the gash on his face looks worse. Juls shifts in his sleep. Lenny feels his forehead. At least there's no fever. She feels a pang of regret for having left him to wake up alone in an empty house.

She takes the leftover sandwich into the kitchen, tossing her purse on the table. She wraps the sandwich and puts it in the fridge. When she closes the door, she notices two Polaroids stuck to the fridge with magnets. The twins must have gotten their hands on her camera. The photos are selfies. In one, the girls are both sticking their tongues out. In the other, Nora is smiling as she cradles Fender in one arm, and Flo is peeking over her shoulder. Lenny runs a finger across the photos. She can see a little of Kendra in Nora's smile.

She misses the twins. Lenny digs her phone out of her purse. No messages. No missed calls. She checks her answering machine. There's one message. It's Flo calling to see if Lenny can bring cupcakes when she comes back tomorrow. She must have called before Juls came downstairs. It's too late to phone them back now. Flo laughs at something. A movie is playing loudly in the background. Nora laughs too. The call doesn't disconnect. Flo must have forgotten all about the phone. Lenny sits on the floor next to the machine and listens to the twins giggling and chatting. It goes on for almost an hour before the cassette runs out on her answering machine. She needed that.

Lenny stands and paces the kitchen. The house feels even more empty and quiet after the sound of the girls' voices. Her beer-soaked mind is restless and begins to swim with everything Sully told her. How Hank was watching Vincent. How he tried to set him up for murder. How he stole money from him.

Lenny grabs the manual from the junk drawer and sits at the table. Maybe there's something in it that can help make sense of her husband's last weeks. Lenny looks through the photos tucked inside the manual. Only now, she takes her time. Vincent at a casino. Vincent at a body shop with another man. Vincent next to a large metal door. Vincent with Reg. Vincent lying on the ground surrounded by police. This must have been when he was arrested. There are photos of a police operation at the body shop and others of some men she doesn't recognize.

Next, Lenny examines the notes written in the margins of the manual. One of them is a password, but there's no hint as to what it's for. All it says is *Password: Natural Blonde*. Her favorite beer back then. She's guessing it's for his work laptop, which she never found. She jots a few things on a notepad—including some names she doesn't recognize. But most of Hank's notes are in a shorthand she can't decipher. She turns to the papers that were inside the envelope with the photos. She scans the obituary.

> Paul Choi. Passed away in a tragic accident on August 14. Son, father, husband. Cherished employee of Tento's Garage.

Lenny cross-checks one of the photos. There it is. Tento's Garage. There's a photo of Vincent talking to a man outside the garage. Maybe it's Choi.

"Who are you, Paul Choi?" she says.

"New case, Detective Bird?" says Juls.

Lenny jumps. She turns to see her grandson standing behind her. He looks like hell.

"He lives," says Lenny.

"Barely," he says. "No one was here when I came down. I figured you took the girls out for dinner. Are they upstairs?"

"They're with Rudi-Rose," she says. "They're okay."

"At the apartment?" he asks. "I should be with them."

"Have you looked in the mirror?" she says. "You'd scare them half to death. Give it a few days. They're fine. They've got their mom."

He nods and lowers himself into the chair beside her. As he settles, he winces in pain. Lenny gets him a couple of ibuprofens and some water. Juls idly runs his finger across the obituary.

"Who died?" he asks.

"I found all this in the glove box of Hank's Jeep," she says.

She points to the items on the table.

"Turns out I was on the right track," she says. "Hank set up your dad for that murder."

"He what?" says Juls, screwing up his face just like Nora.

"He planted evidence in his trunk," she says.

Juls shakes his head.

"No shit," says Juls. "Hank was kind of a badass. Too bad it didn't stick."

"That's not all," she says. "Hank also stole two million dollars from Vincent's trunk."

"What the fuck?" says Juls.

"I only found out tonight," says Lenny. "From Hank's old partner. Hank told him what he'd done, and Sully covered for him."

"That's a fuck ton of cash," says Juls.

"I understand why Hank would want to frame Vincent," she says. "But the money? He had to have known it would put a target on his back."

"Well, no way Reg caught wind," he says. "Someone takes that much from the Caffeys—Reg is coming for them."

But what if he did catch wind? Lenny keeps the thought to herself for now.

Juls looks at the autopsy report. He picks it up.

"What's this guy got to do with it?" asks Juls.

"I don't know," says Lenny. "But it's got to be connected somehow."

"Death by asphyxiation," Juls says, reading the cause of death.

"Maybe he worked for Vincent," offers Lenny.

Juls notices something Lenny has written on her notepad.

"Tony Boxcar," says Juls, reading one of the names. "I know that name. I heard stories about a guy named Boxcar from Billy. He did special jobs for Reg. Contract work. They called him the Sleeper."

"Why was that?" she asks.

"That was his preferred MO," he says, pointing to the autopsy report. "Asphyxiation," he says. "Silent but deadly."

A wave of nausea rises in Lenny's belly and constricts her throat.

"Billy said the dude got pinched years ago," says Juls. "He's doing back-to-back life sentences at Millhaven for a triple murder."

Lenny can't breathe.

Asphyxiation.

That was Hank's cause of death.

43

Lenny knocks on Juls' bedroom door early the next morning. When he lets out a groan, she opens the door. As his body tries to heal and remodel itself, his injuries are morphing through various phases of swelling and bruising, all of which has made him feel worse than he did yesterday. He says he's staying in bed today. She brings him a coffee, then leaves him be.

Lenny's brain also feels bruised. It might be the half dozen beers she drank with Sully, but it's also because of the ominous theory that kept bouncing around in her head all night. She tries to clear the cobwebs with large doses of caffeine, but Lenny can't get the Sleeper out of her muddled head. Or what Juls said about Reg.

Someone takes that much from the Caffeys—Reg is coming for them.

Purely for research purposes, she decides to call Millhaven Institution to ask what the rules are around phone calls to inmates. Apparently, there aren't many. She simply has to leave her name and number. Once the number is approved, the inmate is informed, and they can use the inmate telephone system, or ITS, to call her back.

"The name of the inmate?" asks the prison operator.

"Oh," says Lenny. "I wasn't really—" She hesitates.

"Tony Boxcar," she says.

An hour later, Lenny's phone rings. She picks it up with a shaking hand.

"Hello?" she says.

"Lenny Bird?" he asks. His voice is soft and gravelly. "That a made-up name? You one of them true crime podcasters?"

"No, I'm a grandmother," she sputters, not sure why she said that. "Thank you for calling me back."

"I was curious," he says. "Not many people want to talk to me on the outside."

"You worked for Reg Caffey back in the day," she says. It's not a question.

"Please tell me that motherfucker kicked the bucket." He snickers. "I could use a good laugh."

"They called you the Sleeper, right?" she asks.

He pauses.

"Look, lady, I don't know you, but if you're—"

"My late husband was Hank Bird," she cuts in, trying to keep her voice steady.

"Doesn't ring a bell," he says.

"He died fifteen years ago," she tells him. "Asphyxiation."

Again, he takes his time answering.

"You call hoping for a confession?" he says.

"I want the truth," says Lenny.

"And I want an all-expenses-paid trip to Vegas and a five-dollar hooker," he says.

He belly laughs.

"Did Caffey hire you to kill my husband?" she says.

"Which Caffey? Stallion or gelding?" he asks.

"What are you saying?" she asks.

"I ain't saying nothing, lady," he says. "I'll give you this, you got cullions. You want to talk face-to-face, bring it. But I'm no prat. I know they're listening."

"Who?" she asks.

"Like I said, I'm a handshaker," he says. "Always have been. See ya on the flip side, Lenny Bird."

The line goes dead.

Lenny stares at the phone. *Face-to-face.* She searches Millhaven Institution in her maps app. It's only a two-and-a-half-hour drive. Lenny contemplates all the reasons not to do this.

No driver's license. Check.

The Jeep's likely to conk out halfway there. Check.

He's in prison for triple murder. Check. Check. Check.

I'm too old for this shit. Check.

Lenny looks at the time. It's only eight in the morning. She could be there and back by lunch. Lenny prepares some chicken noodle soup for Juls and takes it up to his bedroom. The coffee she brought him earlier hasn't been touched. As she places the bowl on the bedside table, Juls opens his eyes halfway. She whispers that she's going to visit Silas and she'll be back soon. He nods, then closes his eyes again.

No point in worrying him.

44

Despite the alarming rattle coming from the engine, the Jeep survives the drive to the maximum-security facility. Lenny makes her way to the building marked **Designated Visitation Area** and enters the cramped lobby. She joins a small line of visitors in front of a registration desk. A male guard is checking in the visitors. A female guard stands behind him.

"Next," says the male guard when it's her turn. "Name?"

His fingers are poised over his keyboard, eyes on his computer screen. Lenny panics. She only now realizes she should have called ahead and booked an appointment.

"Eleanor Bird," says Lenny as a hot flash creeps across her body.

"And who are you here to visit, ma'am?" he asks.

"My son, Tony," she says.

Why am I lying? His mother probably visits all the time.

"I mean my nephew," says Lenny. "My sister's son."

The guard looks up at her, then back at his screen.

"Inmate's last name?" he asks.

He's not going to find her name on any visitors' list. She has to think fast. Lenny lets her gaze wander like she's following the path of a butterfly. She's seen Silas do it a million times when he slips into one of his fogs.

"Are you okay, ma'am?" the guard asks.

"Where am I?" she asks.

"You're at Millhaven Institution, ma'am," says the guard, raising his voice.

"Oh, deary me," says Lenny in her best old lady voice. "Did I get the day wrong again?"

"Visiting hours are every day, ma'am. First come, first served," he says.

"Oh," says Lenny.

"You need to tell me the inmate's name, and we'll get you registered," he says.

"Boxcar, Tony," says Lenny.

The female guard raises one eyebrow.

"Probably Anthony," Lenny adds.

"Probably?" asks the guard.

Lenny shrugs.

The guard types. His computer dings.

"He'll be notified," he says. "ID, please."

Lenny hands the guard her Ontario health card since she doesn't have a driver's license. It seems to satisfy him. The female guard steps out of the booth and searches Lenny's purse and hands it back. Luckily, she remembered to put Hank's revolver in the lockbox in the garage before she left.

"Your cell phone will have to stay with us," she says, placing it in a plastic tray. "You can collect it at the end of your visit."

"Wait over there for your name to be called," says the male guard.

He points to a bench.

Fifteen minutes later, Lenny's name is called. She considers running, but she's here now, so she takes a deep breath and enters the visiting room. That's when she realizes she has no idea what Tony Boxcar looks like. There are several visitors already seated at tables across from inmates. What looks to be family, a girlfriend, a brother, a wife. Only two inmates sit alone, still waiting for their visitors. One is a thin man with translucent skin. He's in his twenties, so it couldn't be him. He would have been a kid fifteen years ago.

It's the other man. The one that looks like a bulldog, with sad, deep-set eyes, sagging jowls, and enormous shoulders. Late forties. His thick hands are clasped on the table in front of him. His gaze follows Lenny as she makes her way over. His lower lip is cracked like it's healing from a cut. Lenny sits in the squeaky metal chair across from him. It's bolted to the floor, but it rotates on a pedestal that needs oiling.

He takes her in, his bulldog eyes snooping across her skin.

"That was fast," he says, smiling.

He should scare her, but the oversize prison uniform and the stray tuft of hair sprouting from the top of his head make him look almost childlike. Harmless. Only he's not. He's a killer. His rolled-up sleeves reveal tattoos that snake down both forearms.

Lenny pulls a photo from her purse and holds it up. It's Hank in uniform.

"A cop?" he says, eyebrows lifting. "Wasn't me, doll. I didn't do cops. My gramps was a cop. No women, kids, or cops."

Lenny believes him. Mostly because she gets the feeling he'd take a lot of pleasure in telling her Hank was one of his victims.

"When I asked you about Caffey, you said, 'Which Caffey?'" she reminds him.

"I did jobs for the old man," says Tony. "But this one time, his asshole son reached out for a quickie."

"Vincent," she says.

"Rotten apple, that one." He smiles.

Lenny reaches into her purse for another photo.

"She looks like you. Daughter?" he says.

Lenny doesn't answer.

"Like I said, no women," he says.

She puts the photo of Kendra back in her purse.

"It was some mechanic. Face like a pizza," he says.

Right away, Lenny knows who he's talking about. She can see his face in the photo in the obituary that sits on her kitchen table. Bad acne.

Paul Choi. Cherished employee of Tento's Garage. Hank had photos of him with Vincent. And one of a police operation at the garage.

Then it comes to her. Vincent Caffey's alibi for the night Kendra was murdered was his mechanic. How could she have forgotten that? Boxcar was hired to kill cherished mechanic Choi. Vincent was cleaning up. And Hank was trying to prove it.

"Time," says the guard.

"Wait," says Lenny. "Vincent hired you fifteen years ago, right? In August?"

She can picture the date on the obituary. August 14.

"Yup, sounds about right," he says.

"Vincent was arrested earlier that summer and didn't get out until September," she says. "You're saying he hired you while he was in lockup?"

He smiles.

"You think my story's cap?" he asks.

She doesn't answer.

He ponders her a moment.

"Like I told you on the phone, I'm a handshaker," he says. "Never talked to young Caffey. Whole thing was arranged through some asshole lackey."

"You get a name?" she asks.

"Didn't show me his ID." He smirks.

"What did he look like?" she asks.

"On your feet, inmate," shouts a guard.

Tony rises and joins the line of other inmates filing from the room.

"Come back and see me anytime, Lenny Bird," Tony calls out.

Another inmate whistles like a twittering sparrow.

45

Fifteen years ago

He heard the 10-45 on his police scanner. Report of a death. He recognized the name of the business. He'd tracked his mark there one time. Saw him harassing one of the employees. Figured it was some random shakedown, but now he knows better.

He kept his distance and took out his camera. On scene were a squad car, an ambulance, and a hazmat vehicle from the fire department. An officer sat at the rear of the ambulance. He was being given oxygen by an EMT. Another officer was stringing police tape around the building's perimeter. Three men in coveralls stood out front.

He zoomed in on the men. Tento's Garage *was written on the front of their coveralls, and each man wore a patch on his chest bearing a first name. Remy, Colin, José. The other employees. The mechanic he'd seen before wasn't among them. The one he found out from the license plate in the photo he took was named Paul Choi.*

Two police SUVs arrived. A couple of general assignment detectives he recognized got out of one, and an ident team got out of the other just as the coroner's van showed up. The coroner grabbed her kit and camera and joined the others. A few minutes later, the hazmat team came outside and gave them the all clear. They headed inside. He knew that was how it usually went—the coroner, detectives, and forensic investigators processed the scene as a team. It was an hour before the coroner came back out. She talked to the employees, then she sat in her van making notes. Two EMTs rolled a stretcher out of the garage carrying a body covered by a tarp. They loaded the body into their ambulance and drove away. No lights, no sirens. The hazmat team was long gone, and one of the officers began removing the police tape. The employees looked confused and cold.

A gray van appeared at the far end of the street. He hadn't noticed it before. It pulled out from behind a stand of trees and drove away in the opposite direction. He aimed his lens and snapped a photo. Too far away to read the plate, but he caught a blurry image of a blue-and-yellow bumper sticker. He scrolled through all his shots and spotted the van's wheel partially obscured by a branch in a wide shot he'd taken earlier. The rest of the van was hidden. It had been sitting there awhile. Someone else was watching the scene.

46

The Jeep is Lenny's new best friend. It gets her all the way back to Ottawa from Millhaven. Once she exits the highway, Lenny feels it lurch every time she hits the gas at a stoplight. It's midday. She's made good time, so Lenny makes a quick pit stop to buy a battery for Hank's phone.

As she turns onto Julian Avenue, Lenny spots a car in front of her house. She pulls into her driveway and sees Maya waiting in the car. Lenny parks in the garage, then walks out to greet her friend.

"What the fuck, Lenny?" says Maya, striding toward her. "I got a call this morning from a former colleague. She works in corrections," says Maya. "At *Millhaven*. She told me a friend of mine was visiting a convicted killer. She recognized your name, Lenny. She knew Hank."

There's no way Lenny can tell Maya she's been chasing down a theory that someone put a hit on Hank. Maya would think she's lost her mind.

"It might have been a lapse in judgment," says Lenny.

"You think?" says Maya. "Boxcar is a fucking hit man. What were you doing out there?"

Lenny hesitates. Not sure what to say. It wasn't just a theory that made her drive to a prison. She was drawn there by something that's lurked inside her since she was a little girl. She was drawn to the darkness. Lenny wanted to look into the eyes of a killer. To see if there was something familiar there. Something she might have seen in another man's eyes. Something that might even live inside her. She wanted to see it, feel it, grasp some small piece of it.

"Hello? Lenny?" says Maya.

Lenny snaps back to reality.

"What's going on with you?" asks Maya. "I haven't seen or heard from you in almost two weeks, and now I find out this is what you're up to."

Lenny feels like she's letting everyone down. Her father, now her friend. Maybe Maya *will* understand. She was Hank's friend too.

"I went looking for answers," says Lenny. "Boxcar told me he did a job for Vincent Caffey."

"A hit?" asks Maya.

"A mechanic," says Lenny. "Vincent's alibi."

Maya squints. She's not following.

"His alibi for Kendra's murder," says Lenny.

Maya is dumbstruck.

"How was Boxcar even on your radar?" asks Maya.

"Juls," says Lenny.

"So you thought you'd go interrogate him yourself?" asks Maya.

"Hank was looking into it too," says Lenny. "I found his photos and notes."

"Lenny, this is police business," says Maya. "Listen, I know it was damn fucking hard losing your daughter, but *you* are not a cop."

"Boxcar said someone else arranged the hit," says Lenny. "Vincent's lackey. That's the guy we should be looking for."

"Enough, Lenny," says Maya.

Lenny can't stop.

"Vincent Caffey was in a cell when his alibi witness was killed," says Lenny. "I bet if we checked the logs from back then, we could find out who visited him in lockup. It might be a lead to this lackey guy."

Maya holds up her hand. Lenny stops talking. She's pushed too far. Maya paces the driveway. Then she stops and goes still for a moment.

"Fuck," says Maya. She turns to face Lenny. "Hank asked me that very thing. To look at the visitor logs."

"From when Vincent was in lockup?" asks Lenny.

"I hadn't seen Hank in a while," says Maya. "He'd called a few times asking for a couple of favors. Random stuff. Some traffic footage and plates. Then he called about those logs. I couldn't get my hands on the logs. I tried the security tapes from lockup but came up empty. Couldn't find all the tapes."

"They were missing?" asks Lenny.

"Our filing system wasn't the best back then. The cameras were also glitchy," says Maya. "Could have been a malfunction."

"But Hank was suspicious?" asks Lenny.

"Honestly, I wasn't sure where his head was back then," says Maya. "He was in trouble with the higher-ups. I thought he was trying to dig himself out. I wanted to help. I never believed what they said about him. No one did. When I hit a dead end, he told me to drop it."

"At least you tried," says Lenny.

"He also asked me to get him the name of the owner of a vehicle he saw on that traffic footage," says Maya. "Today was the first time I'd heard the name in years. Back then I had no idea who the guy was, but I know who he is now. Anthony Boxcar."

"Hank was following the same lead," says Lenny.

Maya stares past Lenny like she's trying to sort through everything, from then and now.

"I can take another look," says Maya. "But it was a long time ago."

"Really?" says Lenny. "You're the best, Maya. And you were a good friend to Hank."

"But I'll only do it if you promise me this going-rogue shit ends today," says Maya.

"I promise," says Lenny.

Lenny hugs her friend tight to make up for the lie.

47

Fifteen years ago

He made sure his vehicle was hidden by the field house. It was cool for late summer, so there were no kids swimming in the outdoor pool at Hampton Park. The lifeguards were playing cards at a picnic table. They barely looked in his direction. He watched as the man pushed his young daughter on a swing in the playground beyond the pool. The man was in his mid-thirties. Big, broad shouldered, face like a bulldog.

Through his long lens, he took shots of the man and his kid. He'd been following him for a few weeks ever since getting the license plate number off the automated speed enforcement camera footage Maya tracked down for him. Once they had the van's plates, it was easy enough for her to get his address.

This seemed to be the man's weekly routine. Picked up his daughter on Fridays from the same house in Parkwood Hills. A woman was always at the door saying goodbye to the girl. The man took her to Hampton Park, they hung around the playground awhile, then they went out to dinner at Denny's on Merivale Road before he brought her home. No overnight visits. But no supervision either. Likely the terms of visitation in a divorce.

When the man wasn't with his daughter, he spent the rest of his time at his south-end walk-up or sitting alone at the Riverside Pub. Once in a while, the man drove to the T&T Supermarket. But that was it. The man didn't seem to have a job or friends or hobbies. He never saw the man on a phone. Didn't seem to have one. He didn't see him stop to chat with any of his neighbors. A lone wolf, other than the kid and the local watering hole.

The man drove a gray van with a blue-and-yellow Niagara Falls bumper sticker on the back. The van was registered to Anthony Theodore Boxcar.

48

After Maya drives off, Lenny is about to go inside when she spots Mr. Crawley striding toward her across his lawn. It's too late to escape.

"A word, Mrs. Bird," he says, in his usual crisp tone.

He's holding something.

"Hey, Mr. Crawley," says Lenny, pasting a smile on her face.

"I need you to tell your nephew to stop using my lawn as his personal ashtray." He scowls, shoving his open hand close to her face. He's holding a cigarette butt.

"He's my grandson," says Lenny. "And he would never—"

"This is a quiet family neighborhood, Mrs. Bird," he chirps. "And I for one am not impressed with all the ruckus of late or the steady stream of unsavory types."

"I'm sorry," says Lenny. "We'll try to keep it down."

"Your nephew should be the one apologizing," says Mr. Crawley.

"He's not my nephew, Mr. Crawley," says Lenny.

"Then he's a liar and a lout," he says. "Nearly knocked me over on his way past."

Crawley motions in the direction of her side gate. She stares at the gate. It's resting on the bolt of the latch like someone tried to sneak in quietly but didn't close the gate all the way. Crawley's not talking about Juls. Lenny rushes toward the gate.

"This happens again, don't think I won't call city bylaw, Mrs. Bird," calls out Mr. Crawley.

Lenny is already through the gate. She scans the garden. It's empty, but then she spots the window of her back door. It's shattered. She opens the door. Shards of glass are scattered on the landing. The familiar scent of his aftershave hits her nostrils.

Billy is back.

Lenny steps over the broken glass. Heart racing, she creeps into the kitchen, checks the living room, then rushes upstairs. She opens the door to Juls' room and lets out a sigh of relief. He's right where she left him that morning, still asleep with Fender next to him. The soup bowl is empty. The dog stretches his hind legs but doesn't open his eyes. If Fender's not fussed, Billy must be long gone. Her heart rate begins to calm. Lenny gently closes the door and slips quietly back downstairs.

As she crosses the kitchen, a sound comes from the basement. It freezes Lenny in her tracks. Her heart takes off again. As adrenaline pumps through her veins, it quickly turns her panic to outrage. How dare he come back here after what he did? Clenching her trembling fists, she heads down the basement stairs.

Lenny finds him standing next to the bin where Juls collected the torn pieces from Kendra's wall. Billy is holding something in his hand. A gun is tucked into the back of his pants.

"Should I have a key made for you, Billy?" she asks.

He holds a torn photo and snorts.

"You had no right to touch any of that," she says.

Billy punches the wall. She hears a crack. He's broken something, but his anger seems to numb the pain. Lenny keeps one foot on the bottom step, ready to run, sensing it might have been a mistake to confront him alone and without a weapon.

"You figure it out?" he asks, staring at the photo. "That's what it was, right? Some kind of investigation. That's what the shoes were about? You were trying to pin it on Vinny."

"He did have his alibi witness killed, so if the shoe fits," she says.

He looks at her. His right eye twitches. His skin looks gray.

"What I don't get is why you were trying so hard to prove he did it," he says. "It's not like he can pay for his crime since we both know he's already dead."

Lenny grips the stair rail as Billy takes a step toward her. "See, I got a theory, Mrs. Bird," he says. "I think you wanted to prove Vinny killed her so you can sleep at night, knowing what your husband did to him."

"Hank didn't kill anyone," says Lenny.

"Then how'd this get in your shed?" says Billy.

He pulls something from his pocket and tosses it at Lenny's feet. It's a diamond stud earring. Like the one Vincent always wore in his left ear. Lenny thought it made him look like a pimp. Lenny picks it up as a memory slices across her brain.

She's dragging Vincent from the shed, and his head bumps the doorframe. It must have come off then, and she didn't see it when she cleaned up. She stares at the earring.

This is the proof he was talking about in that note he left her at the Beer Store.

"Just tell me," he says. "Is he dead?"

The strange quiver in his voice surprises her. Billy isn't angry. He's hurting because he needs to know the truth about Vincent. She understands the pain of not knowing. But she can't help him. Lenny tosses the earring at him.

"This could be anyone's," she says.

He kicks the bin. It launches against the wall, and the fragments of Kendra's story explode around his feet. He drops to his knees. His hands frantically searching through the bits and pieces. He finds one and picks it up, then another, then he starts arranging them like a puzzle.

"Billy," she says, as she moves closer. "Billy, what are you doing?"

He's muttering to himself. Lenny gets as close as she dares. Then she sees. He's trying to piece together one of the crime scene photos. The wide shot of Kendra's body on the bathroom floor. He gives up, braces his hands on the concrete floor, and lowers his head. Lenny realizes he's crying when she sees tears drop from his eyes and land on the photo.

"Fuck it," he says.

With a heaving breath, Billy drags himself to his feet, pulls his phone from his jacket pocket, and turns to Lenny. Tears streak his pasty face.

"You want to know so bad?" he says, clutching the phone. "You want *evidence* for your fucking investigation?"

He holds up his phone.

"I got the whole fucking thing on here," he says. "She called me, but I didn't answer."

The words catch in his throat. Lenny backs away from Billy until her calves hit the stairs and she falls back, landing on the bottom step.

Billy puts his phone on speaker and turns up the volume.

You have one saved message. To play your message, press 1.

49

Billy, it's me. I didn't know who else to call. We had another fight, but this one was really bad, and I'm scared. I told him I was leaving him this time for real, and Vin went wild. He said he's going to take Juls away from me. He's gonna tell everyone I'm an addict. An unfit mother. He knows I'm clean, but who's gonna believe me? Reg's lawyers will tear me apart. I can't lose my son. You know how much I love him. I threatened to go to my dad and tell him everything I knew. I only said it to piss him off or scare him. I didn't mean it. He went all quiet and left. Billy, I think I really fucked up. I need you to find him and talk him down. Oh shit. I think he's back. I chained the door. He's going to freak. I gotta hide.

There's a crunching sound on the voice message like Kendra is fumbling with the phone. It sounds like she's running. Her breaths are short and sharp. A door slams, then there's a loud clattering sound like the phone dropped on a hard surface. Bathroom tiles. A distant thumping noise can be heard, then wood splintering and metal clanking. The front door has been kicked in.

"Kendra!" hollers Vincent in the distance. "Where the fuck are you?"

Kendra whimpers like a trapped animal. She's scratching at something. The windowsill. There's more banging. This time louder. Closer. It's a foot kicking at the bathroom door.

"Kendra!" he hollers.

"Go away," yells Kendra.

A loud crash distorts the recording as the bathroom door breaks open and Kendra lets out an ear-piercing scream.

"Please, Vin. Don't," Kendra cries. "I didn't mean it. I won't say a word."

He's panting like he's just run a marathon.

"Why'd you have to go and say that shit?" he whines.

"Juls will be home any minute," she says.

"That boy's better off without you," he says. "I'll make a man out of him."

"He's already more of a man than you'll ever be," says Kendra.

There's a horrible punching sound, and Kendra groans.

"Just get it done, lad," says another voice. It's Reg.

"Please, no." Kendra moans. "Reg, please. Pops. It's me."

"Get on with it, boy. She's your feckin' mess," says Reg. "Now clean it up."

"No, no, no!" screams Kendra.

There's a loud bang. A gunshot.

The recording goes eerily quiet. Then Vincent speaks.

"Jesus, what did I do?" he says. "I'm going down for this."

"Nobody's going anywhere," says Reg. "You're a Caffey."

"They gonna know it was me," says Vincent.

"We can make it look like she offed herself," says Reg. "Or a break-in."

"I think she's alive," says Vincent.

"Get back," says Reg. "Don't feckin' touch her."

"But she's still—" Vincent whimpers.

"Go," yells Reg. "Get the fuck gone."

Footsteps can be heard running. There's a soft wheezing sound. Then a muffled moan slowly weakens.

"Hush now, little bird," whispers Reg.

Then there's nothing.

Footsteps retreat.

After a lingering silence, the message ends with a beep.

To save your message, press 9.

50

Lenny stares at the cracks snaking across her basement floor, imagining herself crawling inside one so she can disappear. But she can't. If she didn't know any better, she'd think Billy had turned to stone. He's standing so still. No tremors. The sickening sounds of the recording linger in the dank air as the crime scene photos flash before her eyes. Billy finally speaks.

"When I heard the message, I got there as fast as I could. I thought maybe she—" Billy chokes on his words. "I was too late."

Lenny remains sitting on the bottom step, holding her knees tight to her chest. She swallows and numbs her heart as she tries to process what she's just heard.

"The police would have known you were the last person she phoned," says Lenny, her voice not sounding like her own. "They must have questioned you."

"They asked me about the call," he says. "I made up some bullshit about her looking for Vinny. Guess it helped lock down his alibi."

Lenny searches through the wreckage of those horrific hours after they found out their daughter was dead. All the wondering and imagining, and now she knows.

"But why didn't you go to the police with the recording?" asks Lenny.

"You think I didn't want to?" he says.

He chews at the skin around his fingernails just like Juls does.

"You don't know how many times I went down to the cop shop, stood there, then walked away," he says. "I couldn't do it."

He turns away from Lenny.

"Reg took me in when I didn't have a pot to piss in. He gave me a job. He even bought me a fucking house," he says. "And Vinny was like a brother to me, and I fucking betrayed him. The Caffeys were the only family I ever had."

"Family? What about *her*?" says Lenny. "She was a mother, a daughter."

"You think I don't know that?" he shouts. "I was a fucking coward, okay? I still am."

With his back to her, Billy shakes his head like he's trying to release pressure. His body vibrates as the tremors return.

"I had no choice," he cries. "What was I supposed to do?"

"The right thing," says Lenny, her words razor sharp. "Instead, you protected those murdering assholes because you were worried about losing your job and your bloody house."

"I wasn't protecting *them*. I was protecting myself," he fires back.

Billy turns to face Lenny.

"That's the fucking truth of it. I knew what would happen if I handed over that recording. Reg would have wormed his way out of it—for the both of them. And even in a world where those two fuckers were sent away, Reg would have got to me."

"You don't know that," says Lenny. "You could have been protected."

He lets out a sharp laugh more like a bark. His body shudders, and he folds his arms tight like he's trying to stop the tremors.

"I was Juls' age when I found out the price of betraying Reg Caffey. These four guys tried to take over one of his territories. He rounded them up. Had them hog-tied at one of his warehouses. He said it was my time to step up. Be a man. He gave me a chainsaw. Told me to cut off their fucking heads. One by one, I did it while the ones I hadn't got to yet watched and screamed, knowing they were next. I'll never forget those fucking screams. They weren't human."

The four horsemen.

Billy paces the basement floor, staring at his feet, arms still wrapped tight to his body.

"So fuck yeah," says Billy. "I made a choice. I chose to keep my fucking head."

Lenny looks at the man in front of her. She realizes all his tics and shakes are remnants of deep trauma. He was broken a long time ago. Another casualty of Reg Caffey's.

"She was gone anyway," he mumbles. "It wouldn't bring her back."

"Why did you let me hear it?" she asks. "Why now?"

He wipes tears from his face.

"Because *I* can't fucking sleep," he shouts. "And it's all your fault. I put all that shit behind me, and now I can't get it out of my fucking head. You keep showing up. I can't stand how much you look like her. I keep seeing her face, fucking everywhere. Then I see it on your wall. When you said I'd end up like the other one, I knew you meant Vinny. I couldn't let it go. I needed to know at least one of those fuckers got what was coming to him. She deserved that much."

Billy might be a fucktard, but because of him Lenny knows the truth about what really happened to Kendra. Reg and Vincent were both there. They killed her daughter. She and Hank always suspected Vincent was involved but could never prove it. Lenny has spent fifteen years searching for this feeling. Kendra is no longer a body in a crime scene photo. She is a girl with braces, a teenager whose knees ached because she grew too fast, a woman who loved her son more than anything in the world. Even if justice is only half done, Kendra is free because her mother knows how she left the world but mostly how she lived in it. This gives Lenny some semblance of peace. The terrible ache eases ever so slightly.

Lenny looks at Billy's face, etched with that same ache—the ache of not knowing. It's a torture she wouldn't wish on her worst enemy—well, maybe her worst, but not Billy. Not the shell of a man standing in front of her clutching his belly like he's dying. All he really wants is what she wanted for so long. Some sort of closure. Some relief from the pain.

"Please, make it stop," says Billy. He sounds like a little boy asking for a beating to end.

Lenny's heart breaks for him despite all he's done. It's a huge risk telling him. It could blow back on her and her family. But Lenny makes a merciful decision. The mother in her can't help it. She decides to make it stop. To tell him her deepest, darkest secret. It's the least she can do after he shared his. Lenny takes a deep breath, looks into Billy's eyes, and returns the favor.

"He came here one day when I was alone. Hank and Juls were away for the weekend. I had stayed behind. My dad was coming over for dinner for his birthday. Vincent barged in when I was making cookies. He'd been released from jail earlier that day. He and I had a slight disagreement."

Lenny hesitates. Billy looks at her.

"He's buried under the wisteria in my back garden," she says.

Billy's mouth hangs open.

51

The moment Lenny's secret leaves her lips, a floorboard creaks above their heads. Lenny races upstairs to the kitchen to find the contents of her purse spilled across the table. The keys to the Jeep are gone. She flings open the door to the garage. The Jeep is already halfway down the driveway, a flurry of golden leaves churning in its wake. All she can do is watch Juls speed away, wind sucking the leaves into the garage where Lenny stands, helpless to stop him.

Out of breath, Billy comes up behind her.

"If he heard *everything*," she says, "we know where he's going."

She turns to look at Billy. He bites his lip, then makes a call.

"Hey, boss, it's me," says Billy, pacing the garage. "We have to meet. There's trouble."

There's a pause.

"I can't say over the phone," he says.

Another pause.

"Nah, best not do this at the club," he says. "I'm at home. How 'bout you come here?"

After a couple of seconds, Billy hangs up. He looks at Lenny.

"He's heading to my place," says Billy. "He'll be long gone before the kid gets to the club."

"But won't Reg just turn around when he sees you're not home?" says Lenny.

"I live way the fuck out in Orleans," he says. "Enough time for me to get the kid sorted. I can deal with Reg later."

She's seen the way Reg treats Billy. He's risking a lot going out on a limb for Juls. But it seems that's something he's always done. Both Juls and Billy said as much.

Billy heads down the driveway. Lenny closes the garage door, then rushes into the house, grabs her purse, and follows him. He's parked halfway down the street. Billy turns when he hears her coming and gives her a what-the-fuck look.

"Don't even try to stop me," says Lenny.

He shakes his head in disbelief.

"Fuck me," he says. Then he nods to the vehicle.

"But I go in alone," says Billy. "I know how to talk the kid down."

As Lenny gets in the car, she ponders their odd alliance. A few hours ago, she could barely stand the sight of him. He's definitely growing on her.

Billy keeps his eyes on the traffic as they make their way across town.

"Why didn't you delete the voice message?" she asks.

He looks at her.

"I guess I saw it as an insurance policy, case I ever got on the wrong side of the old man," he says. "Sometimes I like to listen to it. The first part, anyway—where she's talking to me. I like hearing her voice, you know?"

She does know. Lenny's never been able to erase Hank's voice from her old answering machine. That's how it is when someone you love is gone. You hang on to whatever pieces you have, no matter how painful. Lenny looks over at Billy.

"You were in love with her," she says to Billy.

He keeps his eyes on the road, one hand on the steering wheel, one on his thigh. She notices the damaged skin around his fingernails from chewing at it. Just like Juls. She studies his face. He has a permanent dimple in his right cheek. *Just like Juls.* A realization comes to her.

Billy feels her eyes on him.

"What?" he asks.

"Juls is your son, isn't he?" she says.

He looks away. Billy's brow deepens, and his dimple follows suit.

Lenny can't believe she didn't see it sooner.

He honks at a car, then veers around it.

"She and Vinny were going through a rough patch," he says. "We got close, then she went back to Vinny, like always. We knew he would have lost his shit if he ever found out, so he never did. He thought the boy was his. I kept my distance. It's what she wanted. But once in a while, she'd call me. Tell me about the kid."

Lenny wishes Kendra had told *her*. But she knows why she didn't. It would have been one more reason for them to pressure her to leave Vincent.

"That's why you watch out for him," she says.

Billy doesn't answer.

"Does Juls know?" asks Lenny.

Billy sighs and shakes his head.

"Didn't want to mess him up," says Billy. "Then there's Reg. Don't think he woulda taken too kindly to the notion."

Lenny knows Billy is right. Reg has proven himself anything but kind. And blood matters more to him than anything.

"You should tell him," says Lenny.

Billy nods as they look at each other in a new light. Maybe they're both realizing they're now connected in more ways than one.

The car enters Lowertown, and they get closer to the club. Lenny knows there isn't much time. Billy's guard is down. He's talking about things he shouldn't be. Now could be her only chance to test her new theory. One that came to her after she heard what Reg did to Kendra.

"While we're sharing," she says. "Did Reg kill my husband?"

"Fuck no," he says. "Where'd that come from?"

"I don't know," she says. "I thought maybe he hired someone to do it. But now it's pretty clear he's capable of doing his own dirty work."

"Nah, he was fuming when your old man offed himself," he says. "Reg heard the copper was in deep shit. He was fucking giddy at the thought of him doing hard time. No way he'd waste him. No reason to."

Two million dollars would have been a reason. Billy must not know about the money. Maybe Reg didn't either. No one ever came looking for it except Vincent, and he came alone. She remembers what Sully told her.

When Vincent made a pit stop at a casino, Birdie saw his chance to plant the casing. Said he wasn't thinking when he saw the money. He grabbed it.

That's why no one knew. Vincent couldn't tell anyone Hank Bird got the better of him. Somehow, he must have covered up the loss.

Billy looks at Lenny.

"Listen, Reg spent a lot of time and money looking for Vinny," he says. "In the end, he figured Vinny got mixed up in some shady shit and got disappeared by somebody he screwed over. I know for a fact he didn't think your old man had it in him."

"Hank had a lot more in him than I even knew," says Lenny.

"Reg called him a cop's cop—by the book all the way. Reg knew dirty, and Hank was squeaky clean. He almost admired the fucker—sorry. You bet he looked into him after all the shit with Kendra. Reg is no fool, but nothing pointed to Hank. And he wouldn't risk a cop killing based on nothing but a gut feeling. Besides, we all heard it was the old sewerslide."

Lenny looks away and stares out the side window.

"Sorry," says Billy. "I keep sticking my foot—"

He stops talking when he spots the Jeep up ahead. It's parked in front of the club. Billy cranes his neck as they pass the alley next to the club.

"Reg's car is gone," he says. "Thank Christ."

Billy parks behind the Jeep. Lenny opens the passenger door.

"Hey," he says. "You're waiting here, remember."

She frowns.

"Fine, but leave the car running in case we have to make a quick getaway," she says.

He rolls his eyes.

"Okay, Bonnie Parker," he says. "I'll be fast."

As soon as Billy disappears through the club doors, Lenny shimmies to the driver's side, then taps the GPS screen. She noticed it tracking their route as they drove to the club. A menu of addresses pops up. One is hers, one's the club's, and one is labeled "Home." She taps that one, and a "Go" button appears. She presses "Go," and a map to Billy's house magically materializes. Nora would be so proud.

A half hour later, Lenny is on the Queensway, driving toward Orleans. She can only imagine how angry Billy was when he came back out and found his car gone. She can picture the two of them bursting out of the club. Juls looking like death. Billy's head on a swivel as he scanned the street. She can even hear what he likely hollered.

That broad took my fucking car.

52

Fifteen years ago

From the bedroom window, he watched her hurry their grandson down the front path. The boy had been slow getting up that morning. It was a PD day, so there was no school, and the boy wanted to sleep in. Now they were late for his hockey team's annual fundraiser. It was a car wash and bake sale event that helped the team fund tournaments. He watched as the Camry pulled out of the driveway and headed down the street. They'd be gone all day. Luckily the technician he'd booked for that morning hadn't arrived yet.

She'd seemed surprised that he was still home. They rarely crossed paths in the morning anymore. He mumbled some excuse about roll call being delayed. She gave him that look she often wore these days. Like she didn't believe him. But she didn't bother questioning him anymore. She was long past that. He swore to himself that he'd tell her everything one day. But not yet. He knew she'd make him stop. He couldn't do that.

But he could try to protect his family.

As soon as her Camry was out of sight, he went downstairs and waited at the door for the technician. A half hour later, the guy was running cables and setting up the new DVR in the basement near the fuse box. If she asked, he would tell his wife it was a new internet modem. She was as much of a Luddite as he was. The technician connected and configured and confounded with all his tech talk, but in the end, the app on his phone showed a view from each of the four cameras. The technician said the system was state of the art. The man didn't care. All he wanted was to be able to keep an eye on his family when he was out. The man chose a password for logging into the DVR, then the technician tested the motion settings and showed him how to export and save footage. He even gave the man a free thumb drive.

State of the art was starting to grate on him. They were only half done with the job, and it was close to noon. The final step was to mount the cameras. He grabbed the ladder and showed the technician where he wanted them. Together, they worked fast. Attaching the mounts under the eaves and in corners where no one would notice them. The cameras were small, designed to go unnoticed. At each location, the technician screwed on the mount and clipped the camera to it, then the man checked the view on the app. He got the technician to adjust each angle so the cameras covered all the access points.

When the technician was finally gone, he put away the ladder and buried the instructions and packaging at the bottom of the recycling bin, under all the old newspapers and cardboard.

They came home a few hours later.

He pretended he'd been to work.

It felt like he had.

53

Lenny pulls up to Billy's house in a quiet residential neighborhood in Orleans. Reg is walking down a path alongside the house. Billy's place is a 1970s brick bungalow with an angled roof, double wide front doors, neatly trimmed hedges. A family house. Not at all what she was expecting. Reg looks to be alone. He has something in his hand. Lenny realizes it's a gun when he tucks it in a holster inside his suit jacket. He's probably been combing the property, looking for Billy. She parks in the driveway next to his Mercedes sedan. There's no driver inside the vehicle.

Reg's eyebrows lift when he sees Lenny get out of Billy's Lexus, but he quickly recovers with a big smile. She glances up and down the street. A man is pulling trash cans to the curb a few houses down. A couple jogs along the sidewalk, and a woman is sitting on her front porch swing right next door. Witnesses.

"What brings *you* here this fine day, Eleanor?" he asks.

Lenny wants to rip his heart from his chest, but a quick death won't do.

Instead, she leans on the hood of Billy's Lexus and folds her arms, trying to look casual. When she doesn't answer him, Reg looks her up and down. He mimics her by leaning against his car across from her. He takes his time lighting a cigar. He doesn't like not knowing what's going on, but he's playing it cool.

The problem is, Lenny doesn't have a plan. Everything she's done since hearing that terrible recording of her daughter's death has been drawing her to Reg Caffey almost against her will. His pull has grown stronger. As Lenny looks into his eyes, she sees darkness and knows she really has been dancing with the devil all these years.

"Tony sends his regards," he says.

She's not surprised Boxcar called Reg from prison. He sucks on his cigar and lets the smoke snake from the corner of his mouth.

"How's our boy feeling?" he asks. "None the worse for wear?"

"No thanks to you," she says.

"She speaks." He smiles.

He looks past her. His gaze cruises the sleepy suburban street.

"Did I ever tell you about this dog I once had, Eleanor?" he says. "Wild he was. Springer spaniel. Kept running off. Wouldn't come when he was called. I tried everything. Training, treats. Nothing worked. Not until I got him this collar. It zapped him something fierce every time he wandered out of bounds. That wild dog never strayed again. Hell, even Jesus learned obedience through suffering."

"Is that one of the Twelve Steps?" she asks.

He laughs.

"Something to be said for a man turning himself over to a power greater," he says.

"You mean *you*?" she says with a smirk.

Reg tosses his cigar and approaches Lenny. She doesn't move a muscle. She stays where she is, leaning against the hood of the Lexus, trying to appear calm, cool, and collected even though she feels like she might pass out any minute.

"Are you stalking me?" he says, his words slithering down her neck.

He closes the space between them faster than she expected.

"Bet you could use a good ride," he whispers, his sour breath filling her nostrils.

His lips are close to hers. Lenny tries to twist away, but he places his large hands firmly on the hood of the Lexus on either side of her, trapping her. Lenny squirms, trying to get free.

When she sees the amused look in Reg's eyes, Lenny stops struggling. She won't give him the satisfaction. She's sick of him trying to control her and her family. Lenny holds his gaze.

"You can't break my grandson," she says.

"*Your* grandson," he says with a half grin.

"He was broken a long time ago when his mother was taken from him," says Lenny.

Their faces are inches apart. Reg reaches out and plays with a lock of hair that's come loose from her messy bun. Lenny's cheeks burn.

"Ah, lovely Eleanor," he says. "Tell me what's really got you so hot and bothered."

"I know what you did," she says, trying not to cringe from his touch.

"You heard about my little tourney, did you?" he asks.

"Not that," she says. "What you did fifteen years ago."

Reg licks his lips.

The sound of squealing tires turns their heads.

The Jeep careens to the curb. Juls is out the passenger door before the vehicle even stops. He charges at Reg, shoulders down, fists clenched, eyes wild with rage. Billy races around the Jeep. Lenny stumbles out of the way as Juls grabs Reg by his collar. With brute strength, he slams Reg to the lawn, pins him to the ground, and raises his fist. Billy is behind him, wrenching Juls' arm. Lenny can't move. The ferocity of Juls' attack has stunned her. As Juls fights to get his arm free from Billy's hold, the old man clocks Juls in the mouth. Juls tumbles onto his back. Billy puts a knee on Juls' chest and holds him down. Reg gets to his feet, staggering but no worse for wear. In her periphery, Lenny sees the woman on the porch next door disappear into her house.

"Calm the fuck down, kid," says Billy. "You said you'd be cool."

"Somebody better start feckin' talking," says Reg.

"A misunderstanding, boss, that's all," says Billy.

Juls puts his hands up in surrender.

"I'm good," says Juls.

Lenny wants to run to Juls, but she's afraid she'll fall. Her knees are weak. She suddenly feels feeble and small—no use to her grandson. What was she thinking coming here alone?

Billy releases his knee, and Juls sits up. His lip is split, and blood drips down his chin.

Reg reaches into his pocket and offers Juls his handkerchief. Juls takes it and dabs the blood. Billy stays close to the two men. Reg chuckles as he brushes grass from his suit jacket.

"I know you think I got the tar knocked out of you for a bit of fun," he says. "I admit, things got a touch out of hand. But you did me proud, boyo."

Reg offers a hand to Juls.

Juls looks up at the man he still thinks is his grandfather.

"I knew you were a tough motherfucker," says Reg. "But that shite the other night. That was right savage."

Juls lets Reg pull him to his feet. Billy visibly lets his shoulders relax and backs off slightly. Reg keeps a strong grip on Juls' hand and pulls him in close.

"But don't ever come at me like that again," says Reg.

He lets go. As he does, Juls reaches inside Reg's jacket. The move is so fast, Reg barely knows it's happening until Juls has the muzzle of the gun pressed to Reg's temple.

"Juls, no!" yells Lenny.

Her heart stops.

Everyone freezes. Reg and Juls lock eyes.

"Kid, not the time or place," says Billy, looking around.

As if on cue, a siren wails. It sounds like it's closing fast.

"Juls, please," says Lenny. "Think of the girls."

She moves into his line of vision, forcing him to see her.

Juls' arm is vibrating. He looks at Lenny. She shakes her head.

"We need to go now," she says, voice trembling.

The siren gets louder, backing up her plea.

"Fuck," says Juls, lowering the gun.

Reg lets out a breath. Juls looks at Billy. Billy nods toward the Jeep. It's still running. Juls slowly moves away from Reg, who doesn't take his eyes off him. Juls hands Billy the gun and heads for the Jeep. Lenny grabs her purse from the Lexus and follows him. They drive off.

As they round the corner, a squad car sails past, lights flashing.

54

Juls staggers upstairs without a word as soon as they get home from Orleans. He didn't speak to Lenny the entire drive from Billy's. She takes Fender for a walk, then feeds him. As soon as he's done eating, the dog goes searching for Juls. Neither of them comes back downstairs. She leaves him be. There's a lot she wants to explain, but he needs to rest before he can really take in what she has to say. He's too hurt right now.

As dusk falls, Lenny turns on the porch light, then double-checks that the front door is locked. She goes into the garage, gets Hank's revolver from the lockbox, and puts it back in her purse. Then she remembers the shattered window in the back door. After cleaning up the glass on the landing, she goes into the basement. Using a hammer, she pulls wood slats from an old headboard, then nails them across the window. It's only once she's done that she notices her answering machine flashing. Lenny presses play, expecting a message from the girls or Rudi-Rose, or from Maplelawn, telling her she's won the worst daughter of the year award. Instead, it's a message from Maya.

Lenny, it's me. I might have a lead on a digital copy of that security footage from lockup. I found out that all the old backup drives are stored at the archives building. It might take me a day or two to get out there. Meantime, I put some feelers out around the station. I'll be in touch once I know more. Try to stay out of trouble, amiga.

Lenny would love nothing more than to talk to her friend right now. Tell her about the recording of Kendra's murder. Tell her everything.

Except Lenny doesn't have the recording. Billy does. And what would she say to Maya? That she's already broken her promise. That she went rogue again and teamed up with Reg's number two.

Poor Billy. She wonders what lies he's having to spin about why she was driving his Lexus and why he lured Reg to his house in the first place. She and Billy might have had a momentary meeting of the minds, but Billy Rider isn't on her side. He said it himself; the Caffeys are his family, and Reg has always scared him to death. Will Billy spill her secret about Vincent to curry favor with his boss? She can only wait and wonder.

The old house moans as an autumn breeze kicks up outside. Lenny sits at the kitchen table and busies herself with Hank's phone. The last of his things she hasn't sifted through. She replaces the old battery with the new one she bought and powers it up after a few seconds. She unlocks it easily. His passcode is the year of Kendra's birth. She looks through his old emails, texts, and photos, then checks his voicemail. Lenny finds nothing earth shattering. She notices that all the emails are from 2010, and no new ones appear. The phone must have run out of juice soon after his death, and now it can't connect. Obsolete, she's guessing.

Lenny shoves the phone aside. Of course there's nothing on it. Hank left her nothing.

Lenny paces the kitchen. She can't think about Hank right now. It's too painful, and the smell of Reg's cigar smoke is wafting from her skin. Lenny goes upstairs and takes a long, hot bath. It's nearing midnight when she emerges from the water and dries herself off. As she pulls on her robe and closes the bathroom window that she left open to let out the steam, something catches her eye in the backyard. Someone is out there. She watches him disappear into the thickness of the garden. She knows that gait.

Out back, Lenny finds Juls sitting at the foot of the wisteria.

Fender is nearby, nibbling on a patch of unruly grass.

"We were away at the cabin on that fishing trip," he says. "When we got home, you'd moved this plant to the middle of this clearing. Right where Hank said we could build a fort."

"You were mad I'd ruined your plans," says Lenny.

"I always hated this plant," he says.

Lenny sits on the ground next to Juls. She's barefoot, wearing only her bathrobe. The grass is cool and dewy.

"My dad's been here this whole time," he says, his breath misting the night air.

She didn't want Juls to find out this way. Not about what she'd done or that Vincent wasn't his father. Lenny thought Billy should be the one to tell him, but maybe he'll feel better if he knows.

"I'm sorry, Juls," she says. "But he's not—"

"Sorry I found out or sorry that you did it?" he asks through gritted teeth.

Juls is looking at her like he can't stand the sight of her. Lenny doesn't know what to say that won't get him even angrier. Juls shakes his head.

"You were never going to tell me, were you?" he says with a laugh.

Before she can explain, Juls gets to his feet and starts walking away.

"Juls, wait," she calls out.

He pauses and turns around.

"If something happens to me," he says, "I don't want you to take the girls."

Lenny's heart rips in two. Juls is standing in the shadows. She can't see his face.

"I might not *want* it to be you, but who else is there?" he says. "Ru is fucking useless. No way Reg gets his filthy hands on them. They can't go into foster care with strangers. Between a lot of rocks and hard places, I guess you're it, Lenny. You're all I've got. How fucking sad is that?"

Lenny's chest aches. Words get caught in her throat. When she looks up, he's gone. Fender trails after Juls, leaving Lenny alone in the garden. She lies back, and her robe falls open. The midnight air is sweet and musty, heavy with the scent of decomposing leaves. It smells like death. Lying on her back, half naked, she feels the cold dapple her skin with goose bumps. She's been exposed for who she really is. A sad excuse for a grandmother.

How did she ever think that what she did all those years ago could be forgiven?

55

Autumn 2010

Lenny stood at the kitchen counter. She was making cookie dough. There were eggshells, flour, measuring cups, and utensils everywhere. Lenny wanted to surprise her dad by making her mother's famous oatmeal cookies for his birthday.

Vincent walked right in the back door. No knock. No warning. He'd been released sooner than they were expecting. The Caffey lawyers were good. He helped himself to a beer from the fridge and sat at the kitchen table. He glanced into the living room and asked if she was alone. Lenny scraped down the sides of the bowl with a spatula, then continued stirring the dough with a wooden spoon.

"If you've come to see the boy, he's not here," she said without looking at him.

"I don't give a fuck about the boy!" he yelled.

The sharp edge to his voice startled her. She wanted to run. Instead, she gripped the wooden spoon tighter and kept stirring. She told him Hank and Juls were at the park. They'd be back soon. He snickered like he knew she was lying. Maybe he'd even watched them load their backpacks and fishing tackle into the Jeep and drive off earlier that morning.

She dared to glance at him. He was busy poking a hole in the side of the beer can with his car key. He popped the lid, put his lips to the hole, and sucked all the beer from the can in five seconds flat. He crushed the can and let out a vulgar belch. Lenny eyed the knives in the butcher block. Too far away. She busied herself opening cupboards, reaching for ingredients, adding this and that to the cookie dough, stirring, and trying to hide how badly her hands were shaking. After a few minutes of this, he got sick of staring at her back and told her to *sit the fuck down*.

Lenny brought the bowl to the table where the cookie sheets were already laid out with parchment. She placed it directly in front of him and sat down. He dipped his hand into the bowl, licked the dough off each finger, one by one, then dipped it again. She knew he would. He kept doing this until half the dough was gone. Then he looked at Lenny.

"Where is it?" he said, sitting back, legs wide.

She didn't know what he wanted. When she stayed quiet, he leaned forward and held her gaze. She searched his piercing blue eyes for any trace of empathy or shame or kindness. They were empty. There wasn't a flicker of humanity anywhere in their depths. She realized that even if she *could* tell him what he wanted to know, he was still going to hurt her or worse. She could see that much in his cold gaze. He liked inflicting pain. She wondered if Kendra saw that same look in his eyes right before he shot her.

"I'm only gonna ask you one more time," he said. "Where the fuck is it?"

He cleared his throat. She figured his larynx was beginning to narrow.

"You'll have to tell me what *it* is," she said.

"Don't fuck with me," he replied. Then he coughed.

Lenny shifted to the edge of her chair, bracing her feet on either side, readying herself.

"You know, Kendra never shut up about your perfect little marriage. Her perfect dad," he said. "Hank Bird ain't so perfect now."

Vincent cleared the rising phlegm in his throat.

"Point is, I know he told you everything, so just fucking—" He stopped mid-sentence, grabbed his gut, and winced in pain. His eyes got wide as a bewildering sensation took hold.

It was kicking in now.

Suddenly a mouthful of bile caught him by surprise. He gagged and spat the bile on the floor. When he saw the foamy blood, he was confused. Then he panicked. He stood up fast, sending the chair crashing into the wall behind him. Beads of sweat broke out on his forehead, and froth bubbled at the corners of his mouth. He gripped the table as his insides twisted.

He looked down into the half-eaten bowl of cookie dough.

The head exterminator from the pest control company that got rid of the rats in her garden earlier that summer had given Lenny a box of industrial-grade rodenticide pellets, in case any rats survived and found their way into her kitchen. She'd forgotten all about the pellets, having promptly stored them in one of her upper cupboards after he told her they were fast acting and highly toxic to both humans and animals. She didn't want young Juls or Fender getting into them by mistake. The exterminator also told her they were peanut butter flavored.

Vincent's eyes darted to the sink. He staggered toward the counter, stuck his finger down his throat, and leaned over the sink. He gagged and spat, then he lurched back and started flinging open cupboards.

He found the box of poisonous pellets.

By the time he spun around, Lenny was halfway out the back door.

56

After a night of tossing and turning, Lenny is up before the sun. The look in Juls' eyes is burned into her brain. She stares at the clock in her kitchen. Tick, tick, tick. At exactly 8:00 a.m., she can't stand waiting any longer. Lenny goes upstairs, knocks, then enters Juls' bedroom. He's lying on the bed, wearing only boxers. The duvet is twisted around his feet. There's a bloodstain on his pillow from the split lip Reg gave him yesterday. His face is a dozen shades of awful. A purple bruise darkens his rib cage. If she didn't see the rise and fall of his chest, she'd almost think he was dead.

"Juls," she says, placing a mug of coffee on the table next to him.

He stirs. As he rubs his eyes, she untangles the duvet and pulls it over him. She nods to the coffee. He props himself on the pillows, and she hands him the mug as she sits on the bed.

Long before the sun came up, Lenny decided that even if Juls never forgives her, there will be no more secrets between the two of them.

"The twins are at a motel," she says. "I put them there to keep them safe, along with Rudi-Rose. I convinced her to talk to that journalist—the one that came by the house? Rudi-Rose has been meeting with her. This is how we get Reg."

"Good fucking morning to you too," says Juls.

He tries to take a sip of coffee but winces as the hot liquid stings his lip.

"Ru?" he says, blowing on the coffee. "What could she know?"

"She should be the one to tell you," says Lenny.

"Anything else you want to get off your chest?" he asks.

She figures revealing who his real father is can wait until he's had a sip of coffee.

"I didn't go to see Silas yesterday morning," she says. "I drove to Millhaven to visit Tony Boxcar."

Juls stares at her. He goes to say something but doesn't bother.

"I know, I know," says Lenny. "It was foolish and reckless. I know how ridiculous I am."

Juls sits up a little, resting the mug on his chest.

"Nope, Lenny, you're far from that. You're fucking amazing," says Juls. "I was angry about what they did to my mom, is all. I lashed out. Said things to hurt you. My dad was a piece of shit. You made sure he got what he deserved. What I should have said last night was that I'm grateful to you for that. For everything."

Lenny places a hand on his arm. Her heart swells. The last thing she expected was gratitude. Her throat is tight with emotion. Lenny swallows and looks at Juls.

"Sweetie, I have something else to tell you," she says. "You *are* right about Vincent being a piece of shit. But you're wrong about one thing. He isn't your real dad."

Juls is so caught off guard by her words, he doesn't notice the hot coffee spilling onto his chest. Lenny grabs the mug and places it on the table. She dabs the spill with the duvet. As she watches his face, something flickers in his eyes—a memory, a feeling. Lenny can only imagine what's going on in his mind. He's probably retracing his past, trying to parse through the glances, gestures, words exchanged, all the moments between him and these two men—one he thought was his father, the other who treated him like a son.

"It's Billy," he says.

Lenny nods, resting her hand on his arm again.

Juls touches his chest where the coffee spilled on him.

Suddenly, it's like a haze lifts, and he winces as he feels the burn.

"Stings like a motherfucker," he says.

After getting Juls some ointment for his burn, Lenny decides to give her grandson some space to digest the news about Billy. She goes downstairs, pulls on her running shoes and a light coat, then grabs the dog's leash.

A storm is coming. The air is thick with it. Rain gathers in the dark clouds above the Byron path as Lenny takes Fender for a quick walk before the weather turns. She's hyperalert to her surroundings. So is Fender. His muzzle is in overdrive. He noses through the amber leaves trimming the path. They pass other dogs and owners out for their morning walks. A friendly black Lab circles Fender, and their leashes become intertwined. Farther on, an uppity poodle gives Fender the brush-off despite his gentle attempts to play. Like always, Lenny turns back at the intersection at Kirkwood, and they retrace their steps back to Julian Avenue. The walk reminds her of old routines and how much things have changed in a few short weeks.

Just as they're getting back, the rain releases from the heavy clouds. Fender scurries ahead of Lenny into the house. Juls is coming down from upstairs. He's fully dressed.

"I called Ru and asked her to keep the girls out of school," he says. "I need to see them. Nora's mad as all get-out. She wouldn't come to the phone. Guess I can't blame her."

Lenny removes Fender's leash.

"What about Billy?" she asks. "Are you going to talk to him?"

"Once I wrap my head around it," he says. "Anyway, the girls come first. I need the Jeep."

"Can you drop me at Maplelawn?" Lenny asks.

"Sure thing," says Juls. "How long do you need to get ready?"

Before she can answer, they hear the back gate slam shut. Fender lets out a low growl. The hinge on the gate is tight, and unless you know to ease it gently closed, it makes a loud bang. They look at each other. Juls puts his finger to his lips.

Lenny realizes she's not the only one on edge about the run-in with Reg.

Lenny reaches into her purse on the hall table and grabs Hank's revolver. She holds it out to Juls, who raises an eyebrow but takes it. A rattling sound pulls their attention toward the kitchen. It's the back door. Someone is trying to get in. Juls moves slowly toward the door. Lenny follows. They can't see who it is because of the planks she nailed across the glass. Lenny peeks out the kitchen window but sees no one. Juls motions for her to get back. She flattens against the kitchen wall as he creeps down the steps toward the basement landing. He grabs the door handle, yanks it open, and aims the gun outside with both hands.

"Jesus, what the hell, Sugar?" he says, drawing the revolver back to his shoulder.

Sugar is at the back door. She's wearing jeans and a wet windbreaker. No makeup. She looks younger than the Sugar who pressed her stiletto to Lenny's throat. Her expression is serious and fraught with pain.

"What is it?" says Juls.

"Let's take this inside," says Sugar. "You're going to need to sit down."

57

Fifteen years ago

The morning newspaper sat next to him on the passenger seat. He'd grabbed it when he left the house early. He didn't want her seeing the headline.

> SUSPICION OF EVIDENCE TAMPERING IN MURDER CASE COULD SEE ACCUSED RELEASED PENDING JUDGE'S REVIEW

He watched through the lens as the guy came out the side door of the Full Nelson. The door led to a wide alley where some parked cars and a couple of dumpsters lined one wall. He recognized the guy. He'd seen him at the engagement party and at her funeral. The guy was always around the Caffeys, hanging on the old man's every word. Twitchy kind of guy. The guy lit a cigarette and joined the kitchen staff sitting on overturned milk crates. They welcomed him into their circle, and the guy jumped right into the game of dice they were playing on the pavement at their feet. The staff seemed drawn to him. Their eyes fixed on him, their hands touching his back as he rolled the dice, their voices cheering when he won on his first toss. Some of them feigned heartbreak when he kept winning. One jokingly punched his shoulder, and the guy laughed and waved off the winnings like he didn't want them.

A woman poked her head out the side door. She motioned to the guy. She had something in her hand. A newspaper. She showed it to him, smiling. He stared at it for a second, then he smiled too. She went back inside, leaving the paper with the guy. The game started to break up, and the kitchen staff began heading back inside. As he shared the news with them, they all looked happy to hear it. The guy looked happy too.

When the heavy metal door closed behind the last of them and he was alone in the alley, the guy tossed his cigarette as he eyed the newspaper one more time. He wasn't smiling now. Out of nowhere the guy hollered "Fuuuck" *at the top of his lungs. Then he kicked a milk crate. It crashed into the wall as his voice echoed across the street. The guy shoved the newspaper in the dumpster, shook his head, and disappeared back into the club.*

58

Juls slumps in the kitchen chair as he absorbs the shocking news. Sugar pats his shoulder. Lenny leans against the counter facing them, waiting for the kettle to boil. She can't believe he's dead. Juls stares at the revolver on the table.

"After you and Billy left the club, I followed you," she says. "You seemed pretty keyed up. I thought you might do something stupid. I hung back, but when things got heated, I called it in. A patrol car was close by. I think a neighbor already called. You took off right before these two rookies showed up. I could see Reg laying on the charm. Didn't take long for the boots to drive off, then Reg and Billy went inside the house. After about an hour, I figured I better get back to the club. I was literally starting my car when Reg came out alone. I had a bad feeling. Reg was wearing his black gloves."

Juls looks up at her. Sugar pauses as Lenny brings her the cup of tea she asked for.

"I found Billy sitting in his recliner in the living room," she says, staring at the tea. "I called out, but he didn't answer. Then I saw the blood. When I got closer, I saw his throat was cut. He'd already bled out."

Juls swallows hard and picks at the skin around his fingernails.

"It's my fault," he says.

"This was an execution," says Sugar. "Reg must have thought Billy was the rat. The place had been searched, and he took a hammer to

Billy's laptop and phone. Smashed them to bits. Looks like he was destroying any evidence he figured Billy had been collecting."

Juls and Lenny exchange a glance.

Sugar sips her tea, then turns to Lenny.

"Can you give us the room?" Sugar asks her.

Lenny can't believe she's being asked to get out of her own kitchen. She takes her time. She picks up Sugar's half-full teacup, swishes dish liquid inside it, then rinses it under the tap. She grabs a fresh tea towel from the tall cupboard next to the stairs and dries the cup.

Sugar waits.

"I suppose I could check on my laundry," says Lenny.

She heads to the basement. Once she's down there, Lenny darts over to the washer and dryer. There's an old laundry chute that runs from their second-story hall closet down through the tall cupboard in the kitchen and on into the basement. She and Hank used to joke that it was their intercom system. They could hear each other talking, even if one was on the second floor and the other was in the basement. It was like a magic trick. Something about the way the metal walls caused the sound waves to vibrate down the chute. When Lenny had grabbed the tea towel, she'd left the cupboard door open. Now, standing below the chute, she can hear every word.

"I don't get it. You bust into the club like a raging bull. You stick a gun in Reg's face. Seriously, Juls," she says. "What the fuck happened?"

"It's family stuff," says Juls. "Old wounds."

"Jesus. Do you think he suspects you?" says Sugar.

"I'd be dead, too, if he did," says Juls.

"Listen, I came over because I wanted to tell you about Billy in person," she says. "But there's another reason. The sarge sent me to talk to you. Last night at the club, it got real fucking ugly. When word came in about Billy, everyone was freaking out. You know how much they all love Billy. Reg completely lost it. Totally fucking unhinged. Fell off the wagon, hard. He was scaring the girls, grilling his crew, went after a customer. The guys had to drag him out of there."

"Putting on a show, no doubt," says Juls.

"Oh, it was very fucking real," says Sugar. "He knows he fucked up."

"And he did. I mean, you got him for Billy's murder, right?" says Juls. "You were there."

"It's not that simple," says Sugar. "By now he's dumped the weapon. And if there is any physical evidence that points to him being there, his fucking lawyers will say it's because he's over at Billy's place all the time. Nobody actually saw him do the deed."

"So what are you saying? He gets away with it?" says Juls.

"I've been undercover for a year trying to get something to stick to that motherfucker, but he's smart, and he's careful. Only right now, he's off his game, which makes him vulnerable," says Sugar. "We need you to step up. Get him to confess to Billy's murder, and then we've got him where we want him."

Juls laughs.

"Just like that," he says. "Oh. I see. You squeeze his balls hard enough, and Reg hands you a bigger fish to fry and comes away with a deal. Where the fuck does that leave me? You think he won't figure it out?"

"Listen, I know I brought you in, Juls, but you wanted in," says Sugar. "You wanted an escape hatch. I never forced you. This is what it is to be an informant. As for a deal? That's above my pay grade, but let's nail this prick for Billy. The rest'll wash out how it washes out."

Juls is quiet for a while, and when he does speak, Lenny can barely hear him.

"What's the plan?" says Juls. "He'll search me. I definitely can't wear a wire."

"Arrange a meet," she says. "We'll get a warrant for a long-range listening device. We get within eight hundred feet, we'll hear the whole enchilada. Just get him talking. See where it goes."

Juls doesn't respond.

"Phone him. Tell him you heard about Billy," she says.

There's a long silence. Lenny leans closer to the chute.

Finally, she hears his voice, only Juls is not talking to Sugar. His voice is louder. He's called Reg.

"Hey, I just heard," he says. "Was it you?"

Juls has him on speaker.

"You gotta be feckin' kidding me right now," says Reg. "Billy was like a son to me."

"I had to ask," says Juls.

"When I left his house, he was watching the feckin' telly," says Reg. "But I gotta wonder what you got up to last night. Seems you were itching to cap someone."

Juls doesn't respond.

"*Not the time and place?*" says Reg. "What the fuck was that?"

"Billy knew I was pissed about that fight down at the mill," says Juls. "He was just warning me to chill before I got into it with you. That's all."

Reg huffs.

"I'm thinking that Mississauga gobshite took out Billy," says Reg. "He was making the most noise about losing his wad the other night. I think that arsehole's sending me a message."

"We find the bastards and hang 'em by their balls," says Juls.

"Aye," says Reg. "But we can't go off half cocked. We hit 'em hard, but we do it smart."

"What do you need from me?" Juls asks.

"You lay low for a couple of days. Get that hot head of yours cooled off. I got shit to take care of before we make a move. The pigs want me downtown, seeing as I was the last person to see Billy alive. They're feckin' giddy to get me in a box."

"I can come with," says Juls.

"Nah, they'll keep me there all day, then it's down to the morgue," he says. "Someone's gotta identify the body."

"Shit, that's rough," says Juls. "You okay?"

"Had better days, lad," he says. "Let's you and me huddle when the dust settles on all this shite."

"You got it," says Juls. "Whatever you need, Pops. Text me when you want to meet up."

"I knew you were still my boyo," says Reg.

"I'm with you, Pops," says Juls. "Always. You know that."

"There's a good lad," says Reg. The words sound like they get caught in his throat.

Lenny assumes the call disconnected because the next voice she hears is Sugar's.

"You hear that?" says Sugar. "That's the sound of vulnerability."

Lenny hears the kitchen chairs scrape the floor, then footsteps. Their conversation fades as they move to another room. She goes back up and finds Sugar alone in the living room.

"He's upstairs," says Sugar. "He needed a minute alone. He and Billy were pretty tight."

Fender is sniffing Sugar's shoes. The woman inches away. Clearly not a dog person. Sugar wanders the room while Lenny watches her from the archway.

"Sorry about the whole—" Sugar points to her own throat.

Sugar glances at the framed photos on Lenny's bookcase.

"Is that Juls?" she asks, pointing to the photo of ten-year-old Juls on the dock.

Lenny nods. Sugar's gaze falls on another photo.

"Your husband is something of a legend at the shop," says Sugar. "That's him, right?"

She points to the photo of Hank and Sully at the charity ball.

"The one on the left," says Lenny.

"Who's the guy with him?" she asks.

"His partner," says Lenny. "Sully. Detective Terry Sullivan."

"I've seen that guy before," says Sugar. "Maybe at the station."

"He's retired," says Lenny. "But he's got his own barstool at the Carleton."

"Cop bars aren't my scene," she says.

Sugar nods to the revolver on the kitchen table.

"That police issue?" she asks.

"No," says Lenny. "It was Hank's personal firearm."

"I suggest you store it somewhere safe," she says.

Juls comes downstairs. His eyes are bloodshot.

"I gotta go see my kids," he says.

"I'll drive you," says Sugar. "We can talk strategy on the way over."

"Fine, whatever," says Juls.

Lenny approaches her grandson and touches his cheek. A yellow-and-purple mosaic of bruises is painted across his face.

"Let me cover this up first," says Lenny. "For the girls' sake."

He nods. Lenny goes upstairs to grab some makeup. When she comes back down, Sugar isn't there. Lenny sits facing Juls on the sofa and lightly dabs foundation across his bruises.

"Sugar decided to wait outside?" asks Lenny.

"She took off," he says. "Something came up. Guns and Gangs thinks Reg has a man on the inside. The one who tipped him off about the raid at the warehouse. She got some kind of lead. Had to go."

Lenny examines his face closely. She can't do anything about the cut on his lip or the gash across his cheek, but she's managed to hide the worst of the bruising.

"When I was doing laundry, what did you and Sugar talk about?" Lenny asks, trying to sound casual.

Juls lifts one eyebrow.

"Like you don't already know," he says. "You think I didn't remember your intercom?"

"They're using you," she says.

"I know. But Sugar's right," he says. "This is how we get him."

"There's another way," says Lenny. "The journalist."

Juls shakes his head.

"The cops aren't interested in some write-up in the paper," says Juls. "Besides, if I don't do what they're asking, they'll cut me loose and let the charges stick."

"They can't do that," says Lenny.

"They can do whatever the fuck they want," says Juls. "I'm not one of them. In their eyes, I'm just another shitrat."

Lenny knows there's some truth to what Juls is saying. Hank told her that CIs were rarely respected by their handlers. They only had value as long as they were useful.

"Do you think Reg heard your mother's voice message on Billy's phone?" asks Lenny.

"Could be why he obliterated it with a hammer," he says. "No way to know for sure what Reg got out of him, but I know Billy. He would have kept it all on himself. He always had my back. Always protected me like I was his own—"

Juls bows his head.

"I'm sorry about Billy," says Lenny.

"I gotta do this," he says. "For him."

Juls' phone rings. It's Rudi-Rose. He picks up.

"Shit, sorry, Ru," he says. "We got caught up, but I'm on my way now."

Rudi-Rose says something.

"Why the fuck did you do that?" he asks.

He rubs his forehead as he listens. The foundation smudges.

"Yeah, I get it. I know they've been cooped up," he says. "But there's a lot of shit going on, and—"

He gets cut off. His leg bounces as he listens to his girlfriend.

"Okay, okay, you're right. It's good they're at school," says Juls. "I'll come over anyway. You and I need to talk."

As Juls listens, his jaw tightens.

"The reporter? Yeah, I know about that," he says. "What, right now?"

"Then tonight," he says.

He bites his lip as she answers.

"I need to see my kids," he says.

There's a pause.

"So when is a good fucking time?" he asks.

Juls stares at his phone, then he lowers it from his ear.

She must have hung up.

59

The storm doesn't let up, and the dark day makes the house feel smaller and the hour later than it is. In the early afternoon, Juls goes out to the backyard and stands in the rain. Lenny watches him wander the garden, talking to himself. When he comes back inside, Juls is soaked through, shivering, eyes bloodshot from crying. Lenny heats up a can of minestrone soup while he changes out of his wet clothes. Thunder rumbles in the distance, amplifying the feeling of foreboding she's had ever since they found out Billy was dead. Murdered by Reg. And now it's all on her grandson to prove it. How did it come to this?

When Juls reappears, he makes it as far as the sofa before he has to sit down. She brings him a cup of soup to warm his belly. He has that same look he wore when he first came to live with them all those years ago. The little boy lost.

A loud knock startles them both. Juls peeks out the front window. He looks at Lenny.

"There's a fuck ton of cops outside," he says.

Now what? Lenny answers the door. A man in a suit stands on the front porch. His shoulders are wet. He's about fifty. Lenny can tell he's on the job, but she doesn't know him. Behind him in her driveway and along the curb in front of her house are a couple of police cruisers, an OPP van, and an SUV that looks to be hauling a small excavator on a trailer.

"Good afternoon, ma'am," he says. "Detective Delaney, Ottawa Police Service, Missing Persons."

Lenny grips the door.

"Um, I'm really sorry to bother you, Mrs. Bird," he says.

He knows who she is. Who Hank was.

"Sure is raining cats and dogs." He smiles, but his mouth quivers.

"Can I help you?" she asks, trying to keep her expression blank.

"We got a tip regarding a cold case and the possibility of there being—" He hesitates. "Um, human remains on this property."

Lenny's knees turn to jelly. Billy *did* tell Reg. Of course he did. He was trying to stay alive. And why would he protect her?

"Thirteen Julian Avenue," he says, double-checking the paperwork in his hand.

The paper is shaking slightly. He doesn't want to be doing this.

"You got a warrant?" asks Juls, coming up beside Lenny.

Lenny feels her throat closing. She can't speak. She can't move.

Delaney holds out a paper. Juls takes it when Lenny doesn't. He reads it.

Lenny feels the floor undulate beneath her feet. *It's over. Everything is over.*

"I—that is—*we* are going to take a look in your backyard, ma'am." The detective nods over his shoulder at the group of nine uniformed officers standing at the ready. One holds a dog on a leash. One is pushing something that looks like a lawn mower with a screen attached to the handle. A couple of others are unloading the excavator.

"Like I said, I'm real sorry about this. The chief wants this lead followed. Crossing his t's, I guess," he says. "I promise we'll do our best to get this over and done with ASAP. You okay, ma'am?"

Lenny can't feel her hands, and her face is tingling. When she wavers, Juls supports her and guides her to the sofa.

"She's not feeling well," says Juls. "It's been a rough morning."

"Sorry to hear that," says Delaney as he steps into the front entryway. He's dripping on her floor. Fender licks his wet shoes.

Lenny finds her voice.

"Go ahead," she says. "You can use the side gate. It's not locked."

The detective gives her a sheepish nod and heads back outside.

Juls peers out the front window, then starts pacing the room.

"Fucking Reg must have got it out of Billy," he says. "Now he's singing to the cops."

Juls rakes his hands through his hair.

"It's okay," says Lenny. "Maybe it was always coming to this."

"Fuck that," says Juls.

He crosses into the kitchen and looks out the back window.

"Okay, all you gotta do is play dumb," he says. "You tell them you're as shocked as they are. You have no idea who it is or how someone got buried in your—"

"Stop," says Lenny, coming into the kitchen.

She opens the fridge and grabs them a beer. An IPA called Hazed and Confused. She sits at the table, cracks it open, and takes a sip. It's malty and sweet.

"Looks like they've brought some kind of scanner," says Juls, watching the action outside.

"Ground-penetrating radar," says Lenny.

Juls grabs a beer and joins Lenny. They sit in silence listening to the steady patter of rain on the roof, the muffled voices of the officers outside, and the dull rumble of the excavator. Every so often they hear beeping as the excavator moves in reverse.

Then Juls' phone pings. It's the text from Reg.

The Nelson. 7 A.M. Saturday.

That's all it says. Two days from now. She might not be here in two days.

Juls gives the message a thumbs-up and lets Sugar know the meeting is set. He doesn't bother telling Sugar what's going on at the house. Maybe she's heard.

They stay there at the kitchen table into the late afternoon. It's the only thing Lenny wants to do. There is nothing else that matters but sitting with her grandson.

When it gets dark, they don't turn on the lights. They don't have to. A bright beam angles through the kitchen window from a spotlight the police have set up in the back corner of Lenny's garden. Mr. Crawley must be going out of his mind with curiosity.

About eight hours after the police took over her yard, Delaney finally knocks on Lenny's back door. Juls makes a move to get up, but Lenny squeezes his hand, and he sits back down. She walks to the back door, takes a deep breath, and opens it. The time has finally come, and a part of her is relieved.

Detective Delaney steps onto the small back landing to get out of the rain. Mud streaks one of his cheeks, and he's still wearing his police-issue rubber gloves.

"We're all done, ma'am," he says, batting raindrops from his eyelashes and wiping his nose on the sleeve of his rain poncho.

Lenny nods, bracing herself.

"Sorry for the mess. We had to be sure. Scanned the whole yard so no one could say we didn't do it by the book," he says, nodding behind him. "Turns out it was a wild-goose chase. There's nothing out there. Deepest apologies, ma'am. You have a good night, Mrs. Bird. Hope you feel better, and sorry again about your garden."

Delaney pulls the hood of his poncho over his head and follows the other officers as they make their way around the side of the house with their equipment. Lenny watches them leave, then closes the back door and leans against it.

Juls looks at her and shrugs.

When the last police vehicle has driven away, Lenny and Juls head out into the garden. They don't bother with raincoats. They need to see it for themselves. Much of the garden has been trampled. They find the back corner littered with rocks, broken branches, and soil. The earth around the trunk of the wisteria has been dug up and piled off to one side, creating a deep moat around the tree several feet wide and more than six feet deep. The tree's roots are exposed and scarred from all the digging. Lenny sits on the edge of the pit, and before Juls can stop her, she slides down into it. She bends over and starts scratching around in the dirt like a dog.

"Lenny, what are you doing? They said there's nothing," says Juls. "They would have found him if he was here. Stop."

Dirt flies up behind her as she claws at the roots. Suddenly the rain gets heavier, and the pit begins to fill with water.

"You'll catch your death," says Juls, reaching out his hand. "Please, Lenny."

Lenny looks up at him. She's coated in mud. She takes one more look around, then grabs hold of his hand. He hoists her from the muddy pit. Her body shivers violently.

"This is a good thing," says Juls.

"But how?" she says.

Juls shakes his head. He doesn't know. Lenny lets him steer her back to the house. The downpour washes the mud from her face.

She glances back at the wisteria.

The tree is swaying and glistening in the deluge.

It knows.

60

Fifteen years ago

He waited until 2:00 a.m., when he was certain the storage facility would be deserted. No one had driven in or out of the loading bay since 11:00 p.m. It was a twenty-four-hour operation, but he also knew there was only one customer-service rep and one security guard on the overnight shifts. He'd watched the shift changes in the staff parking lot for two days. He knew where the blind spot was at the rear of the building near the fire exit. He knew the alarm would sound the second he used that door. He parked behind an office building next door as close as he could to the fence surrounding the storage facility.

Then he walked around to the front and headed down the sidewalk, entering the storage facility property on foot, hoodie up, baseball cap hiding his face. There were only two cars in the staff parking. He picked up a rock and smashed the window of one. The horn started beeping. He ran for the building and waited around the corner. He could hear the loading bay door opening. A woman stepped out first. She looked around, then the guard joined her. She pointed toward the car. They both walked over to see what was what. Once they had their backs to him, he made his move. He stayed low and close to the building. He ducked into the bay, ran across it, and made it through the double doors. He hoped the car alarm would cover the sound of the door chime.

He was in. He ran full speed down the hall, found the locker, entered the code, grabbed the hockey bag, checked inside, then zipped it up again. He slung the heavy bag over his shoulder, pulled the locker closed, then took off for the fire exit. He burst out the door and launched the hockey bag over the fence. Then he hopped the fence and threw the bag in the back seat of his waiting vehicle. He kept his headlights off as he made his way toward Carling. He couldn't hear the car alarm anymore. He headed away from the storage facility, turning on his headlights as he sped off, heart racing. He'd done it. His first-ever B&E.

61

After a stormy day of murder and mayhem, Lenny and Juls were totally sapped. They both slept like the dead. When Lenny wakes up on Friday morning, her first thought is that she dreamed it all. Billy is alive. Vincent's still buried in her backyard. In the bathroom, she finds mud under her fingernails and knows it was all real. She looks out the window, down at her muddy, trampled garden. At least the rain has finally stopped.

Lenny can hear Juls talking as she heads downstairs. He almost sounds happy. She finds him standing in the kitchen, pouring himself a coffee. He's on the phone. Juls is smiling. It can't be Reg. He hands Lenny the mug he just filled, then grabs another from the cupboard and pours a second cup for himself. She sits and sips her coffee.

"You're right, Ru. I *should* have," says Juls. "We were both hiding a lot of shit, but no more. I promise."

His tone is gentle. Sounds like Rudi-Rose has filled him in on the truth of her situation.

"Can I talk to the girls before they go to school?" he says. "Yeah, I'll wait."

He joins Lenny at the table.

"Ru's gonna come by after she drops the girls," says Juls. "If that's cool."

A strange sound echoes from Juls' phone. Like a howl. His face goes white.

"Slow down," says Juls. "Ru, slow down."

Lenny can hear Rudi-Rose's high-pitched shouting. Juls stands up, knocking into the table. His mug topples, and coffee spills.

"What do you mean they're not there?" he shouts.

Five minutes later, as the Jeep closes in on the motel, they spot Rudi-Rose. She's standing in the middle of the road. Her eyes are wild. Her hair is wet like she just got out of the shower. She almost gets hit by a passing car. Juls stops the Jeep and jumps out. He pulls her out of the road. Lenny rushes over.

"I told them no," she sobs. "But they must have gone when I was on the phone."

"How long?" asks Juls, gripping her shoulders.

"Like twenty minutes," she cries. "Nor wanted a magazine from the store."

"Where have you looked?" he says.

"Around back, up and down the street," she sobs. "I can't find them."

"That the store?" he says, pointing. "At the gas station?"

She nods. He runs across the street. Lenny guides Rudi-Rose back to the motel. Lenny hears shouting. She looks back at the gas station. A woman rushes from the store. The woman looks terrified. Juls isn't making gentle inquiries. He comes out a few minutes later and runs back across the street.

"The clerk saw them talking to a guy at the pumps," he says, eyes darting left and right.

Lenny's heart sinks. She was hoping they'd just wandered off, but this can't be good. Lenny tries to keep her cool, to think. What would Hank do?

"Make, color, license plate?" asks Lenny. "Anything?"

"He's useless," says Juls. "Can't even describe the guy. Farsighted or some shit."

Lenny's phone rings. They both jump. She pulls it from her purse. No Caller ID. She picks up and puts the call on speaker.

"Hello?" she says.

They can hear someone breathing and fumbling with the phone.

"Who is this?" she asks.

"Where are my fucking kids?" yells Juls.

The call cuts off, but just before it does, someone cries out.

Juls stares at the phone.

"I think that was Flo," says Lenny.

"*Fuuuck!*" screams Juls.

Juls grabs Lenny's phone and taps the most recent call, but the caller has blocked the number, so it doesn't connect. Juls storms toward the motel as Rudi-Rose comes out of the room. Tears streak her face. She looks like a drowned rat. Lenny calls out to her.

"Did you find Nora's phone?" she asks Rudi-Rose.

"Right, her phone!" says Juls.

He tries to track Nora's phone. Rudi-Rose grabs his arm.

"She left it in the room," says Rudi-Rose, holding it up.

Juls rubs his head as he tries to think.

"Reg?" asks Lenny.

"Or one of his guys," says Juls. "The girls wouldn't go with someone they didn't know."

Rudi-Rose collapses against the wall.

"How did he find us?" she cries.

"He must have had eyes on the school," says Juls. "Tailed you here."

"What if they saw me with Christie?" says Rudi-Rose.

Juls kicks the wall, then paces, mumbling under his breath.

"Reg won't hurt them," says Juls.

"He killed Billy," Lenny reminds him.

"He never saw Billy as anything more than a punching bag. He wasn't his blood," says Juls. "I'm the fucking golden boy. He won't touch them until he gets what he wants."

"Billy's dead?" says Rudi-Rose, her lip quivering.

Juls nods. Rudi-Rose begins to weep uncontrollably. She drops to a crouch, face in hands. Juls watches her body shudder. When he can't take it anymore, he goes to her, lifts her to her feet, and pulls her into his arms. She buries her face in his chest.

Lenny can't stop thinking about that awful cry on the phone. She can't imagine how scared the girls must be. She wants to kill Reg.

"This place is blown," says Juls. "Lenny, I need you to take Ru back to the house in case the girls try calling your landline or show up there."

"What are you going to do?" she asks.

"Find them," he says.

They gather the girls' belongings and usher Rudi-Rose across the street and into the passenger seat of the Jeep. She's in no shape to drive. Juls hands Lenny the keys, then grabs the keys to his Mustang from Rudi-Rose.

"You have that revolver on you?" he asks Lenny.

After Sugar took off yesterday, Lenny shoved it back in her purse. She hands it to him.

"Shouldn't we call the police?" says Rudi-Rose, one leg out the open door.

Juls tucks the revolver in the back of his jeans and covers it with his shirt.

"Cops won't do a fucking thing if we don't know who took them or why," says Juls.

"Maybe Sugar can help?" says Lenny.

"They're not gonna blow up the plan now," says Juls. "They want Reg at any cost."

"What plan?" asks Rudi-Rose.

Juls leans into the Jeep and kisses Rudi-Rose, then he closes the door.

He hugs Lenny.

"I'm on my own," he says.

And with that, he rushes back to the motel.

Juls jumps in his Mustang, and he's gone.

62

Rudi-Rose is shaking violently when they get to Lenny's house. She's in shock. Fender doesn't like it, and he retreats behind the sofa. Lenny takes the young woman upstairs and runs her a bath, then comes down to put on the kettle for tea.

The morning sky is clear blue and cloudless. The sun feels too bright. It slants in the windows creating dusty shafts of light. Lenny peers out the front window, scanning for suspicious vehicles while she tracks Juls' phone. He's already at the Full Nelson. He's going to find them and bring them home.

With Rudi-Rose out of earshot, Lenny turns on the TV to see if there's any news about Billy's death. The local CTV morning show cuts to a live report at the top of the hour. A police spokesperson is standing outside the Elgin Street station. She's giving an update. But the story is not about Billy. The banner across the bottom of the image reads **Woman Struck by Car Outside Police Headquarters.**

Lenny gets a prickly feeling as she leans in to listen.

"A woman was crossing the street in front of the station at 474 Elgin at approximately four thirty p.m. yesterday afternoon when she was struck by a red Honda Civic sedan. Witnesses reported that the driver fled the scene. The fifty-eight-year-old was taken to hospital with life-threatening injuries. We can confirm that she is an employee with the Ottawa Police Service, but we will not be releasing her name at this time."

Maya is fifty-eight. Lenny turns off the TV and calls the Ottawa Hospital's main line. She asks if a patient has been registered under the name of Maya Castillo. The administrator transfers the call. Lenny waits on hold for what seems like forever until someone finally picks up. All they can tell her is that Maya is recovering from surgery.

Lenny hangs up. Her mind is reeling. Someone hurt Maya. Someone took the girls.

Could all this be Reg Caffey?

He *was* at the station yesterday. That's when Reg likely pointed the cops to the body. Sugar said he might have a mole in the service. If Reg found out Maya was digging into the past, maybe he went after her too. It's all too much.

Juls won't like it, but they need help. And she knows who to ask. Sully.

Lenny calls him. Sully picks up on the first ring.

"I was hoping you'd call," he says.

"I really need your help, Sully," she says.

"Where's Juls?" he asks.

"He's not here," she says. "Why?"

"You like solving mysteries," he says. "Figure it out yet?"

Lenny is confused. His tone is sour. Maybe he's been drinking.

"Sully, are you okay?" she asks.

"The girls are anxious to see you," he says.

Lenny gasps. His words suck the air from her lungs.

Sully is the caller. He has Flo and Nora.

"It was *you*?" she whispers, her mouth bone dry.

"Come alone," he says. His icy words slice through her.

The call disconnects.

Lenny is shaking so badly, she can barely hang on to the phone. She stares at it in her trembling hand.

A hot flash erupts across her chest, courses up her neck, flushing her cheeks.

Her gaze drifts to the framed picture of Hank and Sully on her bookcase.

The picture Sugar asked about.

I've seen that guy before.

Juls said Sugar left in such a hurry because she got a lead.

Guns and Gangs thinks Reg has a man on the inside.

Lenny drops her phone.

Sully is Reg's man. Not hers.

PART THREE

63

Fifteen years ago

The man was sitting in his usual booth by the window at Denny's with his daughter. Same thing every Friday. They ordered cheeseburgers with fries and strawberry milkshakes like usual. The man was talking, gesturing with his hands like he was telling her a story. The girl was giggling as she listened. She blew bubbles in her milkshake. When they were all done eating, the server came over with the bill and the payment machine. He waved off the machine and paid cash. Outside, he opened the passenger door of his gray van for his daughter. She jumped in. He patted down his pant pockets, then he felt inside his coat. He shrugged and said something to the girl. He closed the van door, left her there, and walked back into Denny's.

This wasn't his usual routine.

With his lens trained on the window, he could see the man crossing the restaurant toward the booth where he'd been sitting with his daughter. The man looked around like he was searching for something, then reached down to the bench and picked up a pair of gloves. The server came by and nodded to him as he left.

But instead of leaving right away, he walked to the back of the restaurant, where he took a seat at a table in the corner where another man sat, his back to the windows. This other man slid a menu across the table. The man who'd just sat down reached for the menu, grabbed an envelope from under it, tucked the envelope inside his coat, then got up and left. The man came back outside, jumped in his van, and drove off with his daughter.

He didn't follow them. Instead, he kept his lens on the other man at the table. The man spoke to the server. Ten minutes later she brought him a plate of food and a beer. Looked like fish and chips. He ate, then he paid with cash too. When he finally stood up, he made his way to the door. The sun had shifted so it was reflecting off the front windows. He couldn't see the man's face until he came out the front door. That's when he lowered his lens. The man walked to his vehicle and drove away. Long after the man was gone, he stayed put. He didn't move. He just sat there, gripping the steering wheel so hard, his hands cramped up.

64

Lenny parks the Jeep in the narrow alley behind Sully's house. Rudi-Rose was still soaking in the tub when she slipped out of the house without telling her. There's a gravel driveway at the rear of Sully's yard that leads into the alley. Both the alley and yard are sheltered by overgrown trees. She can't see any of the neighboring houses from back there. Sully's Ford Escape is parked in a giant puddle left by yesterday's storm. A second vehicle sits under a carport next to the driveway. This one's covered with a tarp. Lenny lifts the tarp and peeks in the windows. The plates are caked in mud. There's a dent in the front bumper, and some of its red paint is scratched off. She checks the make. Honda Civic sedan. Lenny drops the tarp. It's the car that hit Maya.

None of this makes any sense.

Lenny crosses the yard toward the house. There's no movement in the windows. She climbs the back steps as quietly as she can and enters the screened-in porch. She peers in the window. No one in the kitchen. She almost knocks but then thinks better of it. She tries the back door. It's unlocked.

Lenny steps into the small galley kitchen. It smells of garlic and onions. A crusty pot of spaghetti sauce sits on the burner. A few stray uncooked noodles litter the stovetop.

"In here, Lenny," Sully calls out.

Lenny startles at the sound of his voice. He knew she'd come. That her curiosity would trump her fear.

Lenny takes her phone from her purse, sends a location pin to Juls, then turns off the volume. She walks through the small dining room and enters the front room. The curtains are drawn. The room is dark save for the dull glow from a floor lamp in one corner that casts an eerie pool of yellow light on the old hardwood. Sully is seated in a deep armchair. A half-empty twenty-sixer of vodka sits next to him on a TV tray.

"Hey, beautiful," he says, as if she's just walked into the Carleton. He looks past her. "No backup, I see."

Of course he knew she'd come alone. He counted on their friendship clouding her judgment. And he knew she'd do anything for those girls.

"What have you done, Sully?" she asks.

"Take a load off, Lenny," he says.

She can tell he's half in the bag. He nods to a faded leather sofa. She ignores him and heads for the staircase that leads to the second floor. She was only here a few times with Hank, years ago, but the house looks like it did then. Like he only just moved in and hasn't made himself at home yet. Sparse, masculine furnishings, no pictures, books, art, photos. A sad, lifeless, empty place.

"Nora!" she hollers. "Flo!"

Her voice echoes up the hollow stairwell.

"They can't hear you," he says.

A shiver runs through her. Lenny knows for certain it was him. She was hoping she'd somehow misunderstood. He was drunk and lying about the twins. But the blocked ID on her phone wasn't a mistake. How could he do this?

"They're only eight years old," she says, turning to him.

"I said *sit*," says Sully as he grabs the vodka bottle. There's a nasty edge to his voice.

Lenny sits across from his giant TV. She can see herself reflected in its screen.

"The chief called," he says, taking a swig. "Asked me to come down to the station. Said he had some questions about Caffey. Was that you?"

Probably Sugar.

"Tell me what's going on, Sully," she says softly. "This isn't *you*."

"You don't know me," he says. "Not the real me."

"I know you're a good man," she says. "At least you were."

He rocks the bottle on his leg.

"Reg made you take the girls, didn't he?" asks Lenny.

He doesn't deny it. It dawns on Lenny that's why the girls went with him. They knew he was her friend. They'd seen him in Hank's home movies. His picture was on her wall.

"What does he have on you?" she asks.

He shifts in his chair, and that's when she notices the gun next to his hip. He's gripping it in his other hand.

"Your precious *Hank* was as dirty as I am," says Sully under his breath.

"He loved you like a brother," she says.

"Ha!" He lets out a bitter laugh. "Birdie always thought he was better than me."

"If he were here, he'd tell you it's not too late to fix this," she says.

"Who gives a flying fuck what Birdie would say?" he shouts.

Sully flings the bottle, and it bounces off the TV, cracking the screen.

Lenny rises and slowly moves toward him. He grips his weapon. She kneels in front of him. He's trembling. She places one hand on his thigh. He flinches at her touch.

"It's okay," says Lenny, softly. "We all make mistakes, Sully."

"Birdie didn't understand," he says, sniffling.

Lenny realizes this goes way back.

"Tell *me* then. Tell me what happened," she says, leaving her hand on his thigh. "*I* might understand."

He leans back heavily in his armchair, letting out a long sigh. She can smell the alcohol. Lenny can't stand being this close to him, but she doesn't pull away. She can see the past darkening his eyes.

"I used to play the tables to blow off steam after a heavy shift. I'd run into Vinny Caffey a few times at the casino in Hull. This one night, he floated me when I was in the hole. Next thing I know, I'm into him for more than I make in a fucking year. I was beggared," he says. "And my mum was getting sicker. I was covering her expenses on top of my own. Vinny said he'd forgive the odd payment for a little intel. Harmless shit. Nothing that ever put one of my own in the crosshairs."

Lenny realizes she's been chasing Sully. *He's* Vincent's lackey. Sully always called him Vinny. She'd missed it. A clue the two men were close. She'd only ever heard Billy call him Vinny. Lenny keeps her expression warm as she leans closer and lifts her face to his. He takes her hand and stares down at their hands, unable to look her in the eye.

"Birdie didn't frame Vinny," he says, swallowing.

Then Sully looks at her.

"That wasn't how it went down. It was the other way round. Vinny set up Birdie," he says. "I got the bullet casing and made it look like the evidence was messed with. We knew Vinny's lawyers would have a field day, and we knew everyone would be looking at Birdie. Vinny found out Birdie was following him, digging into his alibi. Knew he'd never give up. Never leave him alone. Vinny hated Birdie. He wanted him dead."

Sully squeezes her hand and searches her eyes. She holds his gaze as she listens.

"I couldn't let that happen. I convinced Vinny there was a better play. The frame-up was my idea. Vinny hated how much respect Birdie got because he was a cop. So I played on that. Told him what would really kill Birdie was if everyone thought he was dirty. Vinny liked the idea of bringing him down a peg. Seeing his career and his life go to shit."

"So it was all a lie," she says. "All of it? The money, everything?"

He lets go of her hand and smirks.

"Oh, Birdie took the two mil all right. Not from Vinny's trunk like I said, but he took it," says Sully. "Vinny'd been skimming off Reg for years, moving cash around bit by bit, building a nest egg so he could go off and do his own thing. He fucking hated being under his old man's thumb. Bragged about his plan. How his old man had no fucking clue. Vinny kept his stash someplace only he knew about. Never told me where. Some locker. Day he was released, Vinny went for his money. It was gone. He got his hands on the security tapes. That's when he saw someone pinch the cash. He could tell it was Hank."

"Why would Hank go to all that trouble?" asks Lenny. "You made it sound like the money just fell into his lap."

"Hank knew Vinny was about to be a free man," he says. "My guess is Birdie was afraid Vinny would skip town and never get what was coming to him. But Vinny needed that cash to make a clean break."

"Vincent told you all this?" she says, sitting back on her heels.

"He called me when he saw his money was gone. He was on his way to get it back from Birdie. He wanted to take care of him once and for all," says Sully. "He told me to stand by and wait for his call. Promised that if I helped him clean it up, he'd wipe out my debt and give me a cut of the two million. I called Birdie to warn him, only he didn't pick up."

Lenny knows why. Hank was at the cabin fishing with Juls. No cell service.

"I couldn't go over or leave a message. He'd know I was in with Vinny. I kept trying to get ahold of Birdie. Next day, he phones. He saw the missed calls. But he only reached out to get me off his back. Said he was busy. When I didn't hear from Vinny again, I figured he screwed me over. Got the cash and skipped town. Only part of me knew Birdie wouldn't have handed it over without a fight. He was a tough motherfucker. It needled at me, especially when Birdie kept giving me the cold shoulder. I started to think maybe he got the jump on Vinny. Killed him and kept it all for himself."

Tears glaze Sully's drunken eyes.

"No one was looking for the cash," he says with a whimper. "That was the beauty of it."

Lenny stands up. She can't stand to be near him any longer.

"What did you do?" she asks.

"*I* was the one who changed Vinny's mind when he wanted Hank dead," he says. "*I* saved him. That was me. I never wanted to hurt anyone. Least of all those kids. I took care of them. Lollipops and all."

Sully looks up at Lenny. She can't hide her disgust. He rises from his armchair, holding the gun at his side. He's wobbly legged. She stumbles away from Sully.

"Where's the fucking money, Lenny?" he says. "Hidden somewhere in your house? Safe deposit box? Where'd you and Hank stash it?"

"That's why you took the girls?" she says.

"Ding, ding, ding," he says. "That's right. This is the Terry Fucking Sullivan Show. Reg Caffey has nothing to do with this. He doesn't even know about the money."

He aims the gun at her.

"Take me to the cash, and I'll tell you where I stowed Mary-Kate and Ashley," he says.

Lenny shudders at his words. The girls aren't here in some room in the basement like she thought. All she can picture is the twins curled up in a box in the ground. Lenny shakes off the image. She has to find them before it's too late. She has to make Sully understand.

"I swear on Hank's grave," she says. "He never told me about any money."

"Do not bullshit me, Lenny," he says, moving toward her. "I know how it was between you two. You talk like things were rocky, but I know there were no fucking secrets. *Tell me!*"

Sully lunges at her. Lenny tries to run, but he grabs her arm and yanks her close.

"Why couldn't you just leave it alone?" he says. "You got Castillo poking around, and now the heat's on me at central. You made me take her out."

Lenny knew it was his car that hit Maya, but to hear him say it makes her skin crawl.

"Sully," Lenny begs. "The girls. Tell me where they are."

He squeezes her arm tighter.

"You know, the funny part is, after Birdie died, I didn't care about the money. I thought, *Let Lenny have it. She deserves it after all she's been through*," he says. "And we were friends, you and me. Hell, we could have been more than friends. But now everything's fucked because you had to play detective."

Lenny tries to break free, but his grip is strong. Tears suddenly fill his eyes.

"Lenny, I can't go to jail," he cries. "I need that money. I'll tell you where the girls are, and I'll leave town. I'm begging you. Just let me have it."

His tears enrage her. Lenny slaps him hard across the face. He lets go and staggers back.

"Hank was right about you," she says. "You're pathetic."

He points the gun at her.

Out of nowhere, something hits Sully square in the chin, pitching his head back. He reels backward and lands in the armchair behind him. A marble ashtray crashes into the wall. Lenny turns to see who threw it. It's Juls. He charges Sully. Lenny knew Juls would come the second he got the location pin and couldn't reach her. What she didn't see coming was what happened next. She should have.

Eyes glazed over, Sully turns the gun on himself and fires.

"No!" yells Juls.

Sully's head jerks sideways as the bullet enters, then exits, his brain. His torso slumps over the armrest. Juls grips Sully by the shirt collar and shakes him.

"Where are they?" he screams.

Sully can't answer.

65

Juls storms through Sully's house, ripping open doors, rifling through closets, lifting beds, scouring the basement for any sign of the girls. There's nothing. Juls is terrified. A dead man is their only lead. Sully's phone holds no clues.

Juls didn't find Reg when he crisscrossed the city searching for Flo and Nora. He tried all his businesses, even his private penthouse. And Reg wasn't answering his phone. Juls found out the old man was called in for more questioning. Reg had been at the police station since early morning, so Juls knew he hadn't taken the girls himself. Sugar wasn't at the club. He was told she'd taken the weekend off. Nothing but dead ends.

Juls had entered Sully's house wearing leather gloves. He was a pro.

Lenny isn't even thinking about fingerprints until Juls asks her what she touched. He says it's just a precaution but wants to be sure nothing comes back to her. When Lenny says she touched Sully, Juls shakes his head. Prints don't take to fabric or skin, he tells her. They return the marble ashtray to the shelf where Juls found it, then retrace Lenny's steps. They wipe down the leather sofa, the back door handle, and the edge of the tarp over the Honda. Then they leave Sully's property the same way they came in, under the cover of the backyard trees, checking the alley before making their way to their separate vehicles and driving off.

They meet back at Lenny's house and park side by side in the driveway. Juls waits for Lenny to get out of the Jeep. He leans on his Mustang and lights a cigarette with shaking hands.

"It's been three fucking hours," says Juls.

"We'll find them," says Lenny.

"I'm sorry I didn't bust in sooner. I hung back in the hall," he says. "I figured you'd be more likely to get the truth out of that pissant than me. I heard what he said about Hank."

"I don't know what to believe," she says. "He could have been spinning more lies."

"Tell me more about this Sully dude," says Juls, hauling on his cigarette.

Lenny leans against the Mustang next to Juls. He's right. They have to keep digging. They can't give up.

"He lived alone. Never married. I'm pretty sure he was an only child," says Lenny. "Liked to gamble. Doubt he ever stopped. I'm sure that's how both Caffeys got their hooks in him."

"You think Reg put him up to this?" he asks.

"I think he was the one feeding intel to Reg, just like he fed it to Vincent back in the day," she says. "But this was about the money. I believed him when he said no one knew about it. Sully wanted a way out."

"So where would he take them?" asks Juls. "He said something about his mother."

"His parents are dead," she says.

"Did he ever talk about a cottage, cabin, rental property, anything?" he asks.

She shakes her head.

"Sully was a lot of things, but I don't think he'd hurt them," she says. She only half believes it after what he did to Maya.

"He was still on the job, right?" Juls asks.

"No, he retired a few years ago," she says.

A breeze sends leaves tumbling from the oak in her front yard. Lenny stares at the lawn, trying to think.

"Means he had a contact on the inside," says Juls. "It's how he got the intel to pass on to Reg."

"There's a cop he's always talking to at this bar we hang out at," she says. "If the guy's dirty, maybe *he's* involved or knows something. Maybe Sully promised him a cut if he helped."

"Which bar?" asks Juls.

She doesn't answer. Lenny is gaping at the front door of her house.

"Juls, look," says Lenny.

He turns, following her gaze. The door is sitting half open.

Juls pulls Hank's revolver from the back of his jeans. He moves quickly up the path, then climbs the front steps, revolver at the ready. Lenny stays close behind him. They can't see in through the living room window. Someone's drawn the curtains. Juls gently pushes the front door with his foot so it opens wider. They have a clear view into the house. A river of blood snakes from the front entrance, down the hall, disappearing into the kitchen. It's dead quiet.

No sign of Rudi-Rose or Fender.

Juls aims the revolver and follows the trail of blood down the hall, Lenny at his heels. As they near the kitchen, a pair of shoes comes into view, then legs, a torso, then a blond head.

"Jesus," says Juls as he rounds the corner to the kitchen and lowers the revolver.

Lenny comes up beside him.

Rudi-Rose is sitting on the kitchen floor, back against the cupboards, a large kitchen knife clutched in both hands. It's dripping blood. Not hers. There's a smile frozen on her face. Her eyes are glued to the guy splayed on the kitchen floor a few feet in front of her. He's lying face up, eyes wide, mouth open. Blood stains his jeans. There's a gash in his upper thigh. It looks like she sliced an artery.

Juls looks at Lenny.

"That's Shadow," he whispers. "One of Reg's cleanup men."

Lenny notices a tattoo of a sombrero on the man's forearm.

Juls crosses the kitchen, sidestepping the blood, moving slowly toward Rudi-Rose. He squats in front of her and reaches for the knife. She pulls it close and erupts into a fit of giggles, her body convulsing.

"It's me, Ru," he says softly. "Nobody's gonna hurt you."

She looks at the knife, then drops it. Juls chucks it in the sink and helps her up.

Lenny hears Fender whimpering. She finds him cowering behind the washing machine in the basement. He's not injured, but he won't be coaxed upstairs, so she brings down a bowl of water. Poor thing looks like he's had just about enough of humans. She leaves him be for now.

When Lenny comes back up, Juls and Rudi-Rose have gone upstairs. A while later, he comes down. He tells her that Rudi-Rose has taken one of her sleeping pills and she'll be out for a couple of hours. They stand in the kitchen staring at the body.

"She said he knocked on the front door. Guess he thought it would be that easy," says Juls. "She grabbed a knife when she heard him jimmying the lock. She hid behind the door and caught him off guard. Stuck him and ran. He made it to the kitchen before he bled out."

Juls wraps Shadow in an old camping tarp, then drags him into the garage. He pulls the Mustang inside and lifts the body into the trunk.

Then he drives away.

66

Out the kitchen window, Lenny watches as the sun gets swallowed up by a mass of ominous gray clouds. The dark sky heightens her sense of dread. Her muscles feel stiff from holding so much tension. Flashes of blood and brains won't stop taunting her as she waits for her grandson to get back. When Juls finally returns after a few hours, she's already cleaned up the trail of blood. She doesn't ask where he took the body. She doesn't want to know. Fender has made it to the back landing, but he won't come any farther into the house. Lenny grabs them a couple of beers—an IPA called Rabble Rouser. They sit together at the kitchen table.

"I shouldn't have left Rudi-Rose alone," says Lenny.

"She's a tough cookie. Ru will be okay," says Juls. "Sugar said Reg was on tilt."

Juls pulls a cell phone from his pocket. Lenny doesn't recognize it.

"It's Shadow's burner," he says. "I already took a look. It was a hit. He was sent a location and a photo of the target."

He shows Lenny the phone. There's a picture of her on the screen. Lenny covers her mouth. Shadow was looking for her.

"Reg thinks you're dead," he says. "That's good. Means he won't try again anytime soon."

Juls shows her a text he sent from Shadow's phone.

Tango down.

"Once the hit's confirmed," says Juls, "Reg sends a crypto payment to an account, and that's it. No more contact."

Lenny tries to wrap her mind around it. This has to be payback for Vincent. Even if Billy told him Hank did it, Reg apparently has no qualms about killing her. That connection she thought she had with Reg was an illusion. There was never any mutual respect. No meeting of the minds. But why now? So soon after Billy's murder.

"There's a spotlight on him. Why risk it?" says Lenny. "It doesn't feel like a smart move. Sending the cops over to dig up my backyard I get, but this?"

"He's not expecting blowback," says Juls. "It's why he chose Shadow. The guy doesn't just take people out, he disappears them."

Lenny shivers.

Juls stares at the phone. The wheels are turning.

"I'm guessing he caught wind I was running around town. He probably figured you were alone," he says. "It's classic Reg. It's what he does. Tears people apart so *he* can be the one to put them back together. I think this hit was more about me than you. Controlling me. It's always been about that for him. I did stick a gun in his face. He knows something's up. He might even figure I heard that voice message my mom left on Billy's phone. Billy would have never said as much, but Reg is no fool. And taking what matters most to me is one way to get me back in line."

Juls gets up and crosses to the kitchen window. He grips the edge of the counter and stares out into the backyard.

"You can't go to that meeting tomorrow morning," says Lenny.

"Nothing's changed," he says. "He'll think he has me by the short hairs. But I can handle that motherfucker."

Lenny comes up beside him. She puts a hand on her grandson's shoulder.

"What can I do?" she asks.

He turns to face her.

"You're doing it," he says.

Juls hugs Lenny tight. She wasn't expecting the hug. Or how much she needed it.

"I don't know what I would have done if I'd lost you," he says.

He rests his chin on her shoulder.

"I love you, Lenny," he whispers.

He hasn't said that since he was a little boy.

67

Fifteen years ago

As he aimed the still camera and framed the shot, his heart felt full for the first time in months. The boy stood at the end of the dock, a few feet in front of him. The sun was glistening off the lake behind him. The far shore was obscured in the shadows, nothing more than a silhouetted strip of shapeless balsams. The tin fishing boat bobbed next to the dock. The boy had his finger hooked in the trout's mouth. He was grinning ear to ear. His grandfather took the photo. It was the perfect shot.

They made their way up the rocky trail to the cabin. The boy carried the fish in a bucket. After starting the campfire in the pit, the man went into the cabin and came out with a large cutting board, an onion, a lemon, butter, tinfoil, and a knife. He handed the boy the knife. The boy hesitated before taking it. The man showed him how to hold it. He talked him through each step. The boy inserted the tip of the knife near the tail, then sliced the trout's belly all the way from tail to head. He spread the body and removed the entrails. The boy scrunched his nose but kept going. Together they washed the fish, then cut up the onion and lemon and stuffed them into the belly of the fish with a few pats of butter. Then they wrapped the trout in tinfoil. The fire had burned down to hot embers by that point. The man placed a grill over the coals, and the boy laid the wrapped fish on the grill. The boy turned and high-fived his grandfather.

They sat in their camping chairs as the sun set, listening to the sound of waves lapping on the sandy shore, the tin boat knocking against the dock, the fire hissing and the fish sizzling as it cooked. When it was ready, they grabbed a couple of forks and ate it right out of the foil.

Later, when the boy was asleep, the man sat outside by the glowing coals. A loon's lonely call echoed across the lake. The man gazed up at the night sky. Without the glow of the city, it was brimming with stars. The moon hovered above the dark tree line on the far side of the lake.

It was bloodred.

68

The Carleton is crowded. It's happy hour on a Friday, so the place is bustling. Juls moves slowly through the bar, holding his phone facing the room. He's keeping it low so as not to arouse suspicion. Lenny is watching the video call on her phone. She's in the Mustang parked around the corner. They can't risk anyone seeing her and news getting back to Reg that she's still alive. With Shadow no longer a threat, they figured it was safe to leave Rudi-Rose behind. She was still out cold. Lenny needed to be close by in case something went wrong and Juls needed her to step in. She had more friends than foes in the tavern.

A young woman leaning on the bar in a tight red dress does a double take when Juls walks by. It's probably his battered face, but Juls has always turned heads. The bartender nods to Juls. So far, she doesn't see Sully's buddy, their only lead.

Lenny's stomach is churning, and her heart is beating dangerously fast. Damned high blood pressure. For the second time, she checks to make sure the car doors are locked, careful to stay low in her seat, her hair covered by a nylon scarf so no one recognizes her. At least she has a weapon. Lenny convinced Juls to leave the revolver in the Mustang. Not a good idea to carry a gun into a cop bar.

Juls moves toward the back room. Lenny knows some of the cops playing pool. Then she spots the one named Wyatt. He worked under Hank and knew Sully well. She's seen them having more than one tête-à-tête over the past few months.

"The one in the plaid shirt," she says into the phone.

Juls turns the phone around toward his face.

"I see him," he says, looking into the phone.

"His name's Wyatt," says Lenny.

"Okay, hang tight," says Juls.

Just as he's about to put the phone away, another call comes in on Lenny's phone.

"Hold on, Juls," she says. "Maplelawn is calling me. They never call. Shit, Silas. I'm putting you on hold. Don't hang up."

Before Juls can speak, Lenny connects to the other call.

"Hello, this is Lenny," she says.

"Oh, thank goodness. Mrs. Bird, I'm so glad I got you," says the woman. "It's Chelsea from reception at Maplelawn Manor. I just tried your landline, but no one picked up. Then I remembered you had a cell phone."

"Is it my father?" says Lenny, holding her breath.

"I'm so sorry. I had no idea they were still here," she blurts out. "I was up on the third floor just now, and I happened to pass by Mr. Flint's room. That's when I saw them in there."

"Someone is in his room?" asks Lenny.

Right away she pictures Shadow's twin.

"They arrived with your brother this morning," says the woman. "It seems he's left without them, and honestly, they've been here for hours, and I'm about to go off shift. I was hoping you—"

"Who, Chelsea?" shouts Lenny. "Who's been there for hours?"

"Your great-granddaughters."

Lenny's mind suddenly flashes to something Sully said.

I took care of them. Lollipops and all.

Sully was telling her where he'd taken the girls.

69

Juls races into the room ahead of Lenny. Silas is propped against the pillows on his bed. He looks asleep. The twins are sitting in the armchairs by the window. Nora is reading a *Retirement Today* magazine. Flo has her chin on the arm of the chair. She sees her father first and tumbles from the chair to leap into his open arms.

"Why didn't you call me?" Juls cries, looking at Nora.

Nora clutches the magazine to her chest.

"The man told us he'd hurt you if we called anyone," she says. "He said Lenny was coming to get us."

Lenny remembers her dinner with Sully earlier that week. They'd talked about Maplelawn. He knew her father was here. And he knew they'd be safe.

Flo buries her face in her father's chest.

"We were scared for you, Daddy," says Flo, her voice muffled in his shirt.

He kisses the top of her head.

"I'm okay," he says, tears in his eyes.

"You don't look okay," says Nora, scrunching her nose.

"This?" he says, pointing to his bruised face. "It's nothing. Friendly dustup."

"Did you win?" asks Flo, with a giggle.

"It's not funny," says Nora, sticking out her lower lip.

"I know it's not, honey," he says.

He opens his other arm, beckoning Nora. She hesitates a second, then she crumbles. Nora drops the magazine and runs to her father. He hugs both girls tight.

"You're squeezing too hard, Daddy," says Flo.

Juls tickles them, and squeals burst from the girls.

Silas is awakened by the sound.

"Who's there?" he asks, rubbing his eyes.

Lenny sits next to him on the bed.

"It's just the girls, and Juls is here too," says Lenny.

"Little Julian?" asks Silas. "It can't be. Where is he? Let me look at him."

Juls approaches the bed.

"It's me, Silas," says Juls softly.

Silas blinks at his great-grandson.

"You've got your mother's eyes," he says. "Did you bring her with you?"

Juls glances at Lenny.

"Next time, Dad," she says.

70

Fifteen years ago

He sat on the back steps under the dim porch light. The puppy was across the garden, nosing around in the lilies at the base of the birdbath. The night air was still sticky with humidity despite it being mid-September. The cicadas buzzed, taking advantage of the heat to amplify their mating calls.

He couldn't stop thinking about the security video. He'd played it over and over. The violence of it had shaken him badly. He rarely checked the footage. He could watch the camera feeds live on his phone anytime, and he got alerts if a motion triggered the cameras to record. But he'd been at the cabin with no cell service. He didn't get the alert until he reached the highway. But it was the bruises she'd been trying to hide since they got home that made him check. He should never have left her alone.

When he heard the back door open behind him, he took a deep breath and tried to pull himself together. She came outside and sat next to him on the steps. They didn't speak. Words were hard for them these days. They watched the puppy flipping dirt behind him, digging in the lilies for no reason other than the pure joy of it. The man rested a hand gently on his wife's hand, and they sat in silence for a few minutes. She noticed he was trembling and asked how he could be cold on such a warm night. He shrugged. He couldn't speak for fear he might burst into tears.

She got to her feet and went over to the dog. She'd had enough. She pulled the little pup away from her flowers and filled in the hole he'd dug by the birdbath. The dog kept coming back to the spot, determined to keep at it. She found a stick and distracted the pup with a game of tug-of-war. The man watched her play with the puppy, mimicking the little critter's snarls and dekeing side to side. She laughed as she played.

He watched her with wonder.

His strong, fierce, beautiful wife.

She took his breath away.

71

When they arrive home, Juls drives straight into the garage, out of view of anyone who might be watching the house. He heats up some canned ravioli for dinner. Other than a few arrowroot biscuits, the twins haven't eaten all day. Lenny goes around making sure all the blinds and curtains are closed tight. She flicks off lights that don't need to be on. Rudi-Rose is awake. She curls up in a baggy sweater on the sofa.

Nora doesn't ask about the man who took them or why their dad looks like he's been beaten with a baseball bat or why their mom seems shell shocked. The strangeness of the day gets the better of Flo. She bursts into tears, letting ravioli fall from her mouth. Juls calls an early bedtime. Flo insists he come up and read them a story. He probably hasn't done that since they were little, but he goes. The girls have been through a lot.

Lenny sits on the sofa and turns on the TV. Rudi-Rose stares blankly at the screen. Billy's made the early evening news, only he's not named. It's described as a suspicious death in Orleans. Possibly gang related. The story is brief like his life didn't rate any further details. There's nothing about Sully. Maybe no one's found him yet. Back when Kendra was killed, her neighbors ignored the sound of the gunshot. It was hours later when Juls found her. People don't like to get involved or don't want to believe what they just heard could be anything other than a firecracker. As much as she despises Sully for what he did to the girls,

Lenny can't bear to think of him sitting there, alone, perhaps for days. She decides to call in an anonymous tip to Crime Stoppers.

Lenny reaches for her phone, then stops herself. She can't risk the call being traced back to her number. That could lead to questions. Like why Sully called her. Lenny jumps when the phone next to hers pings. It's a text coming in on Juls' phone. He left it there when he went upstairs. Rudi-Rose doesn't move or blink. Lenny picks it up without her noticing and scoots into the kitchen. She enters his PIN. The year the twins were born. It unlocks. The text is from Pops. Lenny knows that's what he calls Reg.

Change of plans. Midnight tonight at the mill.

He's moved up the meeting. Lenny replies with a thumbs-up like she saw Juls do before.

She waits a few seconds to see if there's a response. None comes.

She deletes the text from Reg. She will not let any harm come to Juls.

And she will not live the rest of her life in fear of Reg Caffey.

Midnight tonight at the mill.

Juls said something about a mill when he phoned Reg.

Billy knew I was pissed about that fight at the mill.

It's where the tournament was held. An idea begins to take shape in Lenny's mind. It's half baked, but it's already cooking.

Lenny nonchalantly places the phone back where she found it and settles onto the sofa next to Rudi-Rose. She turns off the TV, which startles Rudi-Rose from her stupor.

"I know how you're feeling," says Lenny. "It happened to me once."

The young woman looks at Lenny with vacant eyes.

"I had to defend myself," she says. "It'll take time, but you'll be okay."

"I took a person's life," says Rudi-Rose, pulling a tissue from the sleeve of her sweater.

"You did what you had to do to survive," says Lenny.

Rudi-Rose bursts into tears. Lenny squeezes her hand.

"I'm sorry for what you've been through," says Lenny. "I should never have left you alone."

Rudi-Rose blows her nose.

"You got the girls back," she says softly.

"And you're doing what you can to protect them," says Lenny.

Rudi-Rose scrunches her nose. She looks like Nora.

"Oh," she says. "You mean the journalist."

"It's a brave thing you're doing," says Lenny.

"I told Juls everything," says Rudi-Rose. "I'm not sure he can forgive me for lying to him all these years."

"He'll come around," says Lenny. "Juls is good at forgiving. And he knows Reg. You said it yourself. Reg showed his true colors at that tournament out at the mill."

Rudi-Rose pulls her sweater closer as a shiver vibrates her limbs.

"In the video, it looked like a warehouse, not a mill," says Lenny, trying to sound casual.

"It's an old paper mill," she says. "A big place out on Victoria Island."

Lenny knows the island. It's a defunct factory district along the river between Ottawa and Gatineau. Developers bought up most of it years ago and put apartment buildings at one end, but there are still a number of abandoned structures scattered on the island.

"Can't be very private with people living so close," says Lenny.

"The condos are on the other side of a levee," she says. "Reg's place is hidden down by the locks where the river runs loud. You can't see it unless you're right on top of it. It's where he holds his auctions."

Lenny cringes at the thought of young women being sold to the highest bidder.

"I never want to see that fucking place again," says Rudi-Rose.

She tries to dry her tears, but more keep coming.

Lenny lets it go. She got what she needed.

72

Juls comes downstairs around 8:30 p.m., wearing pajama bottoms and a T-shirt. He checks his phone, then grabs a beer from the fridge. Lenny is at the kitchen counter, mixing cookie dough in a bowl. One of her recipe books is propped open next to her.

"*You're* making cookies? *Now?*" he asks.

"I need the distraction," she says. "Snickerdoodles. They were your favorite when you were a kid."

"Haven't we all been through enough?" he says with a fake grimace.

She flicks the spoon at him, and a chunk of dough hits his nose.

He wipes it off with his finger and eats the dough. His eyebrows rise.

"I stand corrected," he says. "But try not to burn them."

"Out!" says Lenny.

Juls holds up his hands and laughs. He joins Rudi-Rose in the living room and drapes one arm around her. She snuggles her head into his shoulder. Juls starts channel surfing. Fender jumps onto his lap. Juls puts his feet up on the coffee table. Lenny knows tomorrow's meeting with Reg must be weighing heavily on him, but it's the first time in days she's seen Juls look relaxed. All he cares about is that his girls are safe.

Juls doesn't notice as Lenny passes through the hall and goes upstairs. She finds Rudi-Rose's sleeping pills by the bed in Juls' room. Benzodiazepines. Lenny was prescribed these same pills when she was having trouble sleeping after Hank's death. They're strong. She remembers missing entire mornings due to their effects. She grabs one pill. That should be plenty.

Back down in the kitchen, Lenny crushes the pill with her rolling pin. She puts half in a beer and half in a hot cup of chamomile tea. Lenny stirs the powder into both, then brings them out to Juls and Rudi-Rose. Juls happily downs the beer in his hand and takes the new one, thanking her. Rudi-Rose accepts the cup and gratefully sips the hot drink.

Lenny goes back to her cookies. She dollops raw dough on a baking sheet, then puts them in the oven, watching them like a hawk so they don't burn.

Some lessons take years to learn.

When the cookies look done, Lenny removes them from the oven. She picks one up, blows on it, then takes a small bite. Success. It's a first.

Lenny transfers most of the cookies to a tin, then takes four on a plate into the living room. She sets the warm cookies on the coffee table. As expected, Juls dives in. The beer and tea wouldn't have been enough, but the added sugar and half dose of benzodiazepine should do the trick. If trouble comes calling, Lenny knows Juls won't be completely incapacitated, but she's hoping for a small window. Just enough time to get everything ready and slip out of the house unnoticed. Juls would never let her leave—even if she said it was to walk Fender. She's supposed to be hiding. Lenny is done hiding.

By 10:30 p.m., they're both asleep.

With her plan now fully baked, Lenny moves fast.

73

Fifteen years ago

She called from her father's house in Kanata. She was staying overnight. The old man wasn't feeling well. A flu bug, she told him. He didn't question it. He'd seen the beating the old man had taken in the video. The boy had gone to an overnight hockey tournament in Kingston. He was rooming with one of his teammates and had gotten a ride from the kid's parents. When he hung up, he knew this might be his only opportunity. He got to work gathering supplies. Once it was dark, he put on rubber gloves and made his way down the garden path.

He knew the spot when he saw it. The earth was freshly turned around the Japanese wisteria. He'd seen her head this way with the spade, hours after the attack. The motion had triggered another recording in the early-morning hours. In that one, she'd disappeared into the shadows, then come back out a while later, covered in dirt, both her and the spade.

First, he dug around the plant, careful not to damage the root ball. Once it was loose, he pulled the plant, roots and all, out of the ground and set it aside. He put on the mask. Then he kept digging until he found him. The body was bloated, and maggots had already been busy feeding. He tugged it from the hole and dragged it to the surface, then rolled it onto the plastic drop sheet. After carefully securing and sealing the plastic around the body with duct tape, he hoisted it onto the wheelbarrow, then maneuvered toward the garage. Once inside, he lifted the body into the back of his vehicle and covered it with a blanket.

Hours later, he returned to the house after sinking the body with rocks in a defunct quarry reservoir on the Quebec side. He went out to the garden and replanted the wisteria, then he washed down the spade and wheelbarrow. By the time he was done, it was already morning.

There was one last thing to take care of. He went down to the basement, found their old TV on the shelf where it had sat for five years, and dragged it over to the DVR. He'd called the technician who installed the security system, and the guy talked him through how to access the footage without his laptop. PSU had confiscated it.

Turns out state of the art *meant the app on his phone did nothing more than basic live streaming. The DVR stored all the footage. To access it, all he needed was a monitor. A TV would do, the technician told him. Once he was connected, he logged into the menu, found the footage of his wife's attack from the day he'd gone fishing, and saved it to the thumb drive. After that was done, he deleted everything else, including the second recording from a few hours after the attack and everything from tonight.*

That's when he heard the front door open. The man yanked the thumb drive from the DVR and shoved it on top of the fuse box in front of him while he quickly disconnected the TV and carried it back to the shelf. She was calling his name as he rushed up the basement stairs.

74

Lenny pulls into the visitor parking lot next to a condo on Victoria Island. A bitter wind bites her cheeks as she gets out of the Jeep. She's glad she wore her heavy winter coat. But even with it she's shivering.

It's 11:15 p.m.

With Rudi-Rose's vague description as reference, Lenny walks a road that leads to the other end of the island. She comes to a bridge over a levee. Farther down the road, she reaches the top of a hill. When she looks down, she sees a large stone building.

This has to be the mill.

It's right where Rudi-Rose said it would be. The four-story limestone building sits near a set of locks. She can hear the water raging down the Ottawa River. A fine mist rises, sparkling in the glow cast by a spotlight near the main entrance of the old mill. There's a **No Trespassing** sign on the side of the building. No cars are parked out front. He's not here yet.

Lenny walks the perimeter of the building, trying to peek in windows, but all of them are blacked out. There's a long metal chute running down one side of the building from an upper window. It looks like a shaft that might have once been used to discard waste or debris.

Coming back around the front, Lenny scans for a hiding spot so she can see how many men Reg brings with him. There's a row of garbage bins near the entrance. She could hide behind them, but she wouldn't have a clear view of the door. Then she spots a small ridge of rocks along the river's edge. She climbs the rocks and discovers a path running alongside the river. Lenny has some time, so she follows the path. It runs along the shore, back to where she parked the Jeep.

A possible escape route.

Lenny retraces her steps, then nestles behind the rocks with a perfect view on the front door of the old mill. She waits.

At 11:50 p.m., Reg's blue Mercedes comes down the road. Lenny ducks as the beams from its headlights swing in her direction. Once they pass, she peeks out. The car pulls up, and the driver gets out. It's not his usual driver. It's the tattooed bouncer she saw at the club when she picked up the girls. He's a beast of a man. Reg has brought muscle.

The big man opens the car door for Reg. His boss steps out. It's just the two of them. They don't go inside the mill right away. Reg pulls out a cigar. The big man lights it for him. They're talking, but Lenny can't hear what they're saying over the boisterous rapids. After a few puffs, Reg unlocks the front door and goes inside. The big man stays outside. He's obviously been told to stand guard and wait for Juls.

Lenny does her final preparations, then takes a deep breath. When the big man turns his back to her and lifts his collar to protect himself from the harsh wind, she scurries over the rocks and heads for him. She clutches the tin to her bosom.

Lesson #1: When in doubt, bring cookies.

Hank used to say that props sold the lie. A thief could walk into an art gallery with a hard hat and clipboard and walk out with a priceless painting under his arm. Props disarmed and distracted people. Made them see things. It couldn't hurt to have Reg's men see *her* as a harmless old woman.

The big man is rubbing his bare hands together to keep warm. He doesn't hear her coming. When she taps his shoulder, he nearly jumps out of his skin. He spins and reaches inside his leather jacket but quickly removes his hand when he sees who it is.

"Christ, lady, you nearly scared the living shhhh—" He stops himself from swearing.

Good sign. Respect for his elders.

"Can I help you with something, ma'am?" he asks, looking around.

He doesn't seem to recognize her from the club. Good.

"I certainly hope so, young man," she says, pitching her voice high and sweet. "You know I used to sleep like a newborn babe, but I find myself up all hours of the night now that my Rupert's no longer resting his lovely bald head on the pillow next to me. Oh me oh my, it's a chilly one tonight, isn't it, son?"

"You lost, ma'am?" he says, wiping his dripping red nose.

"No, no, I live right over that way," she says, waving her hand randomly in no particular direction. "I have to say, you remind me of my grandson."

She looks down at the tin in her hands.

"Speaking of which, would you like a cookie, dear?" she asks. "They're his favorite."

She opens the lid and holds out the tin, smiling sweetly and scrunching her nose.

"Um, no thank you, ma'am," he says. "I'm on the clock. Um, this is private property."

He shuffles from foot to foot.

"Now, don't be shy." She giggles. "These little yummies *were* meant for coffee club at the residence, but there's a pesky bug going around, and they up and canceled the whole thing, and I thought, waste not, want not. So I came out for an evening walk with the idea of leaving them for the ducks. Can't eat them myself on account of the diabetes."

"My auntie has diabetes," he says.

She holds the cookies close to his nose. The smell of cinnamon wafts on the breeze.

"Maybe just one," he says, taking a cookie.

"Snickerdoodles," she says with a smile.

The big man takes a bite, then looks around like he's expecting someone. Juls, no doubt.

"Listen, lady," he says. "This ain't no place for an old—for a grandma."

To the big man's surprise, Lenny tosses the tin of cookies in the nearby dumpster.

"You're right," she says. "I think it's time I went inside."

Lenny stands her ground. The big man furrows his massive brow, probably wondering why she's not moving on.

"Off you go then," he says, sweeping the air with his meaty hand.

"Oh, I meant inside *there*," she says, pointing to the door. "I'm here to see Reg Caffey."

The big man stares at her dumbfounded.

"The name's Lenny Bird," she says. "I believe you helped me get into a cab once."

He blinks. It *has* been over a month since she walked out of the Full Nelson with Flo and Nora, but as she looks at the big man's face, it's almost as if she can see the gears turning as it comes to him. Lenny has no doubt that he caught hell for letting her and the twins escape the club right under Reg's nose. The big man blinks again.

She's pretty sure he remembers her now.

75

When the big man walks through the door with Lenny in tow, Reg squints at them from the far side of the warehouse. He makes his way over. Halfway across, Reg's pace falters as he recognizes the woman in the puffy coat. The woman he thought was *tango down*. Lenny watches Reg quickly recover as a smarmy grin creeps across his face.

"As she lives and breathes," says Reg. "If it isn't the unstoppable Lenny Bird."

He almost looks impressed.

"Says she's here to see you, boss," says the big man with a shrug. "No sign of the kid."

Reg stops a few feet from Lenny. She fidgets with the strap on her purse.

"Juls isn't coming," she says. "It's just you and me."

As Reg steps closer, she discreetly shifts her purse so it's behind her back.

"Well, it surely does warm my heart to see you alive and well, Eleanor," he says. "Now, before we get on with *whatever this is*, Bunny here needs a wee peek inside your handbag."

Lenny was hoping that's where they'd start. She pretends to hesitate, then hands the bag to the big man.

Lenny didn't bring Hank's revolver. Juls had tucked it safely back in the lockbox once the girls were home. And there would have been no point. Lenny figured she'd be searched. She's also never fired a gun, so the odds of her getting the jump on trained criminals were not in her favor.

Bunny roots around inside her purse. She stuffed it with Kleenex and hard candies and lots of loose change. More props. He finds her cell phone at the bottom and hands it to his boss. Reg glances at the screen. A voice memo is set to record. He stops the recording, powers off the phone, and tucks it inside his suit jacket. Lenny suspected he'd do as much. Reg looks at Bunny and tips his chin toward Lenny.

"Um, can you turn around, ma'am?" he says. "And hold out your arms, please?"

Bunny looks sheepish. Maybe the cookies did their job. She turns around. He lightly pats her shoulders, arms, then works his way carefully down the sides of her coat, then down each leg. He finishes by patting her back.

"You can face me now, ma'am," says Bunny.

Lenny turns around, keeping her arms extended. He gently pats across her collarbone, skims her rib cage, trying his best to avoid her bosom, then finishes by patting her stomach.

The big man looks at his boss. Reg folds his arms. He's not satisfied.

"Can you open your coat, please, ma'am?" says Bunny.

Lenny does, and he reaches inside her coat and runs his hands across the back and front of her torso. Then he quickly pulls his hands away.

"She's clean, boss," Bunny mumbles.

Lenny is about to pull her coat closed when Reg elbows Bunny aside and pushes Lenny's coat from her shoulders. She doesn't let it fall, but now her arms are trapped in the sleeves. Reg moves in. Before she knows what's happening, he's running his fingers up inside her blouse, skimming across her bra, then probing inside it, his fingertips grazing her nipples. Lenny bristles at his touch but doesn't move or breathe. His cold hands slither across her chest, down to her belly, then around, lingering on her back. He never once takes his eyes off her.

Then he steps away.

"So she is," says Reg.

Lenny straightens her blouse. She swallows down the shame and humiliation and focuses on getting her coat back onto her shoulders. The big man has his eyes on the floor.

"Shall we, Eleanor?" says Reg, gesturing toward the far side of the warehouse.

Bunny is still holding Lenny's purse. Reg waves him toward the exit.

"But it's cold, boss," says Bunny.

Reg gives Bunny a look. The big man turns tail and heads for the front door.

"Oh, and Bunny?" calls out Reg. "You be sure to let me know if any other surprise guests come waltzing along, won't ya?"

Bunny knows better than to answer. He heads outside.

The warehouse looks brighter inside than it did in the video. Maybe it's because the massive bulbs that hang from metal beams in the high ceilings are turned on. They cast a cold blue light across the cavernous space. There's a makeshift bar at one end, complete with barstools and beer taps. Rudi-Rose filmed the fight from somewhere behind that bar. Metal chairs are stacked along the walls. The concrete floors look like they were recently buffed.

As she follows Reg across the large space, they pass a raised platform at the center of the room. The fighting ring. She's guessing it also does double duty as the auction block where he parades women like cattle. Despite the whole place looking spick and span, the stench of blood and stale sweat lingers like in a boxing gym.

Lenny scans for exits. She spots the metal staircase leading up to the balconied walkway on the upper level, where the spectators watched and cheered. She can see several doors along the walkway. There's light coming from under some of the doors. Then she spots the vehicles parked inside the building under the walkway next to a large garage door. She didn't notice the door when she scouted the building. It must be camouflaged on the outside. The vehicles mean there could be other people in the building, but she and Reg seem to be alone on the main floor.

Reg heads toward the bar. He lifts a panel and goes behind the wood, leaving the panel open. He splays his fingers on the bar as she approaches.

"What's your poison, Eleanor?" he asks.

"Beer," she says, nodding to the taps.

He pours her a draft, tipping the glass expertly so there's just the right amount of foam.

Lenny takes the stool across from him as he slides the glass toward her. Behind him she can see the glow of an exit sign through a thinly curtained archway.

"Where's my boy?" he asks.

"He's hanging out with your friend," she says. "The one with the sombrero tattoo."

He chuckles, then pours himself a healthy shot of whiskey, leaving the bottle on the bar. He raises his glass.

"*Sláinte*," he says, shooting it back.

"So much for a higher power," she says under her breath.

He lets it slide. Lenny doesn't touch her beer. She needs to stay clearheaded. And Reg's disgusting show of power has thrown her off balance. Lenny can still feel him on her skin.

"I take it the lad doesn't know you're here in his stead?" he asks. "Or perhaps this is a little game you two cooked up together, being so tight and all now. I do love a good game."

He pours himself another slug.

"No game," says Lenny. "Like I said, this is between you and me."

"How's that?" he asks.

Lenny reaches into her coat pocket and pulls something out. She slides it across the bar. It's a diamond stud earring. Before she left the house, she'd gone into the basement and searched the floor. It took a while, but she found the earring Billy tossed at her the day he died. It was still there where they'd left it two days ago.

Reg stares at it, then he looks up at her. He knows it's Vincent's earring.

"Seems I've underestimated you all these years, Eleanor," he says, poker faced.

She gets the feeling he wasn't sure until this very moment. Billy likely tried to save himself by telling Reg where Vincent was buried. Reg passed that tidbit on to the police, which is why they showed up at her house. But when his son's remains weren't found, Reg might have thought Billy was lying about the whole thing. And yet he sent a hit man to her house anyway. He wanted Lenny out of the way that badly. He wanted her grandson brought to his knees.

Reg shoots back the second shot of whiskey. The sound of raised voices reverberates from somewhere above. A door opens, and a man shouts. His voice echoes. A woman whimpers, then the door shuts, and everything goes quiet. They're *not* alone. It was foolish to think they would be.

Reg removes his suit jacket and leans his elbows on the bar, relaxed and confident. He's wearing his gun and holster. He wants her to see them. Lenny takes a sip of her beer. She needs it.

"Did I ever tell you how my darlin' wife passed?" he asks. "God rest her soul."

When it came to talking about the past, Lenny had only ever heard Reg mention his wife when he was toasting the dearly departed at gatherings. He seemed to keep details of his marriage close to the vest. It was like his personal life was off limits. Relationships were never mentioned. And Juls once told her that Reg never let anyone into his downtown penthouse except his housekeeper.

"It was Vincent. He took my beloved from me," he says. "She met her end giving life to that boy. He was cursed the moment he came into this world."

Reg pours himself more whiskey, but this one he sips.

"Truth be told," he says, nodding to the earring, "knowing that damnable little shite no longer walks this earth kinda warms my heart."

Reg picks up the earring and drops it into the bottle of whiskey. It sinks to the bottom.

"He'd been looting my coffers for years, thinking I was none the wiser," he says calmly. "I turned the other cheek for his dear ma. I knew he was pissing it away at the tables. Anyone else would have had their nuts in a vise, but turns out blood's thicker than the almighty dollar. Day he walked outa jail and disappeared, I reckoned he owed the wrong person and met a sticky end. Seems I was right."

Reg comes out from behind the bar and takes the stool beside her. Lenny doesn't look at him. Instead, she takes another pull on her beer.

"Vincent was a spineless twat. Spoiled rotten. It was my own fault. Let him get away with too much. I wasn't going to make that same mistake with his son. Not our young Juls," he says, beaming. "Now there's a *laoch* with spirit and heart. That lad's a true Caffey."

Lenny looks at Reg. Time to sling another arrow.

"Only here's the thing, Reg," she says. "He's not. He's not a Caffey at all. He's not your blood."

He blinks but doesn't move or speak.

"Billy is his real father," she says.

The old man lets out a booming Reg Caffey guffaw. The sound echoes off the ceiling.

"That little pox tell you that?" he says, his mouth twisting. "In his feckin' dreams."

He's jealous. Lenny shifts on her stool to face him, letting her coat hang open. She touches the necklace she's wearing. It catches his eye. She can tell he recognizes it. It was Kendra's. Her daughter never took it off. It's a delicate gold chain with a pendant in the shape of a *K*. She was wearing it when her body was found. Hank got it back for them. It had been their gift to Kendra for her sweet sixteen, and ever since her death, Lenny has kept it under her bed in a shoebox.

Until tonight.

After applying lipstick and securing her long hair into a bun, she put on the necklace before leaving the house. It had been in that box for fifteen years, along with every handmade Mother's Day card Kendra ever made for her. Each card adorned with drawings of flowers and butterflies and hearts and lovely words that float around her in this moment.

> I am so grateful for you every single day, mama of mine.
> You are my sunshine and my starshine and my moonshine.
> Thank you for being the best mom in the whole world.
> I am proud to call you my mom and my best friend.

Lenny meets Reg's gaze.

"We're not so different, are we, Reg?" she says.

He opens his mouth to speak, but she doesn't let him.

"And speaking of blood. Billy and Kendra kept their secret from Vincent," says Lenny. "They lied—to him, to you. All those years. But come on, think about it, Reg. Who does Juls look more like? Vincent or Billy?"

That same look that crossed Juls' face when he figured out Billy was his father now ripples through Reg's eyes, twitching the corners of his mouth. Reverberations of the past revealing themselves in seemingly insignificant moments. He sees it. His jaw clenches.

"Billy wasn't man enough for her," he says, his voice cracking.

There it is. She's been waiting to hear it.

The sound of vulnerability. That's what Sugar called it.

Lenny is about to pounce when the front door suddenly bursts open, and Bunny stumbles inside. He's clutching Lenny's purse. He shuffles toward them like his legs are encased in ice.

"I'm getting frostbit, boss," he calls out. "Can't feel my toes."

"Lock the feckin' door and get up to the lounge to warm up," Reg shouts. "I'm in the middle of something."

Bunny bolts the door, then begins slowly clambering up the metal stairs. Reg turns his attention back to Lenny.

"Where were we, lass?" He smirks, leaning an elbow on the bar, knees spread.

The interruption was ill timed. Reg has quickly regrouped. Lenny wants him off his game, and the booze doesn't seem to be hitting him. Pushing Reg Caffey too hard could unleash the devil inside him. Proof of that was on the video Rudi-Rose filmed. But Lenny has no choice. And she knows Reg's pride is his weakness. He wants credit for what he's done.

"I think it was *you* who wasn't man enough," says Lenny.

His eyes seem to get two shades darker.

"Kendra didn't want you, did she?" says Lenny.

Reg tries to laugh, but instead he spits, and drool hangs from his lower lip. Lenny keeps going.

"She let Vincent *and* Billy into her bed but not you," she says. "Not the *big* boss. Too old? A little past your prime?"

Reg slides closer so his legs nudge hers. She flinches as he reaches out and touches her neck, stroking the necklace. Reg leans in and nestles his mouth close to her ear, the stink of cigars and whiskey emanating from his breath. She can't help trembling.

"No one disrespects Reg Caffey," he says in a low, soft voice. "Least of all some junkie whore thinks she's better than me. Vincent might have capped her, but I made sure she didn't take another fucking breath. Slut had it coming."

Reg sits back and folds his arms across his puffed-up chest. Lenny grips the barstool tight, trying to keep her trembling hands from clawing out his eyes.

"Did Billy have it coming too?" asks Lenny.

A smile curls his lips. Reg squints like he's sizing her up or trying to decide something. Reg is enjoying this. He said it himself—he loves a good game. Lenny wonders if he's debating between killing her now or keeping the game going a little longer. Then she realizes it doesn't matter. He's already confessed to murder. An unexpected wave of euphoria washes through Lenny as endorphins flood her brain and release all the tension and fear she's been holding inside her. The trembling subsides.

"Billy, Billy, Billy," says Reg, still smiling. "Unfortunate situation that was, but couldn't be helped. Never should have trusted that lowborn shite. Once a gutter rat, always a gutter rat. Died like one too. Weeping and begging for his pathetic little life. Had to cut his feckin' throat just to shut him up."

Bunny suddenly appears right behind Reg. The big man is no longer wearing his leather jacket. Lenny notices he's in socked feet. That's why they didn't hear his approach. Bunny has gone gray, and his face looks like a deflated balloon. He's clearly distraught by what he's overheard.

"I, I come down to get a shot of bo-bo-bourbon to warm my—" He stammers like he can't make words form in his mouth.

Reg twists his barstool to face Bunny, slowly unfolding his arms and bracing his feet against the lower bar of the stool. Lenny does the same.

"I don't understand. It was *you*, boss?" says Bunny, shaking his head. "You whacked Billy? Nah, man. How could you? It was Billy. You cut—naaah."

Bunny pulls his gun and points it at his boss. Lenny lurches off her stool, nearly falling. She clings to the bar rail. Reg hasn't flinched.

"Get that fucking gun out of my face, Bunny!" hollers Reg.

As soon as Bunny starts to lower his gun, Reg reaches for his holster. Before he gets his hand on his gun, Bunny fires. The bullet misses Reg and explodes a bottle behind the bar. Reg lunges, grabbing Bunny's gun. The two wrestle over the gun. Lenny hears the clatter of running footsteps on the metal walkway overhead. A woman screams. The echo of shouts and footfalls is deafening. Lenny looks for a way out. The front door is too far away. The people upstairs are coming. They'll see her if she runs across the open warehouse. Reg and Bunny are spinning in a crazy waltz as Bunny's socked feet slip and slide. Lenny spots the red glow through the curtains behind the bar. She bolts for it.

As she runs down a narrow hallway, she hears the pop, pop, pop of gunfire.

Lenny pushes open the exit door and finds herself at the back of the building, next to the large chute. Out of nowhere, a girl rockets from the chute and tumbles across the gravel. Lenny runs to her. She's young. Maybe fifteen. As Lenny helps her up, another girl follows, then another. Some of the girls look like they've been beaten. They're terrified. They don't know where to go. More gunfire erupts inside the building.

Lenny looks at the exit, expecting Reg to burst out any minute. She's searching for somewhere to hide the girls when another person drops from the chute. It's one of Reg's thugs. He's come after the girls. He lands between Lenny and the huddle of girls and scrambles to his feet. His brow furrows when he sees her. She's not one of them. He draws his gun and points it at her. Lenny acts like she doesn't see it. Instead, she clasps her hands and gives him a bright smile.

"Oh, thank goodness you've come along, young man," she says. "I was out here looking for my lost cat when I happened upon these lovely young ladies. Now put that silly thing away before you hurt someone and help me find my little Coco."

He hesitates, lowering the gun slightly.

"Beat it, lady," he says. "We're busy."

"I see your mother didn't teach you any manners," she says. "Fine, I'll find Coco on my own."

As Lenny turns to leave, she winks at the girls—doing her best to let them know she won't forget about them. She finds the path. The second she's out of the man's line of sight, she runs.

The moon hangs in the sky like a paper lantern. Its glow ignites the river spray. Lenny's heart pounds against her chest as she jumps into the Jeep and grabs the keys from where she left them under the sun visor. Before she drives away, Lenny reaches into the nest of hair piled on her head. From amid the bobby pins, she pulls out Juls' phone.

She expected to be searched, but Lenny didn't think whoever did the deed would go so far as to poke around inside an old woman's messy hairdo, especially once they'd found *her* phone in her purse. Another prop meant to distract. She knew Reg wouldn't put it past her to try to record him, so Lenny made sure she got caught.

Earlier, behind the rocks, Lenny had set her own phone to record, then she'd tucked Juls' phone deep into her nest of hair. But not before making a call from his phone. When she heard the beep, she knew a message had begun to record. The idea had come to Lenny when she remembered how a few days ago, Flo had accidentally forgotten to hang up after calling her landline. Lenny's old dual-microcassette answering machine had continued to record the girls laughing and chatting for almost an hour.

Lenny ends the call to her answering machine, hoping it got everything. She looks back toward the mill. She knows it's too risky to sit here any longer. Lenny quickly dials 911 and reports gunfire at the old mill on Victoria Island. Then she drives as fast as she can back over the bridge to Ottawa.

It's just past 2:00 a.m. when Lenny pulls into her driveway at 13 Julian Avenue. She stares at the house. She is completely numb. Lenny didn't think she would make it home. She'd gone knowing Reg would probably kill her. All she wanted was for him to admit what he'd done to her daughter. And he did. Lenny touches her necklace. He confessed to killing Kendra *and* Billy. And even if Lenny had met a similar fate and Reg had discovered Juls' phone on her dead body, there was a chance his confession was all there on her answering machine, recorded on a small microcassette. The one she'd rewound to ensure it would record for as long as possible. Lenny had turned off the ringer so the landline wouldn't wake anyone, but she knew Juls would have noticed the flashing light eventually, and then it would have been too late for Reg to undo what Lenny had done.

Lesson #2: Don't fuck with a grandmother.

76

When Juls stumbles into the kitchen the next morning, Flo and Nora are sitting at the table eating granola with yogurt and blueberries. Lenny is sipping coffee across from them. He squints into the sunlight pouring through the window.

"There's a pot on," says Lenny.

"We thought you were going to sleep forever," says Nora.

A gum-eyed Rudi-Rose comes up behind Juls and wraps her arms around his waist.

"Are you and Mommy falling in love again?" asks Flo.

Rudi-Rose yawns.

"We never fell out," she says with a sleepy smile.

"I don't even remember when we went up to bed," says Juls, trying to shake off the cobwebs. He notices his phone on the table.

"Oh shit," says Juls. "What time is it?"

"Daddy said *shit*," says Nora.

"*You* said *shit*, Nora," says Flo. She slaps her hand over her mouth.

"I have to go," says Juls, untangling himself from Rudi-Rose.

He grabs his phone and checks the time.

"You might want to listen to something first," she says.

His eyes narrow. Lenny gives him an innocent shrug.

"What did you do, Lenny?" he asks.

"Lenny's in trouble. Lenny's in trouble," sings Flo.

"Would you mind taking the girls to the park?" asks Lenny, looking at their mother.

"Can we bring Fender?" asks Nora.

Lenny nods, and the girls race off to find the dog. Rudi-Rose looks Lenny up and down.

"Lenny *is* in trouble," says Rudi-Rose. "And I want all the dirt when I get back."

As she leaves the kitchen, Juls folds his arms, waiting for an explanation.

"Lenny, I don't have time for whatever this is," he says. "I'm already late."

Lenny gestures to one of the kitchen chairs, but Juls won't sit down. She waits until Rudi-Rose has herded the twins and Fender out the front door. Then she takes a deep breath and gives him a rundown of her last few hours.

"You drugged us? You went where?" he says. "What the fuck?"

"Just listen to the damn recording," she says.

She crosses to the answering machine and presses the play button. Lenny already listened to the message before anyone came downstairs this morning. It's all there.

Partway through the recording, Juls has to sit down. When it ends, he looks at her. Then, without a word, he heads for the door and goes out into the garden. Lenny pops the cassette from the answering machine and follows him outside. He's smoking, his hand shaking.

"He could have killed you," he says.

"It had to be me," she says. "They need you."

"Dang, woman," says a voice behind them.

They turn to see Sugar entering the yard through the side gate.

She approaches them both, but she's looking straight at Lenny.

"Someone was busy last night," says Sugar.

Lenny can tell from Sugar's tone she's trying to hide her anger.

After listening to the recording on her answering machine, Lenny found Sugar's number on Juls' phone and left her a message. A confession of her own.

"Seems you were the one behind that call for service we got last night at the abandoned mill over on Victoria Island," she says. "Shots fired? Took a few hours to get the situation under control, but in the end, Caffey's crew stood down. And we rescued some of his new girls, so that's something."

"And Reg?" asks Lenny, holding her breath.

She needs to know Reg didn't get away.

"I put the handcuffs on the old bastard myself," she says. "You should have seen the look on his face. Had no idea I was a cop. So that means my cover is blown, and our whole plan to have Juls get a confession out of him is fucked, and he'll probably be out by noon today, all thanks to you, Lenny Bird."

Juls and Lenny exchange a glance.

"Like I said in my message," Lenny explains, "it was me who made that 911 call. I was there when the gunfire started. But that was after I got Reg on tape."

Lenny holds out the small cassette.

Sugar stares at Lenny's outstretched hand, then at Juls, who just shrugs.

"What can I say?" he says. "She's a badass."

Sugar's eyes get wide.

"You got it?" she asks Lenny.

Lenny nods.

Sugar takes the cassette from Lenny and examines it, flipping it over in her hands. When she looks up, her gaze meets Lenny's. Sugar slowly smiles.

"Constable Laura Mastrangelo," she says, reaching out her hand.

The two women shake hands for the first time.

Juls smiles at his grandmother as she brushes aside a strand of hair that's come loose from her messy bun.

77

Fifteen years ago

He sat at the kitchen table and began eating the toasted bacon-and-tomato sandwich she'd made for his breakfast. She had burned the bacon, and the toast was soggy from the juice of the tomato, but he ate it all. She'd looked surprised when he'd accepted her offer of breakfast. He was always out of the house so early. They hadn't had breakfast together in weeks. She topped up his coffee and sat next to him. They could hear the boy upstairs getting ready for school.

When he finished the sandwich, she took his plate to the sink and rinsed it off. As she began cleaning the crumbs off the counter, his eyes lingered on her body. The sway of her hips. The curve of her buttocks. The soft skin on the nape of her neck. The tumble of hair piled on her head. He let his gaze move from her hair all the way to her bare feet. He stood up and walked over to her. He startled her when he touched her waist. She turned around, and he took her face in his hands, pulled her close, and kissed her mouth. It was a long, deep kiss. Then he held her close. At first, she didn't return his embrace, but slowly her arms moved around him. The two of them stood like that for a few minutes, holding each other. He could feel the rise and fall of her chest, the warmth of her body. He missed this. He took her hand in his, letting his other hand find her waist, and they started to dance. At first, she tried to pull away, but he kept hold. Soon she gave in, and he danced her around the kitchen in a slow waltz. He spun her under his arm, and she twirled. She couldn't help herself. She laughed.

That's all he wanted.

To hear her laugh again. To see her smile one more time.

78

Lenny remembers how the frost carved the outside of her father's window with beautiful icy swirls that looked like snowflakes. Many things about that day are etched in her mind.

It was two months after her showdown with Reg on Victoria Island. He'd been denied bail and was awaiting trial for two murders. The recording she'd made had been ruled admissible under one-party consent. Silas was nibbling on an arrowroot biscuit as Lenny picked up the newspaper. She was expecting to find the next installment in Christie Coote's exposé about the rise and fall of local crime boss Reg Caffey and his role in a global human trafficking ring. The journalist's series quoted two anonymous sources from Caffey's inner circle. The articles were syndicated across North America, and the whole thing blew up. International investigations began, indictments were brought, and businesses and properties were seized. A safe full of hard drives loaded with evidence was found in Reg's condo. Surveillance footage from all his businesses that he kept as insurance—something he could hold over his associates if the need ever arose. Footage that turned out to be the final nail in his coffin, seeing as how it also implicated the man himself in innumerable crimes. Caffey's empire was destroyed. Maybe, in the end, Reg wasn't as smart as he thought he was.

But when Lenny looked at the newspaper, the headline on the front page took her breath away. It seemed those associates had come calling.

Accused Mobster Regan Angus Caffey Stabbed to Death in Prison

Lenny let out a small cry. It leapt from her throat without her permission. She had to reread the headline. He was actually dead. Lenny couldn't believe it. But there it was in black and white. A revenge killing ordered by those he'd double-crossed, or maybe some nobody was making a name for themselves by taking out a big dog. It didn't matter why. He was gone.

Lenny slowly put down the paper. It was over. A great weight lifted from her shoulders. She could breathe again. None of them would ever have to testify at that man's trial or watch as he got a reduced sentence or made a deal or ended up back out on the streets and came calling one day when they least expected it. All her worries were washed away by one simple headline.

Silas was staring at her.

"What's wrong?" he asked.

"I'm just happy, Dad," she said.

"That's good, my love," he said, placing his hand on hers.

Blue veins snaked under the translucent skin on the backs of his hands—once strong hands, now crooked and withered. But in that moment, Lenny saw only dignity and beauty in them. They were her father's hands. Hands that had protected her. Hands that had held books and drawn pictures of bugs. Hands that had helped her take her first steps.

The overwhelming love she felt for him in the moment stayed with her the rest of the day.

It's a day she remembers so clearly.

Because it was the last time she saw her father.

Silas Flint died peacefully in his sleep that very night.

PART FOUR

79

Summer 2026

Juls is up on the extension ladder, cleaning out the eaves troughs. The twins are setting the outdoor dining table on the patio. Lenny watches from the kitchen window as Flo ties balloons to the backs of chairs. Nora arranges cutlery on carefully folded napkins. Yellow daisy petals are sprinkled across the pink tablecloth.

As Rudi-Rose prepares a salad at the counter, Lenny stands at the sink listening to the girls' giggles through the open kitchen window. The sound fills her heart.

So much has changed in a few months. Lenny still walks her blind dog every day, enjoys a beer or two in the afternoon in her wicker chair, and sometimes takes her dinner into the garage to be with Hank, but the walls of her fortress fell months ago, and she has no plans to rebuild them. She is surrounded by something much stronger now.

After the charges against him were dropped, Juls and his family moved back into their small apartment. Lenny has the twins for sleepovers as often as she can. Juls is bartending at a pub, and Rudi-Rose works in the admin office of a women's shelter.

Sully's death was ruled a suicide. It was assumed that when he got called into headquarters by the chief, Sully couldn't face being found out. Sugar had seen him with Reg, and an investigation led to the arrest of Sully's buddy, Detective Wyatt, who turned out to have been his inside man after Sully retired. They'd been passing along tips to Reg for years. It was that call from the chief that likely gave Sully the idea to take the girls so he could get the money and run.

On his days off, Juls comes by and fixes up the house for Lenny. He tore down the old shed and built a treehouse for the girls in its place. He's repaired the fence and upgraded the faucet on her kitchen sink. Lenny knows he keeps himself busy as a way of working through all that's happened. He's still trying to figure out who he is now that he's not under Reg's thumb.

Lenny hears Maya's voice.

"Did you hire professionals to decorate that table?" asks Maya, admiring the girls' work.

"*I* did it all by myself," says Flo, bouncing on her heels.

"It looks fabulous, *mija*," says Maya.

"Nora helped a little," she admits.

Nora glares at her sister.

Lenny comes outside with two beers. She gives Maya a hug, and the two friends sit together at the table as Juls and the girls go inside to help Rudi-Rose with dinner.

"Happy birthday, my friend," says Maya with a smile.

Lenny cringes.

"Oh, come on," says Maya. "Think of it like this. You're so far over the hill, you're just picking up speed."

Lenny rolls her eyes.

"How's the hip?" asks Lenny.

"Me? I'll be punching that motherfucking bag before you know it," she says.

They clink cans.

Flo and Nora come racing back outside.

"We made birthday cards for you!" says Flo, dancing over to Lenny.

They hand Lenny their homemade cards. Flo's is a mishmash of wild, colorful splotches. Nora's has a detailed drawing of bluebells in a pretty vase. Words adorn the cards.

Lots of fishes and birthday wishes to the best great grandma in the universe.

Kisses, Flo.

To Lenny,

I hope I am exactly like you when I get really old.

Love Nora.

Lenny hugs both girls. The cards remind her of the ones Kendra used to make. Lenny already knows where she'll keep them.

"I have some news," says Maya. "I'm starting back at work next week."

"Good for you," says Lenny.

The girls take their seats at the table.

"You're a policeman, right?" asks Flo.

"Woman," says Nora, rolling her eyes.

"Actually, I'm a civilian," Maya explains.

"Don't you want to be a police officer?" asks Nora.

"Not really. I love my job, and I'm pretty good at it," says Maya.

"She's being modest," says Lenny. "Maya started out as a junior agent, and now she runs the entire Police Reporting Unit. Hank used to call her his heat-seeking missile. If he needed help finding something, Maya could track it down. She's brilliant."

Juls comes out the back door carrying a platter of salmon steaks, with Fender hot on his trail. Rudi-Rose brings up the rear, cradling a bowl of Caesar salad and a basket of rolls.

"What was he like?" asks Nora.

"Hank?" says Maya.

"Lenny never talks about him," says Nora.

"She talks *to* him, though," says Flo. "Out in the garage."

Lenny blushes. She didn't think the girls knew about that. Juls lightly touches the top of Flo's head as he passes on his way to the barbecue.

"Wha'd I say?" asks Flo, looking at her dad.

"Hank was quite the handsome devil as I remember," says Rudi-Rose as she sets the salad and rolls on the table. "Like his grandson."

She lifts her eyebrows at Juls. He smiles and goes back to grilling the salmon.

"Let's see," says Maya. "Hank was smart. Loyal. Everyone looked up to him. He just had this way about him that put people at ease. He was annoyingly good at his job, but I think that was because he had a secret weapon at home."

She nudges Lenny.

"He could also be infuriating," Maya continues. "Like when he'd get an attack of the sneezes. Instead of blowing his nose and getting it over with, he'd keep sneezing and sneezing."

Maya fake sneezes over and over. The dog barks, and the girls burst into fits of giggles.

"I'd have to whip a box of tissues at his head to get him to stop." She laughs.

"You didn't," says Nora.

"He sounds silly," says Flo.

"He was," says Lenny. "When Kendra was little, his favorite holiday was Halloween. He got more excited about dressing up in a costume than she did. Even after she moved out, he'd still put together some hideous getup and wait on the bench on the front porch. When the neighborhood kids came trick-or-treating, he'd jump up and scare the poor things half to death. I've never heard a grown man laugh so hard watching kids run away screaming."

"And those lame dad jokes," says Maya.

"How do you piss off a robot?" says Lenny.

"Keep pushing its buttons," says Maya, laughing. "Over and over with those same terrible jokes."

"Like his sneezes," says Nora.

They all laugh, and the sound fills the garden. Lenny looks around the table at her family. Hank would have loved this. He never even got to meet his great-granddaughters.

Despite the muggy summer evening, Lenny suddenly feels the chill of Hank's absence.

He is truly gone forever.

And she still doesn't really know why.

80

Autumn 2010

He turned on the overhead light in the garage. The puppy followed at his heels. He'd taken him out of his crate so he wouldn't bark and wake up the house. It was the middle of the night. He gently closed the door to the house behind him.

He found his stepladder and placed it next to the high shelves that ran along one side of the garage. He climbed to the top step, moved a large box to one side, and grabbed hold of a hockey bag that was shoved to the back of the shelf. He unzipped the bag and grabbed an envelope from inside. He held it between his teeth as he pushed the hockey bag back into place and concealed it behind the box again. He got down off the ladder, almost stepping on the puppy, who was trying to climb the first step.

He took the envelope from his mouth and knelt to pet the little dog's head, then he sat at the stool at his workbench. He emptied the envelope, laying out the contents. There was a collection of photos, along with two papers. He searched his workbench for something to write on. When he couldn't find anything, he got up and opened the passenger side of the vehicle. The puppy followed.

He took a pen and the vehicle's manual from the glove box. He went back to the workbench and began examining each photo. He made notes in the margins of the manual. Then he studied the autopsy report and obituary and made a few more notes. He pulled out his phone, looked for something, then added another note. The puppy chewed on the leg of his pajamas. When he was done, he gathered everything back in the envelope. All except one photo. The one of the two men sitting at a table at Denny's. He put that one aside. Then he tucked the envelope inside the manual, then put it back in the glove box.

He grabbed the photo from his workbench, picked up the puppy, turned off the light, and went back into the house.

81

The morning after her birthday dinner, Juls drops by. The girls are at day camp, and Rudi-Rose is working. It's his day off, so he's come to finish cleaning out the eaves troughs. When he's done, Juls tackles the garden, removing great clumps of lilies from Lenny's overgrown beds. Juls labors until midday, when Lenny brings out toasted tomato sandwiches and beer for both of them. He sits next to her and takes a swig as Fender lies spread-eagle on the cool patio stones.

"I uncovered the birdbath your lilies had swallowed up," he says.

"I told you not to bother trying to tame that garden," she says. "Let her run wild."

He reaches into his pocket.

"I almost forgot," he says. "I found this too. It was under the eaves."

Juls places an object on the table between them. It looks like a small pen.

"I think it's a camera," he says. "Like for a home security system. Looks pretty old. Wiring was all frayed, so I took it down for you."

"Must have belonged to the previous owners," says Lenny, sipping her beer.

Juls picks up a sandwich and eyes the burnt edges.

"Did you see Crawley's place next door is up for sale?" he says.

"Can't say I'll miss the nosy old bugger," she says. "Be a great house for you."

Juls rubs his thumb and forefinger together.

"Too rich for my blood," he says.

"By the way, thanks for last night," she says. "As much as I hate birthdays, that one was actually tolerable."

"It was good to hear you talk about him," says Juls.

Lenny nods but doesn't say anything. Talking about Hank still leaves a bitter taste in her mouth. The Hank they reminisced about—the one she thought she knew—wouldn't have done what he did. Lenny examines the small camera. There's a faded sticker on it. She can make out a shield and the letters *LF*.

"I've seen this before," she says.

"The camera?" he asks.

"No, this picture on the side of it." She shows him.

"Maybe the company's logo," he suggests.

Juls pulls his phone out and does a quick search. He finds it almost right away.

"Lex Force," he says, showing her the same logo on the company's website. "Yep, they specialize in home security—alarm systems, cell phone monitoring. Company's been around for twenty-five years."

Cell phone monitoring. It comes to her where she's seen the logo.

"Wait here," she says.

Lenny goes into the house. She grabs Hank's phone from the drawer of his bedside table. She powers it on as she brings it outside. Lenny sits next to Juls and swipes through the apps on the home screen.

"I knew it," she says, holding out the phone.

Juls takes it and looks at the screen. There's an app with the same logo. He touches his finger to it, and the app opens.

"We need a password to log in," says Juls. "Any ideas?"

"Try the year your mom was born," she says.

He types in 1975.

"Nope," says Juls. "Hank have any other go-to passwords?"

"That *was* his go-to because he had such a terrible memory," she says. "Otherwise, he'd have to write it down."

She takes a sip from her beer as she ponders options. Then Lenny looks at the can in her hand and gets an idea.

"I think he did write one down," she says.

Lenny goes into the house again. When she comes back out, she's got the Jeep's manual in her hand. She shoved it in the kitchen junk drawer last year after giving up on finding anything useful in it. She'd all but forgotten about it until now. Lenny places it on her lap and starts leafing through the pages. Juls eats the last bite of his tomato sandwich, watching her.

"So we're definitely thinking this was Hank's," says Juls, looking at the camera.

"Here it is," she says, showing him the words written in the margin of a page.

"Natural Blonde?" says Juls.

"My favorite beer," she says. "At least it was back then."

"Let's give it a whirl," he says, typing the password into the app. "And we're in."

Lenny pulls her chair closer.

"Looks like he set up more than one," says Juls.

A list is displayed on the screen.

Camera 1: front yard.

Camera 2: side gate.

Camera 3: backyard.

Camera 4: interior garage.

"He was covering all the entrances," says Juls.

Juls taps one of the cameras. An alert appears on the dashboard that says Connection Lost. It's the same for the others.

"Back then, the cameras would have been hardwired to a drive somewhere in the house. If there was a power outage or the internet cut out for some reason, the system would have disconnected," he says. "Looks like that's what happened."

Lenny stares at him like he's just spoken Swahili.

"What?" he says. "I'm not as dumb as I look. Reg had cameras all over the club. Back then everything got saved to a drive, but the tech was pretty basic in those days. There was only so much room on each drive. After about a month, footage got automatically deleted to make room for new recordings. Reg didn't like that, so he'd swap out the drives every month. Liked having all that shit in case he ever needed it. His people tried to get him to upgrade to a cloud-based system a few years later, but he wouldn't. Turns out that would have been the smart move."

Lenny's barely listening anymore. All she's picturing are cameras watching her every move. It's infuriating. Another one of Hank's secrets.

"Why would Hank not tell me?" says Lenny.

Lenny feels like her whole house is wrapped in secrets, tangled and shrouded, just like her garden.

"Maybe he set up the cameras to keep an eye on us when he wasn't here," says Juls.

Lenny downs the rest of her beer.

"I want them off my house," she says.

"What?" asks Juls.

"Those fucking cameras," she says.

"Can I finish my lunch first?" says Juls.

Lenny stares at him.

"I'll get the ladder," he says.

82

It takes Lenny and Juls no time to find the other three cameras. The descriptions of each one in the app helped narrow their search. One is tucked under the front porch, another along the side of the house, angled at the gate, and the last one they find inside the garage, pointed at the door leading into the house. Juls was right about them being hardwired. Lenny makes him cut the cables where they disappear into the walls, but she wants everything gone.

In the basement, they check the ceiling joists until they spot where each of the four cables feeds down from the main level. They all lead to the same location right above the fuse box, where they've been tied together, dangling over a power outlet in the wall.

"No DVR. Guess Hank pulled the plug on the whole system at some point," says Juls.

"What's a DVR?" asks Lenny.

"A digital video recorder," says Juls, grabbing a stepladder from the corner. "It's the drive where the footage would have been stored."

"There used to be an old modem plugged in here, I think," she says.

Juls places the stepladder below the cables.

"This does not look safe," says Juls, pointing to Lenny's old fuse box.

Inside the dusty metal fuse box, twisted red and white wires weave around the fuses like spaghetti. Cobwebs blanket the cables leading this way and that.

"At least these wires aren't connected to anything," he says. "I should be able to safely pull them from here."

Lenny watches as Juls reaches up, unties the bundled cables, and tugs on one of them. It begins to release, only held to the wood joists by staples. One at a time, he pulls on each cable, until there's a pile below the stepladder at Lenny's feet. The end of the last cable gets caught on a nail. Juls braces his hand on the top of the fuse box so he can reach higher to unhook it. He knocks something off the top, and it falls to the basement floor.

Lenny picks it up. It's a small metal object.

Juls yanks down the last cable and steps off the ladder.

"Happy now?" he says. Juls spots the object in her hand. "What is it?"

"Part of the fuse box, I think," she says.

He wipes his dirty hands on his jeans, then takes the piece of metal from her hand.

"It's a memory stick," he says.

"A what?" asks Lenny.

"A thumb drive," he says. "For storing files or photos."

"Or video footage?" asks Lenny.

They look at each other.

Minutes later, Juls is out the door. He's gone around the corner to Dollarama to get an adapter for his phone, leaving Lenny to wonder what's on that tiny little drive. *Did Hank hide it there?* Maybe that's what Hank was trying to tell her the night before he died when he was prattling on about the fuse box.

When Juls gets back, they sit together at the kitchen table. He connects the thumb drive to his phone and finds only one file on it. A video file. He opens it, and an image displays across his phone's screen with a play arrow at its center. It's a view of the backyard. There's a date and time at the top.

"September 19, 2010," says Juls. "Time says 15:35."

Lenny gets a chill. No wonder it's called a memory stick. That day is burned into hers.

"What's wrong?" asks Juls.

Lenny has gone white. She's lost all feeling in her hands.

"Lenny?" says Juls.

"Hank knew," she says, her voice barely a whisper.

"Knew what?" he asks. But as the words leave his lips, he understands.

"September. That's when it happened," he says. "The weekend Hank took me fishing."

She nods.

"You think he saw the footage?" asks Juls. "Saw you with the body?"

"That might explain why it's not there anymore," says Lenny.

"Damn," says Juls. "He was covering for you."

"I moved the body later that night," says Lenny. "This footage is from earlier. I can't believe Hank never said anything. He saw what happened between me and Vincent."

"But I thought you were inside when he showed up," says Juls.

"That's only where it started," says Lenny. "In the kitchen with the cookies."

"Shit, woman," he says. "You really laced those cookies with poison?"

Juls has never asked Lenny the details of that day, and she's never shared what really happened. He only knows what he heard her tell Billy in the basement last year.

"I don't know if the poison would have killed him, but when he started to feel its effects, I ran," she says. "He caught up to me in the backyard."

Juls looks at the image on his phone, then at Lenny.

"I need to see it with my own eyes," he says. "I need to see that fucker get his."

Lenny doesn't say a word.

"I won't look at it if you don't want me to," he says.

Lenny gets up and grabs another beer from the fridge. She chooses a pale ale called Warrior Woman. Seems fitting. Lenny leans against the counter, then nods to her grandson, letting him know it's okay. He can look. She doesn't need to watch.

She lived it.

83

Autumn 2010

Lenny lurched out the back door. She was down the steps and halfway across the patio when Vincent caught up to her. He hooked her elbow. She fell forward, landing hard on the patio stones. She flipped over as he came at her, kicking at his shins. He was a rabid dog—eyes bulging, bloody froth sputtering from his mouth. As she tried to crawl away, he kicked her in the ribs. She curled into a ball to protect herself. He stood over her. He grabbed her by the hair and punched her in the face. She crumpled back. He straddled her, pinning her arms, his hands on her throat. She tried to squirm free, but he was too strong. Her mouth was wide, gasping for air. His expression transformed into a kind of twisted euphoria. Her ears popped. She went rag doll limp, closed her eyes so that his monstrous face wasn't the last thing she ever saw.

Then out of nowhere, his hands released, and the weight of him was gone. She opened her eyes to see him careening sideways. A figure jumped over her. It was her father. The eighty-year-old jumped on Vincent and started punching him. The younger man blocked a punch and delivered a crushing blow to the old man's kidney. It stunned Silas, and he withered. The younger man was on him fast. He was striking Silas over and over. Lenny crawled away.

The old man lay bloodied on the patio stones as the younger one got to his feet. Vincent raised his boot over Silas's face. He was about to bring it down when he froze in place, foot in the air. He looked down to see four metal tines protruding from his chest. His mouth fell open. Lenny was behind him, gripping the handle. She yanked the pitchfork. He jerked like a fish on a hook as the gardening tool retracted from his torso. He staggered, turning around to look at her. Their eyes met. Hers was the last face he would ever see. He fell forward, landing flat on his face on the patio. He didn't move.

Behind him, Silas was struggling to sit up. He was bleeding badly. Lenny dropped the pitchfork and ran to him. They embraced. She glanced over his shoulder toward the neighbor's house. She helped Silas get to his feet and motioned for him to help her. She grabbed the legs, and her father looped his arms around the torso. Together they carried Vincent's body down the path and into the garden shed.

84

A week has gone by since Juls watched the footage on the thumb drive. Lenny is out front dragging her garbage bins to the end of her driveway. She's spent the last few days sorting through junk that's been cluttering the shelves in her garage and basement for decades. The garbage bins are overflowing.

It's time to kick the past to the curb. To let go. To let Hank go. She finally removed his clothes from their bedroom closet. They're in a box in the front hall, ready for donation. They hold no clues, just memories.

After his death, she searched the house for weeks but never found anything that explained it. Nothing in his sock drawer or shaving kit. Nothing tucked in the pocket of one of his coats. He left her nothing but a few indecipherable scribbles in a manual, a memory stick of the worst thing she ever did, and a hole in her heart.

For years, it's been killing Lenny. But no more.

Lenny glances over at a young couple standing with Mr. Crawley on his front lawn. His real estate agent is having another open house, and a steady stream of prospective buyers has been coming and going all afternoon.

As she watches the young couple inspect the front facade of the house next door, Lenny's thoughts drift to Juls and his family. Crawley's house would be perfect for them. Much better than their cramped apartment. The landlord who took over the building when Reg's assets were liquidated is threatening to raise the rent. Juls isn't sure they'll be able to afford to stay. They might have to move farther south, to the outskirts of town, where rents are cheaper. Farther from her.

Lenny turns and looks at her house. Maybe there's more she can let go of. She could rent a small apartment in the neighborhood, and Juls and his family could live in *her* house. Her beautiful two-story brick Victorian at 13 Julian Avenue. Her and Hank's forever home, or so they thought.

She remembers the day they came to see it. *They* were the young couple looking to buy their first home. Her gaze wanders across the slope of the roof and follows the ivy that trims to the large bay window at the front. She fell in love with the house the moment she saw it, mostly because of the flower garden in the back. The only thing on Hank's wish list was an attached garage so he could have a place for his tools and maybe build himself a nice workbench. He got his wish. Hank's garage was his happy place.

As Lenny walks back up the driveway, a breeze sends small branches cascading from the large oak that shades her front porch. She picks up the broken branches. The leaves are dry and the bark brittle, despite it being summer. The tree has been in slow decline for years after losing a large limb in a windstorm. She doesn't have the heart to take it down. She only hopes it doesn't fall on her house one day. That large limb took out their power line when it fell.

Lenny stops walking and looks up at the mighty oak as her mind drifts back a week to when they found Hank's cameras. Juls explained how they worked.

If there was a power outage or the internet cut out for some reason, the system would have disconnected.

There *was* a power outage back then. She remembers sitting in the dark for hours with young Juls, trying to make it fun while they waited for someone from Ottawa Hydro to arrive. When a lineman finally did come, he repaired the outside line, then went downstairs to see if there was damage to her fuse box. He told her it was fine but needed upgrading. He cleaned up some wiring and boxed up a few things that were plugged in near the fuse box. He said the devices were at risk of overloading the old circuit and causing a fire. Lenny didn't bother sorting through the electronics. She shoved the cardboard box onto a shelf in the basement, not wanting anything else to go wrong in their lives, like a fire. They'd been through enough. Hank had died only a few days earlier.

It dawns on her what was inside that cardboard box.

The cameras would have been hardwired to a drive somewhere in the house.

A digital video recorder. The drive where the footage would have been stored.

Lenny turns around. She stares at the garbage bins. Lenny walks over and starts digging through the junk jammed inside. At the bottom of one of the bins, she finds it. A gray metal box she thought was an old modem. Lenny flips it over. *DVR* is printed on the top corner. She was right. She *had* seen those letters earlier when she found it in that cardboard box in the basement. Lenny looks at the recorder.

Guess Hank pulled the plug on the whole system at some point.

What if it wasn't Hank? What if that lineman from Ottawa Hydro was the one who disconnected the cameras? Lenny realizes there could still be footage on the metal box she holds in her hands.

There was only so much room on each drive. After about a month, footage got automatically deleted to make room for new recordings.

The DVR might have been recording right up until the day of that power outage.

Someone clears their throat. Lenny realizes she's being watched. Mr. Crawley and the young couple are staring at her from a few feet away. She's surrounded by garbage.

Lenny looks at the DVR, and her mind flashes to the menu on Hank's phone.

Camera 4: interior garage.

Lenny suddenly feels like she's been punched in the gut. Her legs buckle. She sinks to the pavement, still holding the metal box tight. Mr. Crawley and the couple bend down to help her. She tells them it's nothing. She simply felt faint for a moment. She just needs water, and she'll be fine. Crawley seems genuinely concerned. He runs to his house and returns with a glass of water. They fuss over her awhile until she's finally able to stand. Lenny thanks them and escapes into her house.

Once she's safely inside, Lenny staggers into her living room and sits on the sofa, gripping the DVR. Fender trots into the room, sniffing the air. Her dread is palpable. The old dog retreats back to his spot in the hall. He wants nothing to do with it. She sits there awhile, listening to the voices outside her window. Open house visitors coming and going.

After Juls watched the footage of Vincent's demise, Lenny was done with the past. She'd stowed Hank's phone away and told Juls to destroy the thumb drive. But finding that DVR and realizing what might be on it had struck her with such force, it had knocked her to the ground. Lenny has always wanted to know why.

Maybe this is what Hank left her without even knowing it.

Not a note but a recording of his final moments.

Lenny stands on shaky legs. She steadies herself and carries the metal box over to her TV. She kneels, placing the DVR next to her. She lifts the VCR off its shelf and examines the cables. Lucky for her, she still uses old electronics. The cables leading from the VCR into her TV match up with the DVR's. She swaps the cables and turns on the TV. A login screen appears just like on Hank's phone. Using the buttons on the DVR, she enters the password Natural Blonde. A menu pops up. She selects "Playback." Then a list of cameras appears. She chooses Camera 4: interior garage. The display asks for a date. She enters November 13, 2010. A list of files appears, organized by time of day. Two of the video files fall within the window she's looking for. Lenny clicks on the one marked 14:15 and presses play.

The file opens to a full-screen image. At first, the footage is so grainy, she can't make anything out, then a light comes on. It's a wide view from the camera inside the garage. Hank is coming through the doorway from the kitchen. He's right there on her TV.

Lenny pauses the video. Hank freezes.

She pulls herself to her feet, goes into the kitchen, and grabs a beer from the fridge. Lenny needs some liquid courage. She selects a Bavarian lager called Heller Highwater. Seems her beer can always read the room. Lenny heads back into the living room, sits on the carpet and takes a long swig, then stares at Hank's frozen face.

It was a Saturday afternoon. Lenny had left the house just before two. She'd gone to her father's to check on him again. Silas had been in and out of bed over the last couple of months, struggling to recover from his injuries. Vincent had done a lot of damage. That particular Saturday she was bringing Silas more frozen dinners and the renewed prescription for his painkillers. Ten-year-old Juls was at a matinee with friends. Hank was alone at the house from two until she got home just before four.

Lenny takes one more pull of the lager, then presses play.

85

Hank crosses the garage, followed by the puppy. He positions the stepladder next to the storage shelves, then drags the hockey bag off the shelf. He lets it drop to the floor. It lands heavily, and the dog jumps back. Hank leaves it there and heads for the door leading to the garden. The puppy follows. Hank walks like a man on a mission. He disappears outside and, a few seconds later, returns carrying a large metal canister. Hank places it next to the hockey bag. The canister stands about thigh high and widens at the bottom. The puppy sniffs at the dirt staining its base. The top of the canister has a small hole in it. The man flips it over and pulls off a plastic cover from the bottom. The canister is hollow inside.

Next, he grabs the plastic wrap, duct tape, and baggies that are laid out on his workbench. He brings them over, unzips the hockey bag, and begins removing bundles from inside it. As he wraps each bundle in plastic, the puppy noses around in the hockey bag. Once the man has wrapped and taped each bundle tight, he begins placing them inside the metal canister. He shoves them in deeper until there are no more bundles left. Then he puts the cover back on the canister. He struggles with the weight as he turns it upright. He takes a breath, then carries it back out the door to the garden. The puppy trails behind him.

When he comes back inside, the man tosses the hockey bag in the garbage, then wipes his hands on a rag at his workbench before making a phone call. The call is brief. When he hangs up, he picks up a screwdriver and takes his phone over to the Jeep. He opens the passenger door, leans inside, and puts his phone in the glove box. Then he closes it and jams the screwdriver into the lock of the glove box until the lock twists. He tries opening it. It won't budge. He closes the door of the Jeep and locks it.

He leans against the Jeep and pulls a photo from his pocket. He stares at it a moment, then puts it back in his pocket. He crouches down and pets the dog, then takes him into the house and returns a few seconds later, closing the door. Alone in the garage, the man sits down on the step leading into the house, head in his hands. He doesn't move for several minutes.

Then everything goes black.

86

The first video ends, and the next one cues up. Lenny chugs the remains of her beer, then opens the video file. 14:55. When her shaking finger hits play, the video seems to pick up right where the other one left off, only now Hank is standing. Lenny realizes that the camera must have stopped recording because he was so still, but now, he's on the move again.

Hank strides toward the garage door and pulls on the rope to open it.

A car is parked in the driveway. Sully is getting out of it. The two men exchange a friendly embrace. A delivery truck is slowly moving past in the background. It jerks to a stop across the street, and a man slides open the side door and starts sorting parcels.

Hank signals for Sully to follow him inside. They head into the garage, closing the door. Hank keeps his back to Sully. When Hank finally turns around, he's holding the photo from his pocket. Sully's smile disappears when he looks at it. At first, Sully makes a show of looking confused, then he starts pacing and talking with his hands. Hank listens, but something Sully says seems to hit him hard. Hank's whole body shakes. Sully turns and approaches Hank, his eyes pleading. Hank grabs Sully's collar and pins him against the Jeep, shouting in his face. Sully wilts and doesn't fight back.

When Hank lets go, he flips his hand at Sully, and Sully physically recoils. Hank grabs the rope to open the garage door, and Sully comes at him from behind. Sully knocks into Hank, sending him tumbling into some garden tools. Hank spins around and punches Sully in the stomach. Sully doubles over. Hank shakes his head in disgust and goes for the rope again. Still bent over, Sully charges like a bull. Sully's shoulders ram into Hank's midsection. Hank falls back. His head strikes the metal shelf, his neck twisting awkwardly. Hank falls to the concrete and lies there. Sully is panting, clutching his belly. When he gets his wind back, Sully kneels beside Hank. He tries to wake him. Hank's hand moves, but he doesn't come to. Sully stands. He stares down at Hank, then he looks around the garage. He eyes a pair of gloves on the workbench. Sully goes over, puts on the gloves, and starts rooting through the boxes and camping gear stacked on the shelves.

Sully searches behind every box, carefully putting things back in place. He opens the garbage bin and finds an empty hockey bag. He tries opening the Jeep, but it's locked. Sully searches Hank's pockets. He finds the photo, stuffs it in his jacket, then digs out the keys. He opens the Jeep and searches in the back and under the front seats. He tries the glove box, but it won't budge. Something makes him look toward the door sharply like he's heard a sound.

Sully gives up on the glove box and closes the door of the Jeep, being careful not to slam it. He walks over to the door leading into the house and puts his ear to it. He stands there a moment, then he goes back to the Jeep and opens the rear door. He's picked up his pace. Probably worried about someone hearing the dog or coming home. He searches the cargo bay. Nothing. He closes the rear door and kicks the bumper, again glancing at the door. The spare-tire case vibrates. He feels for the release button, opens the hard case, and runs his hand around the tire. He grips the tire and tips it so he can look behind it. Nothing. Sully shoves the tire back inside, closes the case, then leans against it, breathing hard. He looks at Hank, who isn't moving.

Lenny is frozen as she watches the video. There is a look in Sully's eyes. It's that glazed-over stare she'll never forget. The one he had just before he shot himself. Lenny hugs her knees to her chest, hoping Sully is about to revive Hank or go get help. Hoping she's about to come home to confront them or save Hank. Her eyes search for anything on the screen. A crack, a shift, a sign that something else is going to happen instead of what she knows is coming. Because it's already happened. Hope isn't enough to make a dent in the past. She hugs her knees so tight she can't breathe, but she can't look away. All she can do is watch in horror.

Sully bows his head and takes a deep breath that makes his body heave. He walks over to Hank, grabs his feet, and starts to drag him to the driver's side of the Jeep. It takes all his strength to sit Hank upright, lift him over his shoulder, and hoist him up into the front seat. Sully is sweating from the effort. He reaches across Hank, puts the keys in the ignition, and turns on the engine. The exhaust is visible. Sully closes the Jeep's door and stares at Hank through the window for a few seconds. Then he searches the garage and finds a rag. He shoves it in the tailpipe, then walks away.

Sully opens the door leading to the house. Before he leaves, he slowly looks back. Hank's head tips to one side. He's alive, maybe even semiconscious. Sully just looks away, flicks off the light, and closes the door behind him. He leaves Hank there, all alone.

In the shadows, Hank's silhouette rocks forward.

His head comes to rest on the steering wheel.

87

After a few seconds of no movement, the grainy video footage ends, and the next video file in the list cues up to play. Lenny crawls toward the TV. She picks up the DVR and yanks it so hard the cables rip from the back. The screen goes black. She tosses the DVR across the room. It lands, then slides under the kitchen table.

Lenny knows what happened next. She can't bear to see any more of that heartbreaking day play out on her TV. But it does play out, despite her wishing it would stop. It is displayed across her mind in all its vivid horror. Every sight, every scream, every gut-wrenching feeling. She can even taste the fumes on her tongue. She is there.

The sweet, acrid odor hits her when she opens the front door. She calls out for Hank, but he doesn't answer. She almost turns around and leaves, thinking there might be a gas leak, but something makes her stay. She slowly walks to the kitchen, arms weighed down by the groceries she stopped to get on her way home. The puppy is whining and scratching in his crate. She places the bags on the kitchen table and lets the dog out back. When she comes back in, she listens. That's when she hears the engine humming. She opens the door to the garage, turns on the light, sees the rag hanging from the tailpipe. When she spots Hank slumped at the wheel, a tidal wave of panic and horror washes through her.

"No, no, no, no!" she screams, racing around the Jeep.

She pulls open the door. The fumes penetrate her nostrils. She pulls his shoulders back. His head rocks against the headrest, his neck rubber. His eyes are closed, mouth sagging open, lips blue.

She knows, but still Lenny pounds on his chest and breathes into his mouth.

She knows as she tugs on his sweatshirt and hauls him from the Jeep.

She knows as she lays him on the cold floor and begs him to breathe.

She knows as she dials 911 and asks them what to do.

They tell her to turn off the engine and open the garage door. She does.

Lenny sits on the concrete cradling his head in her lap, nauseated from the fumes, but she can't leave him. And she doesn't care. She wants to breathe it in, to smell it, to feel what he felt, to be with him.

The paramedics work on Hank as the responding police supervisor pulls Lenny to her feet. He leads her out to the driveway. She never takes her eyes off Hank. She's watching and waiting for him to come back to life, even though she knows.

Hank is gone. Her Hank is no more.

Lenny collapses on the front lawn as sobs convulse her body. More of Hank's colleagues arrive, including Sully. They all heard the call come in. They know one of their own is in trouble. Cruisers fill the street, the coroner arrives, and neighbors come outside. It feels like the whole world is watching her private hell as Hank's heart refuses to ignite, and Lenny's bursts into flames.

Sully rubs her shoulders as she watches them take photos and write notes and talk in hushed voices. As Hank is taken away in the ambulance, her ten-year-old grandson comes running down the street. The flashing lights reflect in his tear-filled eyes as he races over to Lenny. She's sitting on the lawn. He doesn't say a word. He collapses next to her and clings to her neck.

He knows too.

Death has come calling.

Again.

88

Lenny lies on the carpet weeping uncontrollably. She hasn't shed a single tear since that day, but reliving it all has ripped her heart open, and now she can't turn off the floodgates. She curls into a ball, hugging her knees to her chest, as great sobs heave through her body. Fender inches closer, at first nosing her face and licking the tears from her cheeks. He doesn't back away this time. He stays close. When her crying finally wanes, the dog snuggles his way under her arm.

Juls finds them like that, curled together, the next morning.

He runs into the living room when he spots her legs as he enters the house.

She wakes up, and he eases her to a sitting position against the sofa.

"You scared the shit out of me!" he says. "Did you fall?"

She shakes her head.

"I'm calling an ambulance," he says.

"No," she says. "I'm okay."

"You don't look okay," he says, kneeling next to her.

"I had a shock, that's all," she says.

"Like an electric shock?" he asks, looking around. He spots the cables. "From the TV?"

She points to the DVR lying under the kitchen table.

"I found the drive. I watched the footage from the garage," she says, her voice weak.

He stares at the metal box.

"Where did you—" Then it registers. "Oh damn, the footage from when Hank—" Juls can't say it. "Fuck. It was on there."

"You need to see it," she says.

"*No, no,* I don't," he says, sitting back on his heels and shaking his head. "I can't."

"Juls, you *need* to," she says, touching his knee.

Lenny struggles to get up. Juls stops her.

"I'll get it," he says.

Once he's reconnected the DVR, Lenny finds the video of the moment Sully arrived. That's the one her grandson needs to see.

"You ready?" she asks him.

Juls sits on the carpet next to her. They're shoulder to shoulder. He doesn't want to, but he nods. Lenny presses play, and they watch the video together.

When it ends, Juls is quiet. She lets him process what he's seen.

"If Sully wasn't already dead, I'd kill that fucker," he says, his voice breaking.

"I think I know what happened," says Lenny. "Hank figured out Sully was mixed up with Vincent. He confronted him with evidence, maybe hoping it wasn't as bad as he thought."

"But he found out it was worse, by the looks of it," says Juls.

Lenny nods.

"Hank was so angry," she says. "I think Sully asked about the money. Hank hadn't told anyone about it. Not me, not Sully."

"Hank would have known Sully was rotten," says Juls.

"That's what Sully was searching for," says Lenny. "The money."

Lenny closes her eyes. Juls takes her hand.

"I think I know why he saved that footage from the backyard," says Lenny. "It was proof of self-defense. He kept it in case I ever needed it."

Juls wipes a tear from his cheek with his sleeve.

"I thought Hank was tying up loose ends because he was planning to kill himself," says Lenny. "But it wasn't that at all. Hank was going to turn himself in. That's where he was going. He knew PSU would come digging into Vincent's disappearance. He knew what I'd done. He was protecting me in all the ways he could think to. I bet he would have taken the fall for me if it had come to that."

Juls puts his arm around her.

"Hank didn't leave—" says Lenny, choking on her words. "He didn't leave me."

Tears spill down Lenny's cheeks.

89

A month later, the girls are spending the day with Lenny. The air has been washed clean by a summer storm, and the road glistens. Nora holds Lenny's hand to help her keep her balance. Lenny takes a stride, then another.

"You've got this," says Nora as she lets go.

Lenny picks up speed and starts rolling down Julian Avenue, Flo on one side, Nora on the other. The three of them are decked out in helmets and knee and elbow pads. Flo circles behind her great-grandmother. Lenny wobbles on her in-line skates but stays vertical.

"I'm doing it," shouts Lenny.

"See, you're not too old," says Nora.

"You are Lady Eleanor of Wellington," shouts Flo. "You can do anything!"

Flo spins in circles. Nora stays close as Lenny picks up momentum. She's heading toward the dead end near the Byron path. Lenny is gathering speed. She's passing Nora.

"Use the heel brake to slow down," hollers Nora.

Lenny dips one heel, circles, and careens into Nora. They bear-hug and keep spinning before coming to a stop. Flo giggles as she skates over to them and joins the group hug.

"Look, Daddy's here," says Flo, pointing down the street.

The Mustang is pulling into Lenny's driveway. The girls each take one of Lenny's hands. Together, the trio rolls back toward the house. Juls leans against his car, smiling as he watches them skate over.

"I had to see this with my own eyes," he says.

The girls let go, and Lenny rolls toward him. She crashes into Juls. He catches her.

"Get me out of these things," she whispers in his ear.

He sits Lenny on the front porch steps and helps unlace her skates.

The girls sit on the front lawn to take theirs off.

Juls turns to look behind him as an electrician comes out the front door. The man is carrying a box under one arm, his tools in his other hand. He sets down the box as Lenny signs off on the work order. Inside the box are the dismantled pieces of her old fuse box. Lenny thanks the man, then he heads to the truck parked across the street.

"You finally upgraded," says Juls.

"Figured I'd treat myself," she says.

Juls notices the **Sold** sign on Mr. Crawley's front lawn. He glances over at the house.

"Wow, that was fast," he says. "Looks like he's already moved out."

"Yup, he got a cash offer with a fast closing date," she says. "A hundred thousand over asking. At least that's what I heard."

Lenny removes her helmet and elbow pads.

"She's a beauty," he says, admiring the house.

The girls have removed their helmets, pads, and skates. They run over to Lenny and sit on either side of her as they slip on their shoes.

"What do you think, girls?" says Lenny, looking from one twin to the other. "Shall we go take a look around inside?"

She nods to Mr. Crawley's house.

They both smile and clap their hands.

"Can we, Daddy?" squeals Flo.

Juls eyes Lenny.

"We can peek in the windows if there's no one there," says Juls. "But we're not breaking into some empty house."

"It's not breaking in, Daddy," says Nora.

The girls burst into fits of laughter.

"Can we tell him?" asks Flo, tugging on Lenny's arm.

Lenny nods. Flo looks at Nora, then they both look at their father.
"*It's our house! It's our house!*" the girls chant in unison.
Juls laughs as the girls hold on to each other and jump up and down.
"Very funny," he says.
Lenny pulls a key from her pocket and holds it out to Juls.
He stops laughing.

90

The day Lenny and Juls watched the footage of Hank's final moments was one they'd both never forget. It had changed everything, casting the last few years in a whole new light. A light that not only exposed the truth about Hank's death but also led him back to them.

After Juls had gone home that day, Lenny went into the dark garage and climbed into the Jeep. As she sat there, she listened to the family of crows in her backyard, cawing their last songs of the day before they bedded down together. She thought about Hank and all they'd shared in their roost on Julian Avenue. A home, work, love, tragedy, and secrets. But one of those secrets she would keep just between her and Hank. It was better that way.

Later, under a moonless sky, Lenny made her way out into the backyard, carrying her laundry basket under one arm. She wandered to the edge of her garden and found the old metal birdbath. The one Juls had uncovered the week before. The one whose pedestal she recognized in the footage. It was the metal canister Hank carried into the garage.

It took some effort to get the basin that sat on top of the pedestal to budge, but finally it started turning. She unscrewed it, and when it released, she slid it to one side, letting it fall into the lily beds. Then Lenny began to rock the pedestal. It was heavy, and a few vines were still wound around its base. But eventually, it, too, released, tipping onto its side. She bent down and gripped the plastic cover on the bottom of the pedestal. When she pried it off, she found them inside. There were about three dozen bundles tightly wrapped in plastic, each the size of a small loaf of bread. She loaded them, one by one, into the basket, then carried them into the house.

At the kitchen table, she took a knife and cut open one of the bundles. The first thing that caught her eye was a picture of a canoe printed on the back of one of the brown banknotes. Then she noticed the denomination. One hundred. She opened all the bundles and counted the bills.

All two million dollars' worth.

Lenny would never know for sure why Hank hid the money or what he planned to do with it. As with the things he locked in the glove box of his Jeep, maybe he hoped she would find everything and piece it all together. Or maybe he was planning to tell her about the thumb drive and the money when the time was right. But Lenny knew in her heart that it was more likely Hank hid the money so he could turn it in one day. After all, it *was* dirty money, and at his core, Hank was a good cop, above all else. No matter what mistakes he'd made or lines he'd crossed, Hank always did the right thing in the end.

But she's not Hank.

She is Lenny Bird.

She's used to having a little dirt on her hands.

And at seventy-one, she's learned a few lessons.

Lesson #3: Finders keepers.

Acknowledgments

This is my fourth published novel, yet it proved to be one of the most difficult to write. With my Gus Monet mystery series wrapped up, I decided to shift creative gears, veering into psychological crime territory with a whole new protagonist. I found myself back at square one, navigating without a map, and Gus, who had been living stubbornly in my head for over a decade, kept trying to come along for the ride. She is nothing but relentless. Thankfully I have the good fortune of being surrounded by people who give me space, support, encouragement, and honest feedback, so after many false starts and wrong turns, seventy-year-old Lenny Bird finally showed herself—equally as feisty and unstoppable as Gus, older and not always wiser. Once she and I understood each other, things really started cooking. And I don't just mean the poison cookies.

I am eternally grateful to the lovely folks in publishing who have my back when I need it most. When early drafts had me lost, my agent, David Halpern, helped get me back on track. He was definitely my wingman for this novel. I remember on one particular day, I took a long walk through the neighborhood where the novel is set. I'd sent David the latest version. He called and talked me through the good, the bad, and the ugly of the draft, and by the end of our hour-long conversation, I was excited to get back to my desk and keep writing. David's kindness, patience, generosity with his time, and brilliant editorial guidance helped get this novel to a place where it finally worked. I also want to thank Elizabeth Guthrie for her wonderful notes that helped shape the final manuscript.

I didn't know it at the time, but this novel was the beginning of more than just a new relationship with a new protagonist. It brought a fresh start with a new publisher whose belief in the novel and in me was exactly what I needed. I am so fortunate to have found an editor who embraced the story with such enthusiasm. Liz Pearsons at Thomas & Mercer loved the novel from the get-go, and working with her team has been a joy. Many thanks to Andrea Hurst for her wonderful editorial development of the story and to the entire team at Amazon Publishing for shepherding my novel along, from the beautiful cover design to the attention to detail by copyeditors and proofreaders to the project managers and marketing teams helping get my work out into the world.

I want to thank my friend Chris Tessier, who guided me through the ins and outs of police procedures and jargon, helping to bring authenticity to the world I was trying to create. I also very much appreciate him introducing me to the amazing word *shitrat.*

This novel is dedicated to my father, Joe, who was a good guy like Hank, but who also had a larger-than-life, slightly mob boss presence like Reg. He would have loved this novel.

Writing is my happy place, and other than hanging out with family and friends, there is no place I'd rather be. I appreciate all the book lovers, readers, and bookstagrammers who embrace and share my novels. I'm talking about you, Dana and Lisa of Team Mustard. And to my fellow authors—your love, counsel, and camaraderie mean the world to me. A special shout-out to Tamara, Nadia, Vivi, and Sylvia for always being up for a coffee, a walk, or a chat about all things writing. Another happy place of mine is a book club. You honor me with every invitation, with your enthusiasm, your genuine interest in my career, your incredible insights into my characters—not to mention the Pop-Tarts and doughnuts. Thank you for continuing to share my books.

Buoyed by all your support, I hope to happily write many more.

In fact, one is currently bubbling over as we speak.

About the Author

Photo © 2022 Jill Woodley

Katie Tallo has more than three decades of experience as an award-winning screenwriter and director. After winning an international novel contest, she began writing mystery thrillers. Her debut thriller, *Dark August*, was an instant bestseller, earning acclaim as a *New York Times Book Review* Editors' Choice and an Apple Book of the Month. It also made the Globe 100 list. Since then, Katie has written two more novels in the critically acclaimed Gus Monet trilogy: *Poison Lilies* and *Buried Road*. The author lives in Ottawa, Canada, with her husband.